THE BOOK OF THE DEAD

BOOK THREE OF THE COUNTERFEIT SORCERER

A NOVEL BY ROBERT KROESE

PROLOGUE

Beata's voice came to me on the wind howling through the valley, calling my name: *Konrad... Konrad... Konrad...*

I ran into the wind, my path illuminated by the full moon overhead. Rounding a bend, I saw the shadows of ancient stones jutting out of the ground and I realized where I was: the Maganyos Valley, where lay the ruins of the temple called Romok. Despite the horrors I knew that place held, I did not slow. "Beata!" I cried. "Where are you?"

Her voice called to me again, louder now: *Konrad... Konrad... Konrad...*

I ran toward the sound, which seemed to be coming from a dark tunnel formed by one stone slab resting at an angle against another. I felt for my rapier, but it was not at my side. Cursing, I ran toward the darkness. I got on my hands and knees and crawled inside. As I progressed, the tunnel became narrower, and soon I realized I could neither go forward nor retreat. Then the tunnel began to constrict around me, and I realized it was not a tunnel at all, but some sort of shadowy creature that had seized me: a massive kovet, like the one I had used to blot out the moon during the battle with Voros Korom.

Then the part of the creature that covered my face peeled away, and for a moment I was blinded by the glare of an intense red light. When my eyes adjusted, I saw that it was no kovet that held me, but the giant demon Voros Korom himself, his mutilated eyes illuminated by the glow from a lamp that hung from a chain in the center of a vast underground vault.

"It can't be," I gasped. "You're dead! I killed you!"

Voros Korom laughed. "You killed her too, and yet you come when she calls."

I turned my head to see Beata, my beloved, lying dead on an altar atop a raised dais. Blood poured over the edges of the altar.

"No!" I cried, and found myself released from the demon's grasp. I fell and landed in a pool of slimy muck. Pulling myself to my feet, I saw that I was now in the swamp in Veszedelem where I had met Vili's mother. Zombie-like people trudged through the muck toward the mysterious glow of the temple. I felt the pull as well, just as I had when I had been here before, but this time I was able to resist.

It's just a dream, I told myself. You're not really in Veszedelem.

"That depends on your point of view," said Beata's voice from behind me. I turned to see her standing there, almost knee-deep in the muck, wearing a dirty cotton gown. She seemed to be unharmed, but from the way she looked at me, I knew something was wrong.

"You're not Beata," I said.

"No," she admitted. "I am sorry, I cannot control how I appear to you."

"Who are you?"

"My name is Amira. I am one of the sorcerers in Sotetseg known as the Masters."

"Then this is not a dream?"

"It is a dream. I have come to you while you are sleeping, when your mind is more receptive. With the brand, you have the ability to communicate telepathically with those like myself, but your power is still weak."

"What do you know about me?"

"We have been watching you for some time. We are aware of your dealings with Eben. We know he has asked you to bring him a book."

"Then you know that he schemes against you in your own fortress."

"Eben is of no great concern to us at the moment. It is true that he has gained power over the demons of Sotetseg, but we face a much greater danger. This is why I have come to you."

"You speak of Arnyek the destroyer."

"You know of Arnyek?"

"A sorcerer named Domokos told me about him. Domokos said that Arnyek wishes to destroy the universe in order to end the suffering of the people of Veszedelem."

"That is so. Did Domokos tell you of the history of Sotetseg?"

"He told me of the decay of Veszedelem, and how, in order to save it, the sorcerer Bolond built the keep called Sotetseg. He said that after a devastating attack on Sotetseg by the forces of Arnyek, there was a falling out between Bolond and the few sorcerers who remained alive, called the Masters. Bolond fled to my world, Orszag, and the Masters sealed themselves into an unreachable section of the keep."

"Yes, and since then, the three of us—Foli, Parello and I—have striven to find a way to defeat Arnyek. Unfortunately, we have only been able to keep him at bay, and he grows ever stronger. I fear that we have only a few weeks before he launches an attack that will overwhelm our defenses and destroy Sotetseg. If that happens, there will be nothing to stop Arnyek. All of reality will crumble—including your own world."

"Why do you tell me this?"

"Because we need your help. You must retrieve the Book of the Dead, but you must not give it to Eben. Instead, you must bring it to us."

I laughed. "And why should I trust you any more than I trust Eben?"

"I do not expect you to trust me, but if you believed Domokos, you know what I say about Arnyek is true. We cannot defeat him without the wisdom of Bolond, and Bolond has abandoned us. The Book of the Dead is our only hope."

"You are saying Bolond wrote the book?"

"It is said to be the journal he kept about his experiments with necromancy."

"Then it is true what Eben said? That with the book, Eben could bring Beata back?"

"It is possible. But you must not be tempted. Raising the dead would unleash powers you cannot possibly control."

"But you can control them?"

"We do not intend to use the book for necromancy, but rather to find a way to defeat Arnyek. When Arnyek has been vanquished, we will destroy the book. It is too dangerous to risk it falling into the wrong hands."

"You mean because someone else might try to use it to raise the dead?"

"That, or… you must understand, the book holds secrets that could be damaging to powerful people in your world. We would not see any more bloodshed if we can avoid it."

"I don't understand. What secrets? Whom do they threaten?"

"I do not have time to explain now. I must go help the others prepare for Arnyek's attack before it is too late. Follow Eben's instructions to retrieve the book from under the city, but do not give it to him. Bring it to Sotetseg, and when you are in the courtyard, call out my name. Demons loyal to me will find you and bring you to me. Will you do this?"

"I will get the book," I said. "I cannot make any promises about what I will do with it until then."

Amira in the form of Beata nodded. "I am confident you will make the right choice when the moment comes. I cannot bring your beloved back, but I believe I can rid you of your brand, if you still desire it. Come to me when you have the book and I will do what I can. I'm afraid I can be of no further help to you now. I wish you good luck."

CHAPTER ONE

B y the time I awoke, the dream had already begun to fade, as dreams do. I got out of bed and saw that I was alone in my room at the Lazy Crow. Vili and Rodric must have gotten up already; sunlight poured through the window. They were probably eating breakfast with Ilona in the tavern downstairs. I was tempted to join them, but there was something I had to do first.

I reopened an old wound on my hand to draw blood and then sent my mind to the shadow world, Veszedelem. I no longer needed to seek permission to enter Sotetseg from the unblinking man in the guard tower, as I had mastered the ability of traveling to any location in Veszedelem with which I was familiar. I appeared in the courtyard and then made my way to the room where Eben had left the bell for summoning him. I might have gone directly to the room, but I didn't want to be caught unawares by any demons who might be roaming the passageways. I encountered no one.

Eben appeared within a few minutes, and we went together to the small library where we always met. The odor of mildew had gotten worse since my last visit, and I imagined that some of the books had visibly deteriorated since I'd first come.

"I take it by your visit here that you have decided to bring me the Book of the Dead?" Eben asked.

"I make no promises. If you know where the book is hidden, why did you not retrieve it yourself when you were in Nagyvaros?"

"There are obstacles to retrieving the book. I was able to get close, but my plans were interrupted when the acolytes sent the gendarmes after me. Fortunately, I have learned much in the past few days, thanks to my newly acquired status in Sotetseg."

"What are these obstacles?"

"There are three. The first is the maze of tunnels itself. I have already mapped out many of the upper tunnels, and in fact my own estate in the Hidden Quarter will give you access to them. I have hidden the map in the pages of a book on herbology, which you will find on a bookshelf in my study toward the rear of the house."

"And the second?"

"The second obstacle is the creature called Szornyeteg, which Bolond brought from Veszedelem to guard the cavern that allows access to the lower tunnels. It was the Szornyeteg that prevented me from reaching the book. The creature lives at the bottom of a deep pit and will kill anyone who tries to cross the bridge that spans it. I attempted to cross several times and was nearly killed more than once. Neither magical attacks nor ordinary weapons are of any use against the creature."

"Then how do you expect me to get past it?"

"I have learned how Bolond tamed the monster. There is an enchanted lyre that, when it nears the Szornyeteg, will play a tune that will lull the creature into docility."

"And where will I find this lyre?"

"It is where all relics end up: at Regi Otthon."

"You suggest I break into the Temple of Turelem in Delivaros? I'd be better off facing the monster."

"Are you not allies with the man who now rules Nagyvaros? Surely you can exert some pressure on him to request a relic from the Cult."

"Even if I could, Delivaros is currently under siege by the Barbaroki. It may be impossible to go there."

"You're a clever young man, Konrad. Use the situation to your advantage. Delivaros is in need of aid. Nagyvaros is in a position to provide it."

"The Torzseki will not be anxious to engage the Barbaroki while they are still securing their position in Nagyvaros."

"The Torzseki will not refuse a chance to gain influence in Delivaros and vanquish their old foes, the Barbaroki. They only need a powerful sorcerer on their side to tip the scales in their favor."

"I do not wish to become the court sorcerer for the Torzseki."

"Not even to bring back Beata?"

"Do not speak her name again, warlock. What is the third obstacle?"

"The book is said to be locked in an enchanted box that can only be opened by a certain key. I have attempted to determine what happened to this key, but have had no success. However, if you bring the box to me, I may be able to open it."

I did not tell Eben that I knew exactly where the key was. "What then?"

"Then I will bring Bea—your beloved back from the dead."

"And yourself, I assume."

"Naturally."

"I will kill you again."

Eben smiled. "You are welcome to try."

CHAPTER TWO

I went downstairs to meet Rodric, Vili and Ilona, who were still eating breakfast. Almost no time had passed during my discussion with Eben. Ilona looked relieved to see me; she was the only one of our group besides me who knew about the Book of the Dead, and she'd sworn not to say anything until we could all discuss the matter together.

"Was it that bad?" Rodric asked, looking at my face as I approached.

I gave a grim smile. My visit to Veszedelem had drained me more than I realized. I wearily sat down and tore a piece of bread from the half-loaf that rested on the table.

"I've had discussions with sorcerers in Veszedelem this morning," I said.

"Sorcerers?" Vili asked. "Another in addition to Eben?"

"I was visited in my dreams by someone who called herself Amira. She claimed to be one of the so-called 'Masters,' the sorcerers who once ruled Sotetseg and have sealed themselves off in an inaccessible part of that keep."

"A visitor in your dreams," Rodric said. "If it were anyone but you speaking, I'd think they'd been smoking Troyan milkweed. What did this Amira want?"

I glanced at Ilona, who nodded. "There is a book hidden in the tunnels under Nagyvaros," I said, "called the Book of the Dead."

"This story has an inauspicious start," Rodric observed.

"Indeed," I replied. "But I have actually begun in the middle. Ilona will have to tell you the beginning."

Ilona nodded and then proceeded to tell the story she had told me the previous evening.

"So you believe," Rodric said, "that Varastis was your father?"

"It seems likely."

"Where did he get this key?" Rodric asked. Ilona had removed the chain holding the key and placed it on the table where we could all see it. In the dim light of the tavern, its glow was unmistakable.

"I do not know. Perhaps from Bolond himself."

"And why do you seek the book?"

"My father obviously wanted me to find it. For what reason, I do not know. That is a mystery I hope to solve. What I do know is that I cannot return to Delivaros after all that I have seen."

"You may have to," I said. "According to Eben, there is a monster, called Szornyeteg, guarding the passageway that leads to the book. It can only be passed by one bearing a magical lyre that is in the hands of the acolytes."

"The Lyre of Dallam?" Ilona asked. "It was said to be destroyed along with the rest of the artifacts retrieved from the tunnels three hundred years ago, during the Great Purification."

"I'd bet my bow that's a lie," Rodric said.

"Very likely," I replied. "The acolytes claim to destroy all the artifacts they find, but I'm inclined to believe Eben in this matter. I suspect all the 'destroyed' artifacts are kept somewhere deep inside Regi Otthon."

"Then you think the Cult of Turelem is built on a lie?" Ilona asked. I could hear in her voice that she was trying to muster outrage, but clearly the possibility had already occurred to her.

"I think the Cult of Turelem is primarily interested in promoting the Cult of Turelem," I said. "Whether or not the acolytes approve of their use, magical artifacts have power. I haven't often seen powerful people willingly give up power."

"Why does Eben want the book?" Vili asked.

"He thinks he can use it to recover his physical form, to leave Veszedelem."

"To return from the dead," Rodric said.

"Yes."

"But you're not going to give it to him?" Vili asked.

"No."

"You plan to bring it to Amira?"

"If what she says is true, I may have little choice. But I don't know yet."

"Then you have another reason to seek the book?"

I hesitated. Rodric said, "He wants to bring Beata back."

"No!" Ilona cried. "Konrad, you can't! Perhaps not all magic is evil, but surely we can agree that necromancy is wrong."

"I have made no decisions on the matter," I said gruffly. "Before I do, I would like to see this book."

"Agreed," said Rodric. "There's no use in fighting amongst ourselves, at least not until we know what we're fighting about."

"Then we're agreed that we seek the Book of the Dead?" I asked.

"Aye," said Rodric.

"Aye," said Ilona, with an uncertain glance at me.

Vili hesitated a moment but then nodded. "You freed my parents from torment, Konrad. I go where you go."

Vili's comment cut me like a knife, but I managed not to let my shame show. I wanted to tell Vili the truth, but it was too late. No good could come from telling him now that his parents remained trapped in an endless loop somewhere between our world and Veszedelem. I would have to find a way to free them eventually, even if it meant keeping the warlock's brand. If I brought the book to Amira, would she be able to save them? Perhaps. One more reason to get my hands on the book.

"Even if this lyre is in Regi Otthon, how can we get it?" Rodric said. "With the Barbaroki surrounding Delivaros, we can't get inside the city."

"Eben suggested we appeal to Nebjosa. Offer to help him deal with the Barbaroki in return for getting the acolytes to turn over the lyre."

"Sounds dangerous," Rodric said. "And won't Nebjosa wonder what we need the lyre for? He's not likely to be happy about us sneaking around in the tunnels below his city looking for treasure."

"There may be an easier way," Ilona said. "There are many secret passages into Delivaros, and I know of some of them. I may even be able to get us into Regi Otthon."

"Even so," Rodric said, "if we don't know where the artifacts are kept...."

"I know someone who may be able to help," Ilona said. "Her name is Lara. She is a priestess in the temple. Lara was the closest thing I had to a mother. She often confided to me her doubts about the Cult leadership, and it was her remarks that first caused me to question the Cult's mission. I told her about the key before I left, and she had plenty of opportunity to inform on me to the leadership but did not. I believe I could persuade her to help us."

"Well," said Rodric, "it does sound better than facing this Szornyeteg with bows and rapiers."

"I will need help to get inside," Ilona said. "But there is to be no killing. It is possible the acolytes have misled people for their understanding of the greater good, but they are not evil people. They do much good and rule the city with mercy and justice. We get in, take the lyre, and get out without killing anyone."

"Sounds reasonable," Rodric said. "I have no grudge against the acolytes."

I did not share their compunctions about harming members of the Cult, but I did not argue. "Then it is agreed," I said. "Tomorrow morning, we leave for Delivaros."

CHAPTER THREE

Delivaros, the seat of the Cult of Turelem, was six days' journey to the southeast. We spent the rest of the day buying supplies—no easy feat in a city that had recently been overrun by the Barbaroki. Fortunately the Hidden Quarter had remained mostly untouched by the fighting.

The following morning I retrieved Ember from her stable, and the others mounted the horses they'd secured for themselves. We set out on the well-traveled road that snaked along the eastern bank of the Zold. It would be dangerous for someone marked as I was to approach Delivaros, but Ilona claimed to know a secret way into the city. Hopefully we would not meet any other acolytes on our path.

During the first day of our journey, we encountered several hundred refugees from Nagyvaros, and we were forced to make camp in the wild, as all the inns were full to overflowing. The skies were clear but the nights were cold, and we kept a fire burning to ward off the chill. We met no one who wished to do us harm, however; neither bandits nor Barbaroki. The volume of traffic probably scared off the bandits, and the Barbaroki were undoubtedly fully massed around the walls of Delivaros.

Curiously, neither did we see any sign of the passage of the Fourth Division of janissaries, which had begun pursuit of the Barbaroki two days earlier. The only explanation was that General Bertrek had ordered the division to cut across the marshes to the east to surprise the Barbaroki before they could lay siege to Delivaros.

We met fewer travelers the next day, and fortunately we encountered no bandits either. On the morning of the third day of our travels, we spotted the great stone guard tower that loomed over the north end of the bridge spanning the Zold. Leaving our horses in the valley, Vili and I climbed to the crest of a nearby hill, from which we could make out the taller buildings across the river. We could also see enough of the Barbarok force to gather that they had completely surrounded the city. Nearly two thousand men were camped just out of bow range from the northern tower, and at least another thousand were strewn along the banks of the river for a mile in each direction. Because of the hills and trees, we could only glimpse a few pockets of Barbaroki on the far side of the river, but from what we could see it was clear that the bulk of the Barbarok force was encamped around the walls of the city. We descended the slope to report to the others.

"It is worse than I expected," Ilona said.

"The good news is that they have not yet broken through the walls," Rodric noted.

"Could they be hoping for a surrender?" Ilona asked.

"Unlikely," I said. "The council will never willingly surrender the city, and the Barbaroki know it. But if Nagyvaros could not stand against them, I doubt Delivaros can."

"Then what are they waiting for?" Rodric asked.

We learned the answer to that question later that afternoon. We had skirted the Barbarok camp on the northern side, intending to eventually make our way back south to one of the villages downriver where we could secure a boat to cross the river. Vili, who had gone on ahead to make sure the way was clear, came roaring back down the wooded path toward us. "Barbaroki!" he cried. "Three thousand or more!"

We hastily dismounted and led our horses into the woods a hundred yards or so. Then Vili and I crept back to the trail, where we witnessed the passage of hundreds of Barbaroki on horseback, as well as many scores of carts pulled by two-horse teams. Many of the men seemed to have fresh wounds. When they had passed, we made our way back to the others.

"Who could they have been fighting?" Rodric asked.

"The Fourth Division," I said. "No sign of any janissaries, though. Those Barbaroki were in rough shape, but I suspect General Bertrek's men got the worst of it."

"You think they wiped out the entire Fourth Division?" Vili asked.

"It seems likely. My guess is that idiot Bertrek tried to be clever, cutting across the marshes east of Kalyiba. But there was a thaw last night. The janissary carts probably got stuck in the mud. Barbarok scouts reported to Chief Csongor, who sent a force to crush them while they were bogged down."

"Then there will be no help from the janissaries against the Barbaroki," Ilona said.

"This must be why the Barbaroki have not yet attacked Delivaros," Rodric said. "They were waiting for the rest of their force to return."

I nodded. "Bad news for us. The Barbaroki will be at full strength before sundown. They will likely begin their assault on Delivaros tomorrow. We need to reach Regi Otthon before it's overrun."

"Then we must do it tonight," Ilona said. "Come, there is no time to lose."

Following Ilona, we led our horses back to the trail. Mounting them, we continued south until we reached a small fishing village. Unfortunately, our inquiries of the locals indicated that the Barbaroki had confiscated all their boats several days earlier. We were told the same story in the next three villages. The sun had set when we finally reached a village where a fisherman with a small boat agreed to ferry us across the river, one at a time, for an exorbitant price. Having little choice, we agreed. We went into the village, overpaid for a stable keeper to care for our horses, and then returned to the fisherman. It was well after dark by the time we were all across. The fisherman agreed to return the next morning at dawn to ferry us back, for the same price.

Ilona led us back to the northwest, along the far side of the river, until we reached a group of rocky hills that overlooked the city from the southeast. Ilona led us on a narrow path around one of these hills until we came to a cataract of the river some thirty feet across. From somewhere ahead came the sound of a rushing waterfall. We followed the cataract as it cut through the rocks, snaking back and forth until we came to a cliff from which the water poured in a great sheet to plunge into a dark pool some twenty feet below us. Rather than continuing along the trail, Ilona veered to the left and plunged through the sheet of water. I followed, and for a moment was aware of nothing but the icy blast that threatened to hurl me to the rocks below. Then I was in a dimly lit chamber behind the waterfall. Vili and Rodric came up behind me. There was barely room for the four of us; there seemed to be no way out but the way we had come. Opposite the waterfall was a wall of rock some thirty feet high.

Ilona shook out her hair, splattering the rest of us with water, and then wiped her hand down her face to clear her vision. "Help me up," she said, moving toward the rock wall. Seeing the foothold she was aiming for, I interlaced my fingers to give her a leg up. She grasped a handhold with her left hand and pulled herself up enough to reach another with her right. From where I stood, the wall appeared to be sheer and featureless, but Ilona clearly knew exactly where to put her hands and feet. She had either been here before or had been taught the pattern to follow. When she was near the top, she disappeared entirely. A moment later, something flew toward me from above. I nearly dived out of the way but realized it was merely a rope. I caught the end of it. It was a good, thick rope, with a knot every foot or so. I pulled it taut; the final knot hung at waist height.

"Climb up," Ilona said. I did so. It was easy enough to scale the rock wall using the rope, but even as I did I was unable to identify any of the handholds Ilona had used. Had the acolytes used magic to hide them? Unlikely. Probably they had trained their members to grasp holds that were unusable to bigger people like me and Rodric. Vili might have been able to do it, but even he would have exhausted himself trying to find the barely perceptible irregularities in the rock. It was a better barrier against non-acolytes than any gate would have been.

I found myself in a narrow tunnel, the mouth of which was barely illuminated by the light penetrating through the waterfall from behind me. I could hear Ilona breathing up ahead, and I crawled after her. More breathing from behind indicated Vili and Rodric had come up after me. The tunnel began to narrow, and I felt a wave of panic as I was reminded of the previous night's dream. I forced myself to breathe deeply and focus on the feel of the rock as I crawled forward.

"Stay close," Ilona's muffled voice said from the darkness ahead. "Follow my voice." She started to hum, and I was reminded of Bolond's songs that came to me while I was imprisoned in Nincs Varazslat. I thought perhaps that she was nervous, but when I heard her voice coming from my right, I realized she was guiding us. I had crawled straight forward, following the contours of the tunnel, but Ilona had gone through a raised opening off the side of the tunnel. Clever: we were in a labyrinth, intentionally designed to mislead anyone who wandered into it. I might have avoided the trap if I'd been able to see, but it would have been nearly impossible to carry a torch in that narrow space—assuming I could even have gotten it lit after being drenched by the waterfall. The acolytes had done their job well. I backed up—almost colliding with Vili—and followed Ilona through the opening.

After several more detours from the main tunnel, the passage opened up enough that we could stand, although it remained narrow enough that we had to walk single file. Perhaps a hundred yards further along, I spotted dim light ahead.

Ilona stopped and turned to face me. "There is a guard station up ahead," she whispered. "Let me do the talking. It is unusual for an acolyte to bring outsiders through one of the secret entrances, but we can use the Barbarok siege as an excuse. I will tell the guard Konrad is Nebjosa's court sorcerer, and that you have come to aid Delivaros against the Barbaroki."

"Is it wise to admit to a servant of the cult that Konrad is a sorcerer?" Rodric asked.

"There is no use trying to hide the markings on his face," Ilona said. "If we acknowledge the matter up front, the guard will likely conclude it is a matter for the priests to deal with. The challenge will be preventing the guard from sending a warning to those ahead."

"They use a counterweight relay system?" I asked.

"You know of such things?"

"I've read of them." One of General Janos's books had been about means of communicating long distances, including semaphore, heliographs, and the system pioneered by the Cult of Turelem, which used a daisy-chain of lengths of cord, usually made from horsehair. The end of each length of cord was connected to a curious contraption that was effectively a counterweighted switch. A slight tug on the cord connected to one end of the device would dislodge a carefully balanced weight, causing it to fall downward on a pendulum. This action would turn a gear, creating a tug on the cord connected to the other end of the device. The effect was to turn the weak tug that reached the device into a much stronger tug on the other end. That tug would trigger another device, perhaps a hundred yards away, and in this manner a signal could theoretically travel many miles, through a hundred or more of the devices. After each tug, the switch was reset by an internal spring mechanism so that it could be used again. The reset process took nearly a second, and the relay devices had to be re-wound often with frequent use, so communicating anything more than a very simple piece of information was untenable. Still, the acolytes found it useful for warning systems.

"The guard will be positioned so as to be able to see us coming," Ilona said. "He will give a tug on the relay cord to indicate to those at Regi Otthon that someone has arrived. If it is not quickly followed by the all-clear signal, the temple guards will be put on alert and a contingent will be sent down the tunnel to us."

"Do you know the all-clear code?"

"If they haven't changed it, yes. As long as we can prevent the guard from sending an intruder warning, we should be all right."

Ilona continued down the passage, which soon opened into a great vaulted chamber, roughly dome-shaped and about a hundred feet in diameter. Torches in sconces lined the walls, illuminating the chamber with a dim orange glow. At the far end of the chamber was a continuation of the passage, also lit by torches. To the left of this, from our perspective, was a wooden guard tower, perhaps twenty feet tall, that was just large enough for a single guard to sit and observe the opening through which we'd just come. Ilona was right: there was no way we could have gotten through without being seen; undoubtedly the guard had already alerted the temple that someone had arrived. In the dim light, I could just make out a fine cord that ran along the wall from the guard tower to a pulley at the edge of the far passage. From there, the cord extended out of sight down the tunnel, where it would connect to the first relay box.

"Ho!" cried the guard, the upper half of his body barely discernible through the window of the little tower. "Who approaches?"

"My name is Ilona, fourth tier acolyte. I come with the court sorcerer of the governor of Nagyvaros and his retinue."

The guard spoke a phrase in a language I did not know. Ilona replied in the same language.

"I was not apprised of any such delegation," the guard said.

"There was no time," Ilona said. "I was in Nagyvaros on a diplomatic mission when the Barbaroki attacked. When the battle ended and the Torzseki moved in, Governor Nebjosa approached me and asked that I escort these men to the council to assist in the defense of Delivaros."

"You bring a sorcerer to Delivaros?"

"Konrad is an advisor to Nebjosa. He knows much about the ways of the Barbaroki, and he has sworn not to employ any magic within the city."

"This is highly peculiar," the guard said. "You will wait here while I inform the temple authorities." The guard reached for something out of sight just over his head.

"There is no time for that," Ilona snapped. "The Barbaroki might begin their assault at any moment."

"They've waited a week already."

"Their force was not complete. Just a few hours ago we witnessed two thousand Barbaroki arriving from the northeast. The attack will come soon. We may already be too late. Let us pass."

Again the guard hesitated. "I'm sorry," he said at last, his arm still extended to raise the alarm. "My orders are clear. I cannot let any outsiders pass without explicit approval."

"Damn you!" Ilona snapped. "I've already told you—"

At that moment I heard the familiar sound of a bowstring snapping. This was followed a split-second later by a yelp from the guard.

"I said no killing!" Ilona cried, whirling to face Rodric, who had already strung another arrow.

"Rest easy," Rodric said. "I've only winged him."

It was true: a flicker of torchlight revealed that the arrow had gone clear through the guard's wrist, pinning it to the wall behind him. He was more devoted to his duty than I would have expected, though: already his left hand was reaching for the cord over his head. Another arrow flew, but this one missed the guardhouse entirely. I realized as the two ends of the severed cord fell that Rodric hadn't been aiming for the guard.

"What a shot!" Vili shouted.

Rodric shrugged, embarrassed. "If I'd pinned him to the wall as I'd intended, the second shot would have been unnecessary."

The guard pulled futilely at the cord, which came loose in his hand. "Help!" he shouted. "Intruders!"

"Quiet, you fool," Ilona ordered. "Nobody can hear your yelping from here."

I strode to the cord that hung from the wall and carefully severed a length of it with my knife. "Vili, do you think you could..."

"Gladly," Vili said, taking the cord from me. He wound it up and tucked it into his belt, and then clambered up one of the support posts of the tower. The guard, moaning in pain, was in no state to resist. Vili pulled the arrow from his wrist and the man sank to the floor. Vili threw the man's crossbow and dagger to the cavern floor and then tied his hands and feet. He climbed back down to us. Meanwhile, Ilona took hold of the dangling cord and gave it two tugs, waited a moment and then tugged it twice more.

"Let's hope that's still the correct sequence for the all-clear," Ilona said. "Otherwise I may have just summoned a score of temple guards."

CHAPTER FOUR

Leaving the guard to moan, we continued down the passage for perhaps another quarter mile. Sections of the passage had been hewn out of stone, but in some places it widened into much larger chambers. Some of these had openings that presumably led to other passageways; a proliferation of cords running along the ceiling confirmed the hypothesis. I wondered how many other secret entrances there were to Delivaros.

"We will have to do some more fast talking when we get to the main guard station," Ilona said. "There will be at least six guards, and they will be on edge after receiving the other guard's initial warning. If we cannot talk our way inside Regi Otthon, we will have to subdue them. Above all, we must prevent them from raising the general alarm."

We passed several passages that Ilona said would take us to various places inside the city, continuing toward Regi Otthon itself. According to Ilona, it would be easier to get into Regi Otthon from underneath than from outside its walls. At last she led us down a dark corridor that ended in a sheer wall, against which was affixed a rusty iron ladder. Ilona started up the ladder and I followed, with Vili and Rodric bringing up the rear. There was no way we were going to take the guards by surprise; we would just have to hope Ilona could keep them from raising an alarm.

But when I emerged from the shaft into the well-lit guard room, I saw that it was manned by a single guard who looked no older than Vili. His face was white with terror. The room was

roughly square, about twenty feet on a side, with two torches on
sconces on each wall. Behind the guard was a single door, a
massive oak thing reinforced with steel bands.

"Wh-who are you?" the young man demanded, the tip of his
short sword shaking as he pointed it at us.

"My name is Ilona. I'm a fourth-tier acolyte. I'm escorting
these men from Nagyvaros on an important mission for the
council."

"N-nobody is allowed in," the young man stammered. "B-B-
Barbaroki."

"The assault has begun?" Ilona asked.

The young man nodded. "I j-just got w-w-word."

"Well, that explains the lack of guards," Rodric said. He and
Vili had emerged from the shaft behind us. "They're all on the
walls."

"We need to get into Regi Otthon," I said. "It's urgent."

The young man shook his head. "C-c-can't open the d-d-
door. No k-k-k-key."

"How are you going to get back in?"

The young man shook his head. "I'm n-n-not."

"Well, this could be a problem," Rodric said.

"I think I can handle it," I said, drawing my rapier. "Young
man, I suggest you drop that sword before someone gets hurt."
Rodric trained his bow on the lad. The sword clattered to the
ground.

I sheathed my blade. "Tie his hands and feet. I'll take care of
the door."

While Rodric and Vili bound the guard, I summoned a kovet,
infusing it with the motivation to break through the door. A great
squid-like shadow appeared, adhering the ends of its tentacles to
the stone wall around the door. The center mass of the creature
pulsed toward the door, slamming against it with a deafening
boom that caused dust and loose mortar to shower us. While the
guard lay wide-eyed on the floor, hands and feet bound,
screaming in terror, I backed away from the door to join the
others against the far wall. The kovet drew back and slammed its
body into the door again, even harder than before. This time, one
of the oak beams supporting the ceiling came dislodged, and a

shower of stones fell, nearly crushing the guard, who continued to scream. I moved toward him to drag him to safety, motivated more by my pledge to Ilona not to kill anyone than by concern for his wellbeing, but by the time I got my arms around the guard's chest, the kovet had slammed into the door a third time. The door had splintered somewhat on the previous attempt, and now it burst into a thousand pieces. Not a second later, the kovet began to fade and then disappeared entirely. A stone passageway, half-concealed by dust and debris, was visible beyond.

"Advance!" I shouted, leaping over the guard. "Anyone within a half-mile of Regi Otthon must have heard that." I stepped over the remnants of the door and then sprinted down the passageway; the others followed. Ilona gave me directions as we moved, and we made our way through a maze of passages toward the temple. We heard shouts up ahead, and Ilona redirected us down a narrow hall to our right. We hid around a corner until the guards had passed and then retraced our steps. We did this several more times, sometimes taking long detours from the main route to avoid being seen, until at last we arrived in an antechamber of Regi Otthon. From elsewhere in the temple came shouts and the sounds of people running—presumably either heading to the city walls or shoring up the defenses of Regi Otthon. Ilona led us down a hall to the living quarters of the acolytes and stopped in front of a nondescript door. She knocked, and a moment later the door opened. A small woman with white hair worn in the traditional close-cropped style of the acolytes stood before us in a faded mauve gown. She stared blankly at us for a moment, sighed, and stood aside for us to come in.

We filed into the room and she closed the door. "I expected you to return," Lara said to Ilona. "I did not think you would be accompanied by such fanfare."

"I take it you heard us break through the door," Ilona said.

"You woke the acolytes sleeping in the catacombs," Lara replied. She gazed coldly in my direction. "We thought the Barbaroki had gotten into the tunnels. You are lucky your arrival coincides with their attack. If most of the men-at-arms had not already gone to the city wall, you would not have made it this far."

"I am surprised you are still in your quarters. Shouldn't you seek refuge in one of the secret chambers below Regi Otthon?"

"I am too old to run and too old to live on biscuits and dried meat. Bad for my teeth. If the Barbaroki get this far, so be it. You bring a sorcerer into the temple?" Lara was staring at me, but her eyes seemed to be fixed on my chest, not my face.

"Konrad is a friend. I'm sorry, I do not have time to explain everything. We need your help."

After a moment, Lara nodded grimly and turned back to Ilona. "I assume your return means you did not find what you were looking for."

"Not yet," Ilona said. "Mother Lara, we need the Lyre of Dallam."

"Oh, is that all," Lara said dryly. "You understand that the official position of the council is that the Lyre of Dallam was destroyed in the Purification."

"Yes, and I learned from you that there is some reason to doubt the council's claims on such matters."

"Why do you want an ancient lyre?"

"I need it to retrieve a book that is hidden below Nagyvaros."

"What book?"

"A book that I believe to hold the secret of my past."

Lara seemed doubtful. "And these men? Are they so interested in your past?"

"It is called The Book of the Dead, Mother Lara," I said. "And I believe it holds many other secrets as well."

"Ah, now we are getting somewhere. I have heard of this book. It may well hold answers you do not seek, and which, once you learn them, you wish you could forget."

"What do you know of the Book of the Dead?" Ilona asked.

Lara shook her head. "Pay no attention to the ramblings of an old woman. Listen, the Barbaroki are inside the walls."

For a moment, we were silent. I heard distant shouts and the bustle of men-at-arms, but no certain indication that the Barbaroki had penetrated into the city. I realized, as I watched Mother Lara's face, that she possessed the heightened hearing of someone who had lost the use of one of her other senses: she was blind. A moment later, I heard shouting in the Barbaroki language.

"Please, Mother Lara," Ilona said. "If the Barbaroki take Regi Otthon, all the treasures will be lost."

"And the Cult's secrets will be revealed," Mother Lara said. "Perhaps it is better that way."

"What secrets?" Ilona asked. "You mean that the council has been keeping the artifacts they claim to have destroyed?"

"As you say, there is no time," Mother Lara said, grabbing a wooden cane from where it lay leaning against the corner near the door. "We must get to the vault before the Barbaroki get inside Regi Otthon."

"Then you will help us get the lyre?"

"Preferable that you have it than the Barbaroki. And if the Council manages to repel them… all the better." Mother Lara turned and opened the door before I could ask for clarification of this strange remark. She turned left and headed down the hall, letting the tip of the cane skitter across the floor ahead of her. Ilona shrugged and followed; the rest of our party went after her.

Trusting Mother Lara's uncanny hearing to keep us from running into anyone who might interfere with our mission, we followed her through a maze of corridors until we came to a cluttered storeroom somewhere below the main temple chamber. By this time, the sounds of the Barbarok throng were unmistakable: the war chants and crashing of spears and axes against shields indicated they had Regi Otthon surrounded. The men-at-arms who guarded Regi Otthon couldn't be expected to hold out long. We needed to get the lyre and get out of the temple quickly.

Ilona had taken a lantern from one of the hallways above, although of course Mother Lara didn't need it. Mother Lara pulled aside a curtain to reveal a nondescript wooden door. She produced a key from a pocket in her gown and tugged at the door handle, but it wouldn't budge. She stepped aside and I yanked it open. The door clearly hadn't been opened in years.

Beyond it was another room, dark and musty. Mother Lara went inside, feeling in front of her with the cane, and Ilona came after her with the lantern. I followed, with Vili and Rodric behind me. We were in a large vault lined with crypts. All around us were crates and objects covered with cloth tarps.

"I have not been down here for many years," Mother Lara said, "But if it was not destroyed, it is here somewhere."

"This is hopeless!" Vili cried. "We'll never find it before the Barbaroki get inside!"

"It's too late to turn back now," I said. "Maybe we'll get lucky. Each of us will work from the center toward a corner. Rodric, you take the northeast," I said, pointing in what I hoped was the correct direction. "Ilona, southwest. Vili, southeast. Mother Lara, if you would be so kind, close and lock the door."

"I would be locking you in."

"That's the least of our troubles. Go seek refuge with the other priestesses."

"I have no interest in joining the others," Mother Lara said. "I will wait outside. If the Barbaroki get close to the storeroom, I will knock three times on the door. I wish you luck." With that, she stepped outside and closed the door. I heard the key turn in the lock.

Our search was nowhere near as methodical as I'd hoped, owing to the fact that we had only a single lantern, and that getting to many of the crates required moving others, making it difficult to determine where we'd left off. Slowly, though, we moved toward the corners, uncovering hundreds of artifacts of unknown age and origin: statues, figurines and totems; tapestries and vestments; orbs and crystals; lanterns, lamps and candelabras; cannisters full of mysterious powders and unguents; swords, maces, flails, staves, daggers, spears and axes; and coffers full of jewelry and precious and semiprecious stones. In some cases, chests and coffers we expected to contain some treasure turned out to be empty, suggesting the container itself was an artifact of some kind. Other than their fine workmanship and curious style, few of the artifacts seemed unusual; certainly none of them exuded any noticeable magical aura. None of them glowed or sang out as we touched them. I supposed that very few of the items carried any kind of enchantment, and other than the gems and jewelry, not many seemed particularly valuable. This place seemed more like a storehouse for items of uncertain provenance than a vault of magic artifacts. I don't deny I was tempted to pocket a few of the finer-looking gems, but I resisted the urge—more out of a desire to avoid distraction than respect for the Cult's property rights. I had neither the time nor inclination, however, to ensure the others did not help themselves to any of the treasure.

I was beginning to wonder if Mother Lara had played a trick on us when Vili shouted that he had found a collection of crates holding musical instruments. Already he had unearthed a flute, a set of cymbals and a small harp. Ilona brought the lantern over, and Rodric and I helped Vili open three more crates, which held several more instruments, including a set of small drums that had rotted almost beyond recognition, a collection of brass bells, and three more flutes. At the bottom of one of the crates, under a layer of straw, was a curiously well-preserved lyre. I picked it up and Ilona held the lantern toward it. It was made of wood coated in gold-impregnated paint. The lyre's strings were still intact, and it seemed to hum softly as I removed it from the crate. I strummed the strings, and although I did not know how to play, the notes sounded clear and true. Markings in a strange, ancient language were carved along the lyre's face.

"I cannot read it," Ilona said, "but it's an early form of Gorovic, the language of the Builders. Bolond would have spoken it."

"If it is that old," I said, "the strings should have rotted away long ago."

"Then this is the Lyre of Dallam," Rodric said. "Preserved by magic."

"So it would seem," Ilona said. "Now we just have to—"

As she spoke, three faint knocks sounded on the door.

"Mother Lara!" Ilona cried. "Quickly!"

We might have been better off keeping quiet and hoping that the Barbaroki would bypass the locked room for the moment, but no one objected as I grabbed an axe and moved toward the door. We couldn't let Mother Lara sacrifice herself after what she'd done for us.

A kovet would have been more effective than an axe, but I didn't dare risk hurting Mother Lara. Besides, this door wasn't nearly as formidable as the last one I'd had to break down. Two swings with the axe sufficed to smash the lock. I backed away as Vili pulled the door open. We were too late.

CHAPTER FIVE

Mother Lara lay on the floor a few feet from the door, in a pool of blood, her head caved in by a steel-clad Barbarok club. Four Barbaroki stood facing us.

As I drew my rapier, Rodric loosed an arrow, impaling one of the invaders in the throat. Vili rushed through the doorway, lunging at another man with his dagger in his hand, and Ilona followed on his heels with her fighting stick. So taken aback were the Barbaroki by this sudden onslaught from a motley crew bursting out of the storeroom that three of them were down before I'd even joined the melee. The last man, realizing the odds were now heavily against him, turned to run out of the room, but I managed to hamstring him with the rapier before he could reach the door. He fell to the ground, howling. The man with an arrow in his throat was gasping for breath, the one Vili had attacked was bleeding out, and Ilona had knocked her opponent unconscious.

As the man I'd injured dragged himself toward the door, I was tempted to silence him with a blow to the head from the flat of my blade, but I realized it was unnecessary: my ears were now filled with a deafening roar that seemed to be coming from all around us. "Let's go!" I shouted, not sure if I could even be heard over the sound.

Glancing back to make sure the others were following, I left the room, holding my rapier in my left hand and the lyre in my right. Retracing our steps, I headed back toward the guard room that led to the tunnels. I heard Ilona shout something from behind me; I thought she was asking what the noise was, but I couldn't be sure. The noise was even louder here, like unrelenting thunder. I had an idea what it might be, but I wasn't about to stop to conjecture. Our best bet was to get to the tunnels as quickly as possible.

But as we rounded a corner, I found myself facing a score of Barbaroki running toward us. They were some fifty feet off, but there was no other exit from the passage. "Run!" I shouted, unnecessarily. In the time it took me to turn back the way we had come, I saw that the Barbaroki were not alone: they were being pursued by men wearing the uniform of the temple men-at-arms. Had the tide turned?

We had no time to speculate. Ilona now led the way as we fled from both the Barbaroki and the temple guards. As we continued through the maze of passages, the noise grew still louder, until we burst out of a door that led to a plaza outside Regi Otthon. But if Ilona hoped that we could escape through the city, she was mistaken. We saw now what the noise was: a hailstorm had struck the city, raining thousands of fist-sized chunks of ice down on the streets and buildings all around Regi Otthon. If it weren't for a sloped overhang over our heads, we'd be getting pelted. Many dead lay in the street, but whether they'd been killed in battle or by the hail was impossible to say. Most of them appeared to be Barbaroki, but some were civilians or temple guards. Visibility was limited to about a hundred feet; I couldn't tell whether the hailstorm encompassed the whole city or if it was confined to the vicinity of Regi Otthon. Either way, a hailstorm happening to strike just after the Barbaroki hit the temple was an eerie coincidence.

"It's a miracle," Ilona shouted, watching as the ice accumulated on the pavement.

"It's definitely something," I replied.

A man-at-arms emerged from the door next to us, his sword drawn. Two more men came after him. They began to move toward us, and I went for my rapier.

"Help those people out of the street!" Ilona shouted, pointing into the hailstorm. I saw now that a woman and a young boy were huddled in the lee of a building, pinned down by the hailstorm. After a brief conference, the three men ran into the street, holding their shields over their heads.

"This way!" Ilona said, continuing along the wall to the right. As we reached the corner of the temple, she pointed to a long stone retaining wall that ran along the base of a low cliff, on which were perched the houses of the wealthier merchants of Delivaros. She shouted, "We need to get to that wall! Preferably before the hail stops!"

I nodded. Men-at-arms now approached us from along both walls, and many more were taking shelter nearby. The Barbaroki who hadn't been killed by the men-at-arms or the hail seemed to have fled, which would make it all the more difficult for us to escape.

I summoned a kovet large enough to shelter the four of us and imbued it with the motivation to protect us from the hail. "Ready? Go!"

We ran as one to the wall, the hailstones bouncing harmlessly off the shadow canopy overhead. It dissolved the moment we were safely in the lee of the wall. As long as the wind didn't shift, we were safe. I led the way north along the wall, the others following. Glancing back, I saw a group of perhaps half a dozen men trying to follow us, their shields over their heads, but the lead man slipped on the accumulated ice and fell, dropping his shield, which had been beaten beyond all recognition. The next two men stumbled over their comrade, who had been knocked unconscious by the hail. While they struggled to help him, the rest of the men ran to the safety of a nearby building.

By the time we reached the end of the wall, nearly two hundred yards away, the hail had begun to let up, so we ran down an alley and continued along a street to the east, doing our best to shield our heads with our arms. Hundreds of dead Barbaroki, as well as several dozen civilians and gendarmes, lay dead in the streets.

We reached the city wall without incident. Ilona claimed to know of another tunnel that could be accessed through a trapdoor in a building about a half-mile to the north, but it turned out this wasn't necessary: we came to a place where the Barbaroki had broken through the wall with a ram, and we slipped through just ahead of a crew of gendarmes who were running to shore up the city's defenses in case the Barbaroki regrouped. The Barbaroki, however, seemed to have scattered. The sudden, inexplicable hailstorm had spooked them. The Barbaroki were renowned as fierce warriors, but they were also a primitive, superstitious people who feared the Cult of Turelem. In the fervor that succeeded their assault on Nagyvaros, their leader had been able to convince them to overcome their qualms, but a freak hailstorm that seemed to have been sent by Turelem herself had been enough to send them running. No doubt they would rally eventually, and possibly renew their attack, but for now there was little danger.

Ilona found a trail through the wooded hills to the east of the city, which we followed until we reached the river. We traveled along the river for several miles, encountering no one, and arrived at the rendezvous point well before dawn. To our relief, the fisherman returned as promised and ferried us across the river. We got a few hours' sleep at an inn in the village and then retrieved our horses and headed out once again for Nagyvaros.

CHAPTER SIX

A week later, we were back at the Lazy Crow, sitting in the tavern and going over our plans. The tavern was busier than usual—a fact I attributed to the destruction of residences in the other parts of the city. Now that we possessed the lyre, we had within our reach everything we needed to overcome all three obstacles to retrieving the Book of the Dead. We would rest for the evening and then head to Eben's secret lair to find his map and enter the tunnels. We would have to trust that between Eben's map and Ilona's key, we could find our way to the chamber guarded by the Szornyeteg. As there was little more we could do to plan the expedition, our conversation turned to the mysterious hailstorm that had repelled the Barbaroki.

"I never put much stock in the Cult's teaching," Rodric said, looking at Ilona, "but I must admit that storm was fortuitous. If your goddess is capable of such feats, it is no surprise that her followers are so devoted."

"If indeed Turelem was behind the storm," I said.

"What other possibility is there?" Vili asked. "Surely you don't believe it was only a coincidence."

Ilona remained silent, but I suspected her thoughts echoed my own. "What some call a miracle," I said, "others refer to as magic."

"You don't mean to suggest that summoning one of your little shadow creatures is on the same level as controlling the weather?" Ilona asked.

"Not on the same level, no. But perhaps in the same category. You have said yourself that the Cult's opposition to magic is due to its belief that sorcerers meddle in powers reserved for the gods. Is that not an admission that Turelem is in effect a powerful sorceress? Perhaps she is immortal, like Bolond, and the Cult's efforts to stamp out sorcery are just an attempt to eliminate the competition."

"Blasphemy," Ilona muttered, but her heart wasn't in it.

"Do you really believe that?" Vili asked.

I shrugged. "It would not be the strangest thing I've heard since I got involved with this whole business. In any case, it is all the more reason to steer clear of the Cult. If they realize that we've taken…" I trailed off, realizing something wasn't right: sometime in the past few minutes, the tavern had gotten too quiet. At a few of the tables, men continued to speak in normal tones, but the rowdy buzz that had filled the place had died.

"Konrad?" Rodric asked, seeing the look on my face.

"Rodric, do you remember the time we pursued a Barbarok raiding party through Keskeny Pass? We reached their camp only to find it had just been abandoned. I ordered the squad to pursue them to the east, but Artok spotted a trail leading south."

"Certainly I remember," Rodric said. "They'd seen us coming and set up an ambush. If we'd continued east, they'd have had us surrounded."

"It seems I didn't learn my lesson that day."

"I don't…ah," Rodric said, glancing behind me. "Yes, it does seem you could have been more careful."

"Was that situation as bad as I remember it?"

"Worse, I think. There were at least seven men to the south."

"And another five to the north."

Rodric nodded. "Remind me how we got out of that situation at Keskeny?"

"We ran," I said.

"That was a good idea. Sometimes discretion is the better part of valor."

"Women and children first," I said.

Ilona and Vili, who had begun to catch on, nodded.

I lowered my voice. "Vili, get the lyre. Go out the window and wait at the stables. We'll find you. Ilona, wait upstairs. Rodric and I will try to lead them away from the inn."

"I'm not—" Ilona started. She broke off as I felt a heavy hand on my shoulder.

"Konrad the Sorcerer," said a deep voice from behind me. "You would not have to worry about eavesdroppers if you accepted the governor's offer to allow you to stay in the palace."

"Or at least I'd save them a trip across town," I said. "What are you doing here, Davor Sabas?" The hand left my shoulder and I turned to see that it was indeed Davor Sabas, the right hand of Chief Nebjosa of the Torzseki. Behind him stood four other men armed with axes. They were disguised as ordinary villagers, but they were clearly Torzseki. Turning around, I saw the seven I'd spotted earlier also getting to their feet. It seemed that half the men in the tavern were against us. Those who remained seated had gone deathly quiet and pretended not to watch the unfolding drama. I stood and faced Davor Sabas.

"Governor Nebjosa suspects that you are plotting to loot the treasures the lie beneath his city," Davor Sabas said. "I wish I could report he was mistaken, but I have heard you speaking."

"Nebjosa and I are allies," I said. "I would not take anything that belongs to him."

"Then what is this book you seek?"

"Something of use only to a sorcerer," I said. "It is of no value and of no concern to the Governor."

"That sounds like something for the Governor to decide."

"He is welcome to come and speak to me about it in person."

"The Governor has empowered me to summon you to his palace."

I smiled. "The Governor possesses no such power. Surely you recall our battle with Voros Korom. You and your men are no match for my magic."

"Perhaps. But you would do well to remember whose city you are in. You will not be able to remain here for long if the Governor decides you are unwelcome. Now, tell me where he is."

"Who?"

"The man you met in Delivaros. The one who will take you to the book."

I was unable to follow this turn in the conversation. Had Davor Sabas misheard us? Was he referring to Eben?"

"We met no man in Delivaros."

"I heard you speak of a man, without whom you cannot get to the book. Although why you would trust such a man, given the way you speak about him, I cannot guess. You called him the liar."

Rodric laughed. "The lyre is not a man. It's a—"

"A woman," I said. "I'm afraid your comprehension of Szaszokish is lacking, Davor Sabas. It is true that we sought a woman in Delivaros, but she was killed in the Barbarok assault on that city. We did not refer to her as a liar, but rather by her name, Lara."

Davor Sabas regarded me sternly, trying to decide whether I was playing a trick on him. His knowledge of Szaszokish was actually quite good for a Torzsek, but it wasn't inconceivable that he'd misheard *Lara* as *liar*. I doubted he knew the word *lyre* at all, which would explain his initial confusion.

"You said she was in your room upstairs," Davor Sabas said. He glanced to the man on his left, who nodded. In all likelihood, the other Torzseki's Szaszokish was worse than Davor Sabas's.

"I am sorry, but you misunderstood. There is no one upstairs. We would have brought Lara back here, but as I say, she is dead."

"I think one of them did say something about a woman killed by the Barbaroki," one of the men behind Davor Sabas said.

Irritation swept across Davor Sabas's face. "Innkeeper!" he shouted, and the old woman, who had been studiously drying glasses with a towel while we spoke, looked up. "Did these four arrive with someone else?"

"Not that I know of, sir," said the innkeeper, who obviously recognized Davor Sabas.

"You'd better not be lying to me."

"Yes, my lord. I'm not, my lord."

"What room are they staying in?"

"They have numbers four and five, upstairs."

"Karel, check the rooms. Break down the doors if you have to."

"No need for that, sir," said the innkeeper, pulling a large keyring jingling with keys from her gown. "Door at the end of the hall and the one just to the right of it."

Karel took the keys and went upstairs. We waited anxiously, surrounded by the Torzseki, until he returned.

"Well?" Davor Sabas asked.

"Nobody in any of the rooms. I checked the rest of them too. They're all empty. I did find something strange, though. Look."

As Karel approached, I saw that he carried the lyre in his hands. It seemed almost to glow in the yellow light from the fireplace. My innards tightened.

"What is it?" Davor Sabas asked.

Karel strummed the strings with his fingers, filling the room with the reverberating sounds. "A musical instrument," he said. "We'd call it a harfa. I don't know what the Szaszokish word for it is."

The innkeeper started, "It's a—"

"Harp," said Ilona. "It's the harp I brought from Delivaros. Mother Lara gave it to me when I was very young."

The innkeeper frowned. "If I'd known you were keeping a fancy *harp* in your room, I'd have charged you more."

"Fine," I said.

"Another three ermes a night."

It was an absurd price, but I nodded curtly.

"It looks valuable," Davor Sabas said, taking the lyre from Karel.

"Only to me," Ilona said. "It's the only thing I have to remember Mother Lara by. That is probably why you thought I was referring to it by her name."

Davor Sabas frowned, growing increasingly frustrated. "Then you can play it?"

"Of course," Ilona said. "Although it has been years since I've had the chance."

"I would like to hear you play it now."

"Please, I would rather not. As I say, I am out of practice. We only just retrieved it from Delivaros and I have not had a free moment to play since then. I would not insult the ears of the Governor's most trusted advisor with my clumsy attempt at music."

"If you wish to keep the harp, you will play," Davor Sabas said.

"I beg you not to insist," Ilona said. "Your men have given me a fright. Look how my hands shake. Perhaps if you return tomorrow, after I have had a chance to prepare—"

Davor Sabas's face was turning red. I could see we were not going to get out of the inn without Ilona attempting to play the lyre. "Do as he says, Ilona," I said. "Do not worry that you are out of practice. Music is like magic. It comes when it needs to." My hope was that the lyre's magic was not limited to soothing monsters; perhaps it would sense the danger we were in and provide a song, despite Ilona's lack of facility with it. I did not think this was very likely, but it was the best chance we had.

"Very well," said Ilona, reluctantly taking the lyre from Davor Sabas. "I will do my best," she said, catching my eye, "but you should be prepared to be disappointed in case it goes wrong."

I gave her a slight nod. Ilona held the lyre against her breast and began to play. The first few notes were tenuous, and I realized the lyre was not going to offer any assistance. It was a beautiful instrument, but its magic—if it truly possessed any—was not for charming irritated tribesmen in a shadowy tavern. Ilona was on her own.

But as her fingers continued to strum, a melody began to take shape. It was slow and simple at first, but there were no false notes. Ilona's playing picked up speed, and the bittersweet melody grew more complex. Those in the inn no longer pretended not to be watching us; every eye and ear in the place was turned to Ilona. It was difficult not to be moved by the song; it reminded me of Beata's singing. By the time it ended, more than a few of those present—even some of the Torzseki—were fighting back tears. She finished the song and set the lyre down on the table. The tavern was absolutely silent.

"You were overly modest about your skill with the harp," Davor Sabas said.

Ilona gave him a nod. "You are very kind."

"It is a wonderful instrument," Davor Sabas said, running his fingers along the gilded frame. "It looks to be quite old. Do you know who made it?"

"I do not. It was a gift from Mother Lara, as I said."

"I believe Governor Nebjosa would like to see such an instrument."

"He is welcome to come see it," I said. "Perhaps Ilona will even deign to give another performance."

"You would be wise to watch your tongue, sorcerer," Davor Sabas said.

"And you would do well to remember that your chief is a Governor, not a king—and one with a tenuous hold on the city, at that. He should think carefully before offending his most powerful ally."

Davor Sabas seethed at this but did not speak. "We will be watching you, sorcerer," he said. "If you take anything belonging to the Governor, we will know."

"I do not intend to do any looting within Nebjosa's domain," I said.

Davor Sabas glared at me, knowing what I was implying but not willing to speak it aloud: whatever treasures remained under the city were out of Nebjosa's reach. He grabbed his mug from the table, downed the contents, and then marched past us to the door. The rest of his men silently followed.

When the last man was out the door, Ilona, Vili, Rodric and I breathed a collective sigh of relief. The other patrons, realizing the show was over, went back to their beer and conversations.

"I didn't realize you could play," I said after some time.

"All acolytes learn an instrument. I was never very good, to be honest. It's a very fine harp."

"Liar," I said.

CHAPTER SEVEN

The next morning, we made our way to the secret entrance to Eben's lair, taking care to avoid being followed. The hidden doorway was in an alley not half a mile from the Lazy Crow, but we spent the better part of an hour meandering all over the Hidden Quarter just to be sure.

While Vili acted as a lookout, I located the catch that opened the door. Rodric and Ilona went inside, and I gave Vili a whistle. He ran down the alley and we disappeared into the maze of shrubs, letting the door close behind us. It had been several weeks since Eben's death, and the shrubs were now completely overgrown, making it difficult to discern the path through the maze, but I eventually found the way to the fountain at its center, where I had confronted Eben. It took us another half-hour to find the exit at the far end.

The shrub maze opened up to reveal a ramshackle estate that was nestled against the cliff wall that marked the northern boundary of the Hidden Quarter. It was less an estate than a collection of seemingly unrelated buildings constructed on top of each other. Earth seemed to have been backfilled against the cliff to allow construction in several tiers, with the buildings on the upper level looking out over the sprawl of the Hidden Quarter. I realized, regarding the buildings, that I had seen them from below many times, thinking they were the residences of some of the wealthier merchants in the Hidden Quarter. I never realized they were all part of the same estate, owned by the mysterious warlock Eben, and apparently accessible only via entrances (for surely there was more than one) known only to him. To the east, south and west were high walls that blocked our view of the rest of the city.

The estate was overgrown with weeds and in general disrepair, although Eben had only been exiled to Veszedelem a few weeks earlier. I wondered if Eben had fallen on hard times sometime before I encountered him. I opened an unlocked door and we entered the main building that occupied nearly the entire bottom tier of the estate. The place was more impressive from the inside: despite external appearances, it had clearly been constructed with an overall design in mind. The front door opened to a vast, vaulted entryway with twin staircases at the far end that led up to the next level. Doorways to the left and right led to other rooms on the main level. The floors were of stained hardwood, and the walls were of granite, with marble accents. Beautiful tapestries of Troyan or Sammerian make hung on the walls, and Prendish carpets ran along walkways. We could have spent the entire day exploring that camouflaged mansion, but we would have to be content with a short visit to the library.

I led the way through the door centered between the two staircases, which opened to a hall that was lined with doors that opened to many more rooms. We were concerned only with the door at the end of the hall, which led to the library.

The library was vast, containing hundreds of books on dozens of topics, most of which were in languages I couldn't even identify, much less read. Although the room was deep within the mansion, it was lit by sunlight that streamed through angled shafts over our heads. Following Eben's instructions, I located the book in which he'd hidden the map of the tunnels under Nagyvaros. I opened the book and several sheets of paper fell out. I re-shelved the book and spread the papers out on a desk in the center of the room. As it turned out, there were five different maps, each of them describing a network of tunnels beginning at a different starting point. The maps were labeled only with letters of the alphabet, which evidently corresponded to locations in or around the city. As we didn't possess the legend, the maps would do us no good, but it was clear which one we needed: inside a rough circle at the far end of it someone—

presumably Eben—had written *Szornyeteg*. I spent a moment memorizing the map and then gave it to Rodric to carry. After six years in Nincs Varazslat, my visual memory was such that I wouldn't need to refer to it again.

With the map in hand and Ilona carrying her key, we were as prepared as we were going to be for what lurked below the city. I led us back down the hall to a doorway that opened to a stairway leading downwards. I lit a lantern and we went down, finding ourselves in a large cellar. To our left was a doorway that led to a tunnel that disappeared into shadow. To our right, a long wooden ramp led upwards; a faint smattering of sunlight was visible on the upper part of the ramp. Against the wall behind us leaned dozens of shovels, picks and various other tools. I realized that at one time Eben must have employed a small army of excavators to dig from his estate to the network of tunnels under the city— yet somehow he had managed to keep the estate a secret. I suspected I didn't want to know what happened to the workers after their task was finished. The ramp also explained where the earth had come from to build the tiers against the cliff: Eben must have begun the excavation process before the estate had even been built.

Near the doorway were benches on which lay more tools, as well as supplies for sojourning into the tunnels: torches, lanterns, waterskins, ropes, and chalk—presumably for marking passages to prevent getting lost. I didn't see anything we would need that we hadn't already thought to bring along, so I held the lantern before me and entered the tunnel.

The walls of the tunnel were earth, supported by ribs made of pine planks. These looked old and many were rotted, but I supposed they would hold for a few more hours. I advised the others to be careful not to brush against them—more of a challenge for me than the others, as I was the tallest and broadest-shouldered of the group. I had to keep my back bent to avoid banging my head against the lower beams.

For the rest of the morning we traveled this way, occasionally stopping so I could lie down and work the kinks out of my neck and back while Rodric refilled the oil in the lantern. After about two hours, we reached the end of the "new" tunnel that Eben had dug; it suddenly opened up into another, somewhat larger passage that ran roughly perpendicular to it. This passage was supported not by wooden beams but by arches made from the mysterious aggregate for which the Builders were famous. Following the map, we turned right and continued for another hundred yards before coming to a series of passages that broke off from the main. The third passage on the left was clearly marked on Eben's map, so I continued down this passage, with the others following. This passage too was lined with openings, and I again followed the map's guidance. I made several more turns, with Rodric insisting that we stop to double-check each one on the map. There must have been miles of dead ends and circuitous passages, but these were marked only with Xs. At one point, Eben must have mapped them all, but a complete map of the labyrinth would have taken several sheets of paper. It quickly became clear that the map we possessed was neither complete nor to scale; it was merely a rough guide for getting from the cellar to the chamber where the Szornyeteg dwelt.

At last the labyrinth ended, and we were once again following a long tunnel that descended steeply while following a wide leftward spiral. By this time, I was thoroughly turned around, but I suspected that we were somewhere beneath the palace. After an hour of this, we stopped for a brief lunch of dried meat, biscuits and water, and then continued for another hour. We had to be a good half mile underground. The sheer scope of the tunnels was staggering, and we hadn't even touched any of the tunnels spreading out from the access points marked on Eben's other maps.

I was beginning to wonder if the spiraling passage would ever end when it suddenly opened up into a cavern so vast that the ceiling, floor and walls were all lost in the darkness. A rope bridge lined with wooden slats extended as far as we could see across the chasm. We had reached the end of Eben's map: the circular region labeled *Szornyeteg*.

Ilona, whose key now glowed so brightly that she no longer needed the lantern to see, removed the lyre from her pack. The instrument glittered in the light, but it showed no sign of coming to life.

"Should I play it?" she asked.

"Not yet," I said. I wished I had gotten more specific instructions from Eben. This had to be the cavern where the Szornyeteg lived, but I wasn't sure how the lyre was supposed to help us get past it. I stepped out onto the rickety bridge, holding the lantern before me. The lantern illuminated the bridge some distance ahead but did nothing to pierce the surrounding gloom. The cavern was completely silent. Was the monster dead? Sleeping? Or merely lying in wait?

I'd have liked to douse the lantern, but I didn't trust the bridge enough to cross it in the dark. I would have to risk waking the Szornyeteg. "Stay close," I said. "Try to step where I step." I was the heaviest of the party; if the slats didn't break where I stepped on them, the others were probably safe. I started slowly across the bridge, with Ilona right behind me. In her right hand she carried the lyre. In her left was the key, which she used to illuminate the bridge in front of her.

The bridge creaked and swayed as we crossed, but the slats held. I wondered who had built it. Not the original Builders, surely. Their constructions—at least the ones that had survived until now—were of stone or the strange stone-like aggregate of which they were the masters. On the other hand, perhaps the dry, sterile air of the cavern had preserved the bridge since the time of Elhalad.

Other than the slight bowing of the bridge, there was no way to know how far across it was. We had gone about fifty paces and seemed to be reaching the nadir of the bow when I heard something like a low moaning that seemed to come from all around us. I thought I felt the air moving. As if harmonizing with the profundo moans, the lyre suddenly began to play, its strings resonating as if plucked by invisible fingers.

"Keep moving," I said, continuing to put one foot in front of another. The lyre and the Szornyeteg fell into a song, and we moved with its rhythm. Intent on placing my feet, I didn't notice the monster until Ilona gasped. I looked up to see something huge and black slithering through the air just to my right. At first I thought it might be a great winged lizard or wyvern, but there was no beating of wings. The thing was like a gigantic snake, but instead of scales it had flat black skin that looked more like stone than something alive. The thing undulated along with the lyre's melody, slowly receding into the blackness. Then I caught sight of another one to my left. And another, a little further ahead. At first I thought this one was a smaller specimen, only a foot or so in diameter, but as it curled itself over the bridge a few paces ahead of me, I saw that it tapered to a point: I was seeing the thing's head, or maybe its tail. But as the things continued to writhe in concert, I realized they were not individual creatures but rather tentacles—appendages of a single creature that lay at the bottom of the cavern: the Szornyeteg. The monster was a hundred times bigger than I'd imagined.

I pressed on, trying to ignore the undulating tentacles that now seemed to be all around us. Occasionally one would wrap itself around the bridge either ahead of us or behind us, but I noticed that they never actually touched the bridge. Was the bridge protected from the Szornyeteg by some kind of enchantment? That would explain why the monster had not torn it apart.

The magic of the lyre's song seemed to be working. The tentacles came within a few feet of my torch, but the monster didn't touch me. We were now on the uphill part of the bow; I estimated we were nearly two thirds of the way across. We were going to make it.

As the tip of a tentacle passed so close in front of me that I could have reached out and touched it, I heard a scream from behind. I turned in time to see Vili disappear into the darkness, the end of a tentacle wrapped around his midsection.

CHAPTER EIGHT

I went for my rapier, but something cold and hard wrapped around my wrist before I could reach it. The thing's strength was unimaginable; it was like having my arm stuck in a stone block. I did the only thing I could think of: I swung the lantern to smash it against the tentacle. Rodric had just refilled the lantern, and the receptacle shattered and splashed oil along the length of the tentacle for several feet. I doubt I hurt the creature, but I startled it enough to loosen its grip for a moment. I jerked my arm away and backed up, bumping into Ilona, my shirt sleeve blazing with burning oil. I patted at it wildly as the tentacle continued to writhe in front of me, dripping with burning oil. It did not try to seize me again, although I doubted the fire had done any real damage.

"Rodric, huddle close!" I shouted. "Stay near the lyre!" I was a fool not to realize it earlier. We were protected only as long as we were near the lyre. Glancing back, I saw Rodric had already caught on: he was standing with his back against Ilona's shoulder as she held the lyre high. He had an arrow nocked. Boards creaked beneath us. The fire on my sleeve was out; I drew my rapier.

From somewhere up ahead, I heard Vili scream again. All around us, barely visible in the dim light of the key in Ilona's other hand, giant tentacles continued to writhe. The tentacle I'd splattered with oil retreated, disappearing into the darkness. A moment later, Vili reappeared, dangling a few feet over the bridge directly in front of me, the tentacle still wrapped around his chest.

His eyes were wide with terror. I took a step forward, aware that another tentacle lurked just to my right, waiting for me to get far enough from the lyre to strike.

"It's baiting us," Ilona said.

"Agreed," I said. "But we have no choice. We have to save Vili. Stay close, or I'm going to be lost as well."

I took another step forward, with Ilona and Rodric following close behind, but Vili receded as we moved. "Konrad," Vili gasped. "Please… help… me…."

"Damn that thing," I said. "It's toying with us. I'm going to have to lunge at it. Rodric, be ready with your bow." I took another step forward, avoiding a board with an ominous crack in it. Ilona and Rodric crept forward as well. Then, moving as quickly as I could, I leapt forward and lunged with my rapier, hoping to penetrate the monster's thick hide with its point. But the tentacle moved nearly as fast as I did, and I barely nicked it. Vili screamed as he shot upward and away into the dark. A board under my forward foot splintered and I fell, sprawling forward to avoid plummeting straight down. I lost my grip on the rapier and it skittered along the slats and then fell over the side.

As I grasped frantically at the slats, another tentacle swept over my head before curling back toward me. An arrow shot over me from behind, so close that I felt my hair ruffle from the wind. The arrow lodged in the monster's hide, but the creature showed no sign of noticing. The tentacle wrapped itself around me and began to tighten, the arrow sticking out toward me. I gripped the shaft of the arrow with both hands and plunged it as deep as I could. Something cold and sticky oozed over my hands, and I felt the tentacle shudder. I put my sternum against the end of the arrow so that by tightening its grip, the creature would be pushing the arrow farther into itself. As the arrow's blunt end dug into my chest, I consoled myself that although I might die, I'd at least cause the monster a little pain. The butt of the arrow gouged my skin as it sunk the rest of the way into the Szornyeteg. The massive tentacle constricted around me, pressing my arms against my chest and squeezing the air from my lungs. I was on the verge of blacking out when suddenly the thing's grip loosened. A moment later, it was gone, retreating into the darkness. I fell onto my back. Ilona was leaning over me, holding the lyre in her hand, the glowing key hanging from her neck. Rodric was a few feet behind her. The lyre continued to play.

Still out of breath, I opened my mouth to warn Rodric about the shadow moving toward him from behind, but was unable to make a sound. Rodric had served in the janissaries with me long enough, though, that he could read the warning on my face. He threw me his bow, along with the arrow he had nocked, and then whirled around and dived toward the tentacle, grabbing hold of Vili's ankle before the monster could jerk him away again. Ilona ran toward Rodric as the tentacle lifted him off the bridge. Rodric managed to hook his right foot under the guide rope, snaking his foot around one of the vertical cords to secure the hold. The monster lifted Vili and Rodric, pulling the bridge upward. The deck of the bridge pitched to the side, nearly throwing me over the edge. Ilona lost her footing but grabbed a rope with her free hand. All the while, the lyre continued to play. The bridge had gone taut and Rodric screamed from the strain. As the monster continued to pull Vili upward, I wondered which would give out first: the bridge or the sinews in Rodric's leg.

Ilona crawled up the now steeply-angled bridge toward Rodric, holding the lyre before her. The monster seemed to hesitate, as if torn between its duty as guardian of the bridge and its compulsion to obey the song of the lyre. I managed to wedge myself against the side ropes, still holding Rodric's bow in my right hand and the arrow in the other. I nocked the arrow and drew it almost to the breaking point. I let the arrow go and it plunged into the tentacle a few inches from the tip, where I hoped its hide was thinnest. The tentacle quivered slightly and Vili slipped from the monster's grasp. With the tension on the bridge gone, we fell.

I thrust my arm through Rodric's bow and grabbed onto the guide rope as tightly as I could. I saw Ilona scrambling to get a better hold. Then the bridge went taut again. The guide rope I was holding snapped at the end where we had entered the cavern, and I fell until the rope went taut again. My shoulders were pulled nearly out of their sockets, but I did not fall. I hung over the abyss with the bridge above me.

I felt a jerk as Vili reached the nadir of his fall, and Rodric howled again as Vili's weight as well as his own threatened to pull his leg out of his hip. They were now both hanging upside down, with Vili swinging like a pendulum and Rodric gripping Vili's ankle with both hands. Ilona, by some miracle, had one arm wrapped around the intact guide rope while the other continued to clutch the still-singing lyre.

Rodric was probably close enough to the lyre to be safe from the Szornyeteg, but Vili was not. I looked on helplessly as a tentacle swept toward him. Before it could get a hold on him, though, the other railing snapped, and once again we were falling. We swung until we slammed against a hard wall of rock at the other end. For a moment, I was too dazed to notice that the music had stopped. Had Ilona fallen?

Looking down, I still saw the glow of the key below. Ilona was still there, along with Rodric and Vili, a short distance farther down. But the lyre was gone. For the moment we were all still alive, but we no longer had any protection from the Szornyeteg.

If I were a true sorcerer, I might have had a spell ready to save us, but my facility with magic was limited. I could perhaps summon a kovet to carry us to safety, but there was no time. The Szornyeteg would throw us into the abyss before I could complete the summoning. I could not fake my way through this.

Or could I?

It occurred to me, as I hung there in the near-darkness, waiting to be swept off the wall by the Szornyeteg, that the song with which the lyre had charmed the monster had seemed familiar. It had the same tune as one of the songs Bolond had sung to me when I was in Nincs Varazslat. What if it was not the lyre itself that charmed the monster, but simply the melody? It was certainly worth a try; I had nothing to lose but my dignity.

I took a deep breath and resumed the song, reciting the lyrics as best as I could remember.

"Konrad!" cried Rodric from below. "I can't hold on much longer! You have to do something!"

"Just sing!" I shouted. I became aware of a tentacle moving hesitantly toward me.

"What?"

"Sing!"

"I don't know the words!"

"Just... hum the mel... ody," I sang. "Buy me... a little time."

Rodric began to hum, and Ilona along with him. Vili was too terrified to add much to the chorus. It didn't seem to matter. My plan was working: the creature's tentacles undulated all around us, just out of reach.

I could not, however, sing and summon a kovet at the same time. I would just have to trust that Ilona was close enough to protect me with her singing. I stopped singing and sent my mind to the in-between, summoning a kovet as I had done several times in the past. As the kovet came into being, however, I became aware that one of the tentacles was getting dangerously close. I only needed a few more seconds, but I was not going to make it. The tentacle began to tighten around me. I let go of the rope.

I slipped through the monster's grasp and continued to fall, barely missing Ilona and then continuing to plummet past Rodric and Vili. At the same moment, Rodric lost his grip on Vili, and Vili let out a scream. We fell together in the inky blackness for several seconds, not knowing how far it was to the bottom. Then I hit something soft and spongy, and Vili and I tumbled together like marbles at the bottom of a bag. The kovet, having broken our fall, began to rise like a giant jellyfish. Above us, I saw the dim light of Ilona's key. Ilona had taken over singing, and Rodric hummed uncertainly. He had untangled his leg from the rope and he let himself onto the kovet as it passed. Ilona jumped on as well. Then the four of us, singing and humming, floated up past the forest of tentacles to the far end of the bridge.

We got off onto a small stone shelf that jutted out into the cavern. A few paces away was the opening to another passageway. On either side of it were large iron loops affixed to the stone, from which hung the guide ropes of the bridge, now dangling into the chasm below. The kovet dissolved and I led the way into the passage, keeping up the song until I was certain we were out of the Szornyeteg's reach. As I no longer had a lantern, I allowed Ilona to take the lead, holding the glowing key before her.

"We didn't need the lyre at all," Ilona said. "If your friend Eben had just told us about the song...."

"I doubt Eben knew," I replied. "I don't know where he gets his information, but it's often rather sketchy. I don't think he knows anything about your key, for example. And he is most certainly not my friend."

We followed the passageway as it meandered back and forth, gradually leading us deeper below the city. After perhaps another mile, Ilona suddenly stopped.

"What are you—?" I started.

"Shhh!" she hissed. "What is that?"

We were silent for a moment, listening. From somewhere up ahead came a dull murmur, like the sound of a distant crowd.

"Is that... people?" Rodric asked.

"Sounds like a river to me," Vili replied.

To me, it didn't sound quite like either. Ilona shrugged and proceeded toward the sound. We followed.

It turned out that Vili and Rodric were both right: after another hundred paces or so, the passage came out to another shelf overlooking a cavern even larger than the one in which the Szornyeteg dwelt. It was illuminated by patches of what seemed to be luminescent fungus of dozens of different colors, scattered randomly all over the walls and ceiling. Through the middle of the cavern ran a fast-moving stream, which appeared to have been widened into a shallow pool for about a third of its length. Clustered around the stream were hundreds of stone buildings. The buildings near the stream were squat, single-story affairs, but the buildings grew taller as one neared the perimeter of the roughly circular cavern, forming a rough bowl shape. Just across the stream from us, near the shallow pool, stood a glittering crystal palace whose spires nearly touched the stalactites hanging down from the top of the cavern. The palace seemed to be constructed of quartz or glass, and it refracted the multicolored light from the lichen patches in a million directions. I realized after a moment that some of the light came from within the structure; there seemed to be lamps of some sort inside the palace that illuminated it from the inside and cast a cold glow over the buildings around it.

Across the cavern, perhaps a quarter mile away, we could see that the "buildings" along the perimeter were just caves that had been dug out of the walls. Catwalks ran along the walls at irregular intervals; these were connected to the ground (and often each other) by ladders and stairways. Everywhere one looked, there were people going about their business, building more structures or tearing them down, carrying goods to market, washing clothes, cooking, and performing a hundred other tasks. The cavern was filled with the sounds of blacksmiths hammering, masons chiseling, children playing, and people calling greetings or admonitions to each other. I even saw farmers tending to herds of some sort of subterranean worm-like animals.

"By Turelem's teats," Rodric murmured. "It's an entire city!"

Ilona glared at him and he muttered an apology.

"There must be thousands of people down there!" Vili exclaimed.

"Ten thousand, at least," I said. "An entire city hidden underneath Nagyvaros. It seems that the Builders never left. They just fled underground."

So awed were we by the spectacle that we did not notice we were cornered until it was too late.

"Stop right there, sun-dwellers!" shouted a gruff voice in a barely comprehensible accent, and we turned to see that a half dozen men in finely crafted plate armor had emerged from the tunnel, blocking our way. How they had gotten behind us—to say nothing of how they had managed to sneak up on us while wearing such armor—was a mystery. The man who had spoken, wearing a shoulder crest that marked him as the captain, stood to the side, his palm on the pommel of a short sword, while the others pointed spears at us. Just below each spear tip was a ring of what looked like glass, about three fingers thick, that glowed greenish-yellow, brighter than the lichen hanging overhead but not so bright as a torch. We could see only their faces, which were deathly pale and irises so colorless that they appeared almost white.

We could not retreat without falling a hundred feet or more to the city below. My rapier was lost, and Ilona and Vili were armed only with daggers. Rodric had his bow, but it was strung across his back. We backed toward the edge of the shelf as the men advanced toward us. I'd never summon a kovet in time.

The captain shouted an order in a language I didn't understand, and suddenly the men planted the butts of their spears on the ground and fell to their knees. For a moment, we stood facing them, unable to make sense of the situation.

"Forgive me, Keybearer," the captain said, looking up to Ilona. "I did not know. It would be an honor to escort you to the palace."

CHAPTER NINE

We were escorted back down the passage from which we had come for about fifty paces and then directed through a hidden tunnel that led to a spiral staircase leading downward. We took the staircase all the way to the bottom of the cavern and emerged, sweaty and breathing hard, onto a something like a narrow city street, lined with peculiar stone buildings. Many had no roofs—after all, why bother with a roof in a place where it never rained? Pale-skinned people with big, sunken eyes stared at us as we passed. The clothing they wore was little more than rags, and most of them were bald or nearly so—even the women. Some had thin clumps of hair that could have been white or pale blond, but the strange light made it difficult to tell.

The captain, who called himself Emil, was cordial but refused to answer any but the most basic questions about the city. The name of the place, we learned, was Fold Alatt, and it had indeed been founded by refugees from the battle of Elhalad nearly a thousand years earlier. Originally these caves were easily accessible from the city above, but after the destruction of the Temple of Romok, the upper caves were abandoned and most of the access points deliberately collapsed. Only about a tenth of the population of Elhalad had survived to flee to Fold Alatt; most had been killed in the battle or died within a few weeks, unable to survive on the surface. If Emil knew about those who had been trapped between the two worlds, manifesting as wraiths in the Maganyos Valley, he did not say.

Word had obviously reached the palace before we got there: we were escorted directly through the open gate and into a large hall inside. I saw now that what I had taken to be lamps were in fact globules of the same sort of luminescent material that formed the bands on the guards' spears. These globules hung from silver chains attached to the ceilings of the palace, causing the walls to glitter with a rainbow of colors. Even directly under one of the globules, though, there was not so much light as there is on an overcast day on the surface world. The Builders could not tolerate sunlight, and their descendants had adapted themselves to an existence underground.

The hall was already occupied by some two dozen men and women in fine clothes—at least by the standards of Fold Alatt— who seemed to be eagerly awaiting the start of a ceremony for which they had practiced many times. These people lined the sides of the room; we were directed to stand at the near end of the hall, facing a raised dais on which stood a crystal throne.

We had just taken our places when a herald announced the arrival of King Berrant. A small man wearing a white gown and a silver crown entered the room through a door behind the dais and took a seat on the throne. The man looked to be at least a hundred years old. He was completely bald and his skin was gaunt and so white it seemed almost blue. Everyone in the room fell to their knees, and we followed suit.

The whole ceremony was so bizarre that it was all I could do not to burst out laughing. Next to me, Rodric concealed his chuckle with a cough. Ilona's expression was unreadable; Vili seemed genuinely awed by the spectacle.

"To your feet," the king said after a moment, in a pleasant, gravelly voice, and everyone rose. "Who comes bearing the Key of Bolond?" He spoke Szaszokish in an accent so thick I could barely understand it. I wondered if this was how people spoke a thousand years ago, when Elhalad was still a city. Among themselves, the people of Fold Alatt spoke another language entirely, which I did not recognize.

"Your Highness, I am Ilona, an acolyte of Turelem. My father was the sorcerer Varastis."

"Varastis lives?"

"He was killed six years ago. But he left the key with me. It led me here."

"When Varastis left," the King said, "he told us that if he was unable to return, he would send someone with the key who would fulfill the prophecy of Bolond. Are you the one he spoke of?" The question seemed as much a matter of ceremony than a genuine request for information.

"I... believe I am," Ilona said. Her declaration was met with uncertain murmurs from those assembled.

"Bolond foretold that one would come from the surface world to retrieve the Book of the Dead, and that this person would deliver the Book to those who can use it to save our people. Are you the one of whom he spoke?"

Ilona hesitated.

"I cannot let you have the book unless you are the one foretold of in the prophecy," King Berrant said. It came across as less a threat than a helpful nudge from an indulgent guardian.

"Yes," Ilona proclaimed. "I am she."

Dubious murmurs continued, but Berrant drowned them out with his own proclamation: "Then all is as it should be! You shall be given the Book and our salvation will soon be at hand. Come!" Berrant abruptly stood and motioned to the door behind the dais.

Ilona paused, gesturing toward me.

"Yes, yes, your friends too. Come!" He opened the door and went through. We followed, finding ourselves in a small sitting room. The king removed his crown and tossed it onto a nearby chair. "I apologize for the ceremony," he said. "If I didn't go through the motions, I'd never hear the end of it. This way please."

I glanced at Ilona, who shrugged. We followed Berrant down a narrow hall to a door, which he unlocked with a key from his pocket. We continued through the door, finding ourselves in a cylindrical room about twenty feet in diameter. The entire ceiling glowed faintly, illuminating a bas-relief that covered the entirety of the walls. I realized after a moment that it depicted the destruction of Elhalad and the founding of Fold Alatt. In the center of the room was a pedestal, on which rested a tattered leather book. The book was protected by a dome of such fine crystal that it was nearly invisible. Just under the lip of the dome, on the side of the pedestal facing us, was a small keyhole.

"How long has it been here?" Ilona asked.

"Since Varastis left, twenty years ago," Berrant said. "He came to us bearing a map of the tunnels, which showed passages even we were unaware of. He led us to many hidden treasures, the greatest of which was the Book of the Dead. We believed him to be the one foretold of by Bolond's prophecy, but Varastis said the time had not yet come. He placed it here under an enchantment. If the glass is broken, the room will be filled with fire, destroying the book and the one who seeks it. He said that if he could not return, he would send someone with the key. And here you are."

"Forgive my boldness, Your Highness," Ilona said, "but it seemed to me that you were not entirely convinced I was the one you were waiting for. You haven't even asked why I want the book. We could be treasure hunters who stole the key from its rightful owner."

"What matters," Berrant said, "is that you have the key. You will take the book from this place and we will be rid of it."

"Has it brought you misfortune?"

"Some would say so. I would not. In my opinion, it has brought us nothing. To be perfectly honest, I am not certain I believe the book has any great power. What I do know is that it is not healthy for a civilization to live this way. For a thousand years we have muddled through, living underground like worms. Nothing changes, nothing grows. Our survival is too delicate to allow for innovation, and our environment too limited to allow for population growth. We have no contact with other civilizations, no frontiers to explore. Fold Alatt is in stasis, like a book that cannot be read because it is locked away. Is the Book of the Dead our salvation? Perhaps. Perhaps it is our doom. Perhaps it is nothing. But we cannot go on this way much longer. You will take the book, and perhaps something will change. At the very least, we will have something new to wait for."

Ilona nodded. "I think I understand. Very well, then. Let us open it."

"Wait," said King Berrant. "If the book is our salvation, I will find out eventually, or perhaps I will die first. But if it is nothing but a source of false hope, I think my heart will break. Worse, I will go on living, knowing the book to be a fraud, and I will be forced to lie to my people or pretend that we are saved. Allow me to leave the room before you open the case. I will await you in the sitting room." With that, King Berrant went out, closing the door behind him.

"He is a strange man," Rodric noted.

"This is a strange place," I said. "Let's get this over with. Hopefully this isn't a trap to burn us all alive."

"Ach, I hadn't thought of that," Rodric said.

"You may wait outside as well, if you like," Ilona said.

"No, we remain together as always," Rodric said. Vili and I nodded.

"Do it," I said.

Ilona inserted the key into the keyhole and turned it a half-turn to the right. There was a soft click. Rodric and I stood on either side of the crystal dome, pressed our palms against it, and lifted. The dome came cleanly away, and there was no blast of fire. We set it on the floor and breathed a collective sigh of relief. A faint musty scent filled the air.

Ilona gingerly opened the book to reveal scribbled handwriting covering yellowed parchment. "I cannot read it," she said.

"Nor can I," I said, looking over her shoulder. "I do not even recognize the language."

"I suppose Eben could read it," Rodric said. "Or the sorcerers you call the Masters. If you could get it to them."

"I think I could," I said. "I know now how to shift physically to the shadow world, and I am able to bring clothing and other items with me. It seems to be only metal that I cannot take. I do wish, though, that I could get some idea what was in the book before I entrusted it to someone else."

Ilona had been turning pages while we spoke, and she came to what appeared to be a rough sketch of the layout of a building. The next several pages were filled with more sketches, of the foundation, columns, plinths, arches, and other parts of the structure. I realized that I recognized some of them—not as a

whole, but as individual elements. I had seen some of them
before, strewn about the floor of the Maganyos Valley.

"It is the temple called Romok," I said. "It once stood at the
center of Elhalad, the city on whose ruins Nagyvaros was built. It
was torn down and the ruins dragged to the valley." Vili, who had
been entranced by the bas-relief on the wall, suddenly took an
interest in the book. He walked over to get a better look.

But the next several pages held only text, which we could not
read. As Ilona continued to work her way through the book, she
came to a page entirely filled by a diagram of a naked woman,
with unreadable labels connected by lines to various body parts.
It did not escape my notice that the woman wore her hair in the
style of the acolytes of Turelem.

"That isn't..." Rodric said, obviously thinking the same thing.
He was looking over Ilona's other shoulder.

"A coincidence, I'm sure," Ilona said, although she didn't
sound convinced. She hurriedly turned the page. The writing
remained inscrutable, but the diagrams and illustrations began to
tell a story. What we were looking at was a recipe for
necromancy—the raising of the dead. Eben had been telling the
truth, or at least part of it. With this book, he might be able to
bring Beata back.

"How old is this book?" Rodric asked.

"Hard to say. Presumably Varastis's enchantment preserved it
from decay, but we don't know how it was stored before he
found it. A few hundred years at least, judging from the
yellowing."

"Could it be a thousand years old?"

I realized suddenly what Rodric was thinking.

"I suppose," I said cautiously. "If the drawings on the
preceding pages truly were the blueprints for Romok—and not
merely an attempt at reconstruction—then presumably that
section at least was written before the temple was built, over a
thousand years ago."

"And the Masters said that the book was written by Bolond?"

"That was the implication, yes."

"Then this book could very well be Bolond's notes on his
first attempt at necromancy, before the rise of the Cult of

Turelem. Look here, does the altar on which the body lies not look like the same altar that was sketched earlier in the book?"

"What are you getting at, Rodric?" Ilona asked.

"You saw that first picture of the woman," Rodric said. "The acolytes are said to wear their hair in an imitation of the style favored by Turelem. But if this book was written a thousand years ago, there were no acolytes yet. If the book was hidden down here around the time of Elhalad, then there's only one person that picture could be."

"Be very careful what you say next, Rodric," Ilona said. "I may have my doubts about some aspects of the Cult's teachings, but I will not listen to outright blasphemy."

"Call it what you like," Rodric said. "You know as well as I do who that woman is that Bolond so painstakingly drew—first as a corpse and then, a few pages later, as a live person. Is it not the teaching of the acolytes that Turelem was cast into the Zold and then miraculously returned from the dead?"

"Miraculously!" Ilona cried. "Not through necromancy!"

"What is the difference?" Rodric asked. "You called the hailstorm that saved Delivaros a miracle. Konrad called it magic. To me, they're both just words."

"Words that mean something! Turelem returned from the dead because in her purity, she was able to transcend the bonds of death. She returned to teach the ways of righteousness to others, and so that the world would have proof of her purity! Claiming that a sorcerer brought her back from the dead through magic makes a mockery of our faith!"

"It is not I who mocks your faith, Ilona," Rodric snapped. "It is that book, the meaning of which is clear even though none of us speak the language in which it was written. Your own father— a sorcerer, mind you—led you here. Perhaps this is what he wanted you to discover!"

"No," Ilona said, shaking her head. "It is too much. Why leave me with the Cult if this is what he intended? And why would Bolond wish to resurrect Turelem in any case? It makes no sense. They were enemies!"

"I cannot answer the first question," I said, "although I'll note that it was only your connection with the Cult that allowed us to acquire the Lyre of Dallam. As for the second, it is true that

Bolond and Turelem were enemies at first. But what if Bolond had a change of heart? I thought Bolond insane because he seemed to be playing every side against the others, but what if there is reason in his madness? Eben told me that it was Bolond who trained the first sorcerers. What if he decided that was a mistake, but it was too late for him to stop the propagation of arcane knowledge? Maybe he decided the only way to keep magic under control was to put in motion a countervailing movement?"

"You're suggesting that the Cult of Turelem was founded by Bolond?" Vili asked.

"I'm suggesting it was started by Turelem and her followers, with a lot of help from Bolond."

"You mean raising her from the dead."

"Raising her from the dead and perhaps planting in her mind the idea that she was chosen by the gods to eradicate magic from the land."

"This is absurd!" Ilona cried. "Why would Turelem go along with such a scheme?"

"She may not even have been aware Bolond was behind it," I said. "He appears to be quite adept at manipulating people without their knowledge."

"Has it occurred to you," Ilona snapped, "that he may very well be manipulating you?"

"It has indeed," I replied. "But denying that he has done so to others in the past does not help my situation. I can only hope I figure out what he is up to before he is through with me."

CHAPTER TEN

King Berrant insisted that we stay for dinner to celebrate the impending salvation of the people of Fold Alatt. Nobody told us what this "salvation" was supposed to look like, exactly, and we didn't ask. Did the people expect that we would use the book to make the surface world habitable for them, or perhaps to transport them to Veszedelem, the world from which their ancestors hailed? It was all very unclear, and I got the impression that the various noblemen and functionaries with whom we dined in the palace were not eager to have the matter clarified. Probably they, like the King, had their doubts about the power of the book and were simply glad to be rid of it. Additionally, I suspect many of them wondered whether they would remain at the top of the social strata after the people were "saved."

The cuisine of Fold Alatt left a lot to be desired (specifically flavor, texture and variety), but it was palatable if one didn't think too hard about the various giant insect-like animals we had seen in pens on the way to the palace. I was preoccupied with the concern that with the bridge destroyed, we would have to rely on a kovet to carry us all the way across the cavern—while doing our best to mimic the song of the Lyre of Dallam so that the Szornyeteg wouldn't consume us. Halfway through the dinner I broached the subject with King Berrant, who assured us there was another way to the surface.

Berrant strongly encouraged us to stay the evening, but by the end of the dinner we were more than ready to leave that strange, stifling place. The people of Fold Alatt could never have survived aboveground, and I suppose they had adapted quite a bit over the many generations since the abandonment of Elhalad, but I could certainly sympathize with their desire for something better. Humans are not meant to live that way, stopped up in a bottle.

After dinner, the king led us to another room, near the rear of the palace. The room, whose walls were made of the same translucent crystal as most of the rest of the palace, was lit by a single luminescent globe hanging from the ceiling. In the far wall was an arched doorway, beyond which nothing was visible but blackness.

"That is the way back to the surface," King Berrant said.

"A tunnel straight out of the palace?" I asked.

"Not a tunnel. A magic mirror, created by Bolond himself. It is one of a pair, the other of which is somewhere in the surface world." I walked to the frame and saw that it was not a doorway at all, but rather a mirror hanging on the wall.

"Somewhere?" Rodric asked. "You do not know where?"

"Not precisely. The last we knew, it was in Nagyvaros, but it has been dark for many years. We cannot know for certain where it is without going through, but we dare not risk revealing ourselves to the sun-dwellers. There is no easy way for us to return here."

"You can't just go back through the mirror?" I asked.

"Each pair of mirrors allows travel in only one direction. There used to be two pairs, but the mirror that led here was destroyed after the battle of Elhalad. We suspect the mate of this mirror survives only because those who possess it do not realize what it is."

"How do you know it has not been destroyed?" asked Ilona.

"When one of the other pair was destroyed, the second one shattered as well. The fact that this one is still intact implies that the other survives."

"But it could be in a cave somewhere," Rodric said. "Or buried underground, or at the bottom of the ocean...."

"It could be," the King agreed, "but it is unlikely that someone would dispose of a finely crafted mirror in such a way, and without breaking it. In any case, you are welcome to take your chances with the Szornyeteg."

I shook my head. I wasn't at all certain I could summon a kovet that would last long enough for all of us to get across the abyss; nor was I confident we could charm it again without the help of the lyre. "We go through the mirror," I said. "Whatever is on the other side, the odds are in our favor."

"Ilona, Vili and I should go through," Rodric said. "You should go to the Masters with the book."

"We have not yet decided on that course of action," Ilona said.

"Fine," Rodric said. "Then go to Veszedelem, but return to the Lazy Crow. You said you can do that, right?"

Rodric had a point: I'd figured out how to transport myself to an arbitrary location in Veszedelem, and from there to an arbitrary location in Orszag. It would require a great deal of effort, but essentially, I could shift from Fold Alatt to the Lazy Crow by traveling through the place between worlds. "Theoretically," I said.

"Then you should. The book is too valuable to be allowed to fall into the wrong hands."

"As much as I hate to admit it," Ilona said, "Rodric is correct. If you can, take the book to the Lazy Crow. We will go through the mirror and meet you there when we can."

"No," I said. "I do not know for certain the book will even survive the journey through the in-between. In any case, we are in this together, and you may need my help to get back. We go through together."

Rodric nodded, acknowledging the point. Ilona sighed. "Very well, then. King Berrant, we thank you for your hospitality. I very much hope that we can find a way to use the book to help your people."

"As do I," said the King with a grim smile.

I gave the king a bow, clutched the book to my chest, and stepped into the mirror.

Finding myself in complete darkness, I took a cautious step forward to get out of Ilona's way. She came through a moment later, and suddenly the room was lit with the dazzling glow from the key. We seemed to be in a kind of exhibition hall, filled with statuary and sculpture. The stone walls were covered with paintings and tapestries. The air was cold, still and musty. I took a few steps further into the room to give Rodric and Vili room to come through. Soon our party had been reunited.

"Well, we're not underwater, so that's a relief," Rodric said.

"Where are we, though?" Vili asked.

"Judging from this collection, somewhere in Nagyvaros," I said. I recognized the style of most of the works as dating from the early days of the city's founding. "Either below the Governor's palace or in a private collection somewhere nearby."

"King Berrant said the mirror had been dark for some time," Ilona said. "Perhaps we're in a room under the palace that the Barbaroki and the Torzseki never found."

"We'll find out soon enough," I said. "Stay close." I moved through the forest of statuary toward the door at the far end of the hall, wishing I still had my rapier.

"Wait," said Ilona. "I've got the light. I'll go first."

I reluctantly let Ilona past me to the door. She turned the handle: it was unlocked.

Ilona led the way down a dark passage. We turned a corner to find that the ceiling had caved in. The passage was littered with stone and earth. It didn't seem to be completely blocked; dim light penetrated a small gap near the top of the rubble, and we could hear muted voices in the distance. But there was no way Rodric or I were going to be able to crawl through that space.

"Can you summon one of your shadow things to widen the gap a little?" Rodric asked, peering toward it.

"I could," I said, "but without knowing how far the cave-in goes or what's on the other side, I might make things worse. Kovets don't respond to commands; the best I could do is tell it to push its way through to the other side. It could easily block the way out by accident or even cause another cave-in."

"Also," Ilona added, "we don't know who or what is on the other side. Pushing a few tons of debris out of the way is going to make some noise."

"I can go through," Vili said. "I'll find out what's on the other side and report back."

"That sounds incredibly dangerous," Rodric observed.

"It is," I said. "But it may be our only chance. Vili, that opening looks pretty tight. Are you sure you can do it?"

"I crawled through tighter spaces when I was living under the ruins of Romok."

"What if it collapses on you?" Ilona asked. "Konrad, can you do something to protect him?"

I held up my hands. "My grasp on magic is still pretty limited. I could summon a kovet to try to hold up the ceiling, but I think it would just get in Vili's way."

"I'll be fine," Vili said. He'd already removed his pack and knife. "Just give me a few minutes."

Vili carefully climbed up the pile of rubble then disappeared headfirst into the gap. The space was so small that his body entirely blocked the light from the other side. For some time, all we could see by the light from Ilona's key were the soles of Vili's boots, slowly wriggling away from us. Then he disappeared entirely into the darkness. We waited, holding our breath for another minute, until suddenly light streamed through again.

"Made it," said Vili's voice quietly from the opening. "Nobody on the other side. Going to do some reconnaissance."

Again we waited silently, listening to the murmurs of distant voices. Several minutes later, we heard Vili's voice again.

"We're below the palace."

"Oh, wonderful," Rodric said.

"The good news," Vili continued, "is that the only thing nearby other than storerooms is the kitchen. There were some Torzseki eating in there a moment ago, but they're gone now. I don't think anyone will hear us. The collapsed area is about twenty feet long, and there's another twenty feet or so of clear passage beyond that. If you push a man-sized opening straight ahead, you should be able to get through."

"Good work, Vili," I said. "Back up and I'll try to clear a way through. I'd say to warn us if anyone is coming, but I can't stop the kovet once it gets going. Just stay out of the way and be alert. Rodric and Ilona, you'd better back up as well."

They did as instructed, and I summoned a kovet just large enough to make a man-sized hole in the rubble and infused it with the will to move straight through the hole Vili had crawled through. I had no doubt the thing would have the strength to push aside the stone and earth; my worry was suddenly moving that much rubble would cause another cave-in. Earth rained down as the shadowy creature shoved its way through the opening, but there was no major collapse. The kovet faded and I saw Vili waving from the other side.

I set Vili's pack just inside the opening and then took off my own and placed it just behind his. Then I shoved them both as far as I could reach and climbed in after them. It was tight going, and more earth fell as I crawled, but I made it to the other side. I pushed the packs through and then Vili helped me navigate the rubble as I emerged from the hole. I stepped aside and gave the others the go-ahead. Rodric and then Ilona crawled through without incident, and we were once again reunited.

This part of the passage had a much higher cciling than the part we had just left, and it was dimly lit by small windows far above. Straight ahead about twenty feet, steps led up to a door. Vili went up the steps, opened the door a crack, and then motioned for the rest of us to follow.

We went through the door and found ourselves in a storeroom that seemed to have been mostly emptied of foodstuffs and anything else that it might have contained. Empty shelves lined the walls and the debris from broken barrels lay strewn across the floor. Either the Barbaroki or the Torzseki had cleaned the place out, but evidently none of them had been intrepid enough to dig their way through the rubble to the hidden treasury. I assumed the collapse happened during the battle, but for all I knew the treasury might have been blocked off for years.

The storeroom opened onto the kitchen, which was in almost as much disarray as the storeroom. Clearly Nebjosa was struggling to get his nomadic army to adjust to life indoors. As we were familiar enough with the palace from our previous stay to know the way out, we followed a passage from kitchen to the entry hall. Vili opened the door a crack, peered out, and then closed it again.

"Two guards with halberds at the main door," he said. "They're wearing the uniform of the palace guards, but they look like Torzseki."

"Did they see you?"

Vili shook his head. "They're watching the door."

"Worried about people breaking in, not breaking out," Rodric said.

"Good," I said. "We can make this work for us. Wait here." Before they could protest, I opened the door and went through.

The hall was some forty feet wide and sixty feet long, with a vaulted ceiling and high windows that provided enough light to see where I was going. There were several passages off the side walls and one set of large double doors in the far wall. On either side, facing each other, were men in the uniform of a palace guard, bearing halberds.

They stiffened as I strode toward them. "Who approaches?" the one on the left demanded in a Torzsek accent.

"Do you not know me?" I asked. "I am Konrad, the court sorcerer."

"You are the warlock who was with the Governor the night we took the city," said the one on the right.

"I work for Nebjosa now," I said, now halfway across the hall. "I am on an important mission for the Governor and cannot be delayed."

"I was not told anything about a court sorcerer," said the one on the left. "Stay there while I—"

The man gave an involuntary grunt as all the air left his lungs. He dropped his halberd and fell to his knees. The man on the right ran toward me, but he made it only a few steps before he also fell. The two men writhed on the floor for a few seconds, clutching at their throats, and then were still. I turned and beckoned to Vili, who was peeking out the door at me. He and the others came running toward me.

"They won't be out long," I said, staggering and nearly falling to the floor myself from the effort of casting the spell. "Get their uniforms off and tie them up. We'll have to drag them to the storeroom."

We managed to get them undressed and tied up before they could put up any serious resistance. We had nothing with which to effectively gag them, but fortunately they spent the first minute or so gasping for breath. By the time they had the energy to start shouting, they were locked in the storeroom. Vili and Rodric put on the uniforms (Vili looking rather absurd in his, as both men were significantly larger than he) and we went back out into the hall. Ilona opened the door and we strode into the courtyard, with Ilona leading the way. I feigned having my hands tied while Vili and Rodric walked on either side of me, looking menacing with their halberds. We could only hope that anyone who saw us would assume I was a prisoner who was being turned over to the acolytes by the Torzseki.

The courtyard was empty except for a few more guards, who gave us only a passing glance. We were nearly to the gate when it suddenly opened and the guards stepped aside to let a procession through. I realized, with sudden terror, that it was Nebjosa himself, flanked by half a dozen Torzsek warriors. There was no place to hide, and no chance that Nebjosa wouldn't recognize me. The sun had set and the light was fading, but a score of torches rested in sconces all around the gate. As we came within ten paces, I lowered my face, wishing I knew a spell to get out of this mess. If I'd had the energy, I might have summoned another kovet or shifted outside the gate, but I was exhausted from the spells I'd already cast. I could barely put one foot in front of the other.

"You there, acolyte," said Nebjosa, now standing just inside the gate. "Where are you going with that man?" He knew Ilona was an acolyte from her dress and close-cropped hair, but didn't seem to recognize her.

"This man is a known dabbler in magic," Ilona said, deepening her voice in an attempt to disguise it. "We're transporting him to the city gates, where a cart is waiting to bring him to Nincs Varazslat."

"On whose orders?"

"Davor Sabas's, your excellency."

It was a bold move on Ilona's part; Davor Sabas did not seem to be among Nebjosa's party, and it was not inconceivable that an acolyte would have arrived while Nebjosa was out, to retrieve a prisoner who was being kept in the dungeon below the palace. One look at my face, though, and the ruse would fall apart.

"Who is this man?" Nebjosa demanded, coming closer. "Davor Sabas didn't—"

"Governor Nebjosa!" called a man running across the yard toward him. "News from Delivaros!"

"Yes?" said the governor, irritably. "What is it?"

"The Barbaroki are on the move, Your Excellency. They have regrouped and are heading north."

"Fools! Cowards!" growled Nebjosa. "They leave Nagyvaros to seek weaker prey and then come running back after a little snowfall. Very well, we will be ready for them. Assemble the war council. And find Davor Sabas!" While this discussion was going on, the men with Nebjosa clustered around him, shoving Ilona and the rest of our party out of the way. Ilona took advantage of the situation to quietly lead us closer to the gate. The chief glanced around as if he had forgotten something, shook his head, and then hurried toward the palace, trailed by his retinue. I let out a sigh of relief.

Ilona strode boldly toward the gate, which had not yet been closed.

"Hold on," said the guard nearest the gate. "Who are you? Where are you going?"

"You must be joking," Ilona snapped angrily. "Did you not just hear my conversation with the Governor?"

"It is not my custom to eavesdrop on the Governor's conversations."

"I'm an acolyte of Turelem," Ilona said irritably, as if this were the hundredth time she'd had to say it today. "This man is a prisoner. We are escorting him to the city gate where a cart waits to take him to Nincs Varazslat. How many more times am I going to have to go through this? I heard that the Torzseki were doing a poor job of running this city, but I had no idea it was this bad. What is your name, young man? I will be sure to include it in my report to the Council."

"You don't need my name," said the guard cautiously. "But I will need to verify with my superiors that you have authorization to take this man out of the palace."

"Governor Nebjosa just gave me authorization, not two minutes ago, right in front of you. Are you deaf? In case you are, let me fill you in: the Barbaroki are returning to attack Nagyvaros, and Nebjosa just called an emergency meeting of his war council to address the threat. But if you really want me to call him back to have him repeat *what he just said....*" Ilona turned and cupped her hands over her mouth as if to shout to Nebjosa, who was about to disappear into the palace.

"No, no," said the man hurriedly. "It's all right. Just go."

Ilona nodded curtly to the man and then continued walking out the gate. "Hurry up, you two!" she snapped. "We were supposed to be on the road before dark!" We hurried after her. The gate closed behind us and we made our way across the city to the Lazy Crow.

CHAPTER ELEVEN

The next morning, Rodric rudely shook me awake. "Konrad!" he said, "Wake up! Something is wrong!"

I waved him off and sat up slowly, still tired from the previous day's adventure. It was dark outside. "What is it?"

"Vili is gone," Rodric said.

I groaned and flopped back into bed. "He probably couldn't sleep and got up to skulk around the way he does. Maybe he'll steal us some breakfast."

"I don't think so," Rodric said. "Look." He pointed to my pack, which lay on the floor beside my bed. In my sleep-addled state, it took me a moment to realize what he was telling me. I had placed the Book of the Dead on top of my pack before going to sleep.

I sat up again. "He took the book?"

"It seems that way."

"What for?"

Rodric shrugged. "Nothing good, I'm afraid."

"Have you spoken to Ilona?"

"Not yet."

"Come." I got out of bed and got dressed, and we went across the hall and knocked on Ilona's door. She was no happier to be wakened than I was.

"Vili is gone," I told her. "He has taken the book."

"What?" Ilona cried, backing away from the door to let us in. "Why would he do that? Has he been working against us this entire time?"

We entered the room and I closed the door. "No," I said. "Of that I am certain. But… I am afraid this may be my fault."

Rodric met my gaze, knowing what I was thinking. He shook his head tiredly.

"Your fault?" Ilona asked. "How?"

"I lied to Vili," I said. "I felt I had no choice at the time, but there is no putting a pretty face on it. I swore to him that I would see that his parents were at peace, but I failed. They are trapped in a sort of vortex between our world and Veszedelem. I still intend to find a way to free them, but I didn't think Vili could bear knowing that they suffer. I thought he needed to hear they were at peace. Or perhaps I simply did not want him to know I had failed. I see now that I was wrong."

"This is only your guilt getting the better of you," Rodric said. "Perhaps you made a mistake, but how could Vili have found out? And what possible use does he have for the book?"

"I do not know. Some clue he came across in Fold Alatt? He was examining that fresco pretty closely. As for why he did it, maybe he hopes to find someone who can use it to bring his parents back."

"Where would he take it?" Ilona asked.

"I have no idea," I said. "Only a sorcerer would know what to do with the book. Vili cannot reach Eben. Bolond is in the wind. Varastis and Domokos are dead."

"You don't think he intends to destroy it?" Rodric asked. "Just to spite you?"

"No. He will preserve the book as long as he believes there is a chance it will help his parents."

"Then what do we do?" Ilona asked.

"I don't see that there's much we can do," Rodric said, "other than wait here and hope he returns."

"There is one thing I can do," I said. "I only hope it is not too late."

*****

I sat on my bed and sent my mind once again to the courtyard of Sotetseg, the mysterious keep on the plain of

Veszedelem. I went down to the passage where I generally met Eben and rang the bell he had left there. After several minutes, I rang it again. I waited for an hour—as time is reckoned in Veszedelem; less than a minute passed in Orszag—but Eben did not come. I considered exploring the passages under Sotetseg in an attempt to find him, but I suspected this would be for naught. I returned to the courtyard, which remained deserted. "Amira!" I called. "It is I, Konrad." I hoped I was not overheard by one of the servants of Eben, although I am not certain how much difference it would have made at that point.

A small demon, with leathery wings and the stumps of horns on its head, shot overhead and then landed with a thump behind me. I turned to face it, expecting a fight, but the thing simply beckoned to me and then trotted off across the courtyard.

I followed it through a doorway and up a steep, narrow flight of stairs. At the end of a long corridor, it opened a door with a key and then stood aside for me to enter a room lit by a single lamp resting on a small table against the right-hand wall. Directly ahead was doorway into another room of similar size. There was something slightly off about the doorway, and I was trying to figure out what it was exactly when the door closed behind me. The imp was gone. I tried the door, but found it was locked. I cursed and turned back to the only other way out of the room.

But as I approached, I realized it was not a way out at all: what I had taken in the dim light to be a doorway was in fact a very detailed painting. I couldn't help laughing: why would someone go to the trouble of painting a picture of an empty room? The painting had no subject, to speak of. It seemed to be a mirror image of the room I was in, down to the single door and the table with the lamp. The only thing missing was the confused and frustrated man standing in the middle.

Was the painting a magical artifact, like the mirror in the crystal palace of Fold Alatt? I put my hand to the canvas but found it to be solid. Perhaps I needed to demonstrate more commitment. I closed my eyes and attempted to walk through to the other side, but succeeded only in smacking my forehead against the wall.

"I give up!" I shouted to no one in particular. I received no answer. I supposed the Masters were watching me even now, wondering if I would solve the riddle. Or perhaps there was no riddle, and this was only a waiting room. If so, how long would I have to wait? And why hadn't the imp told me what I was to do? The so-called Masters were toying with me, and I didn't like it.

"I don't have time for these games!" I shouted. "I have retrieved your book. If you want it, let me out of this room or I'll…." I trailed off. I was about to threaten to return to Orszag (an idle threat in any case, as there was no way I could find Vili without the Masters' help), but it occurred to me that I could just as easily transport myself to somewhere else in the keep. I had found that I could travel anywhere in Veszedelem I had been before; all I had to do is focus on that location and project my mind to that place.

But did that imply that I could only project to places I'd already been? Could I not also go to places that I'd only *seen*? I regarded the picture again. It was a near-perfect rendering of the room I was in, but it was reversed, like a mirror. And as I looked more closely, I saw another subtle difference: the door through which I had entered was marked with a symbol, a circle with a horizontal line over it. The door in the painting was marked with a different symbol: two vertical lines. I didn't have any idea what either of the symbols meant, but I deduced one thing: although the painting was a close rendering, it did not actually represent the room I was in. It was a painting of a different room entirely.

There was only one rationale I could imagine for creating such a painting and hanging it where it hung: the painting was a doorway, of sorts. Not a magical doorway, but a doorway that could only be accessed via magic. The painting depicted another room, nearly identical to this one, somewhere in the palace— perhaps directly on the other side of the wall. Of course: when the Masters had sealed themselves up in a secret part of the keep, they would have made sure access was limited—at the very least—to those capable of magic. The painting served the same purpose as the handprint on the outside of the guardhouse. The imp hadn't given me instructions because the answer was supposed to be obvious to me. I was embarrassed it had taken me so long to figure it out.

I examined the painting carefully for nearly a minute and then closed my eyes, picturing the room before me. I willed myself into the room and then opened my eyes to find myself staring at exactly the scene I had just been observing—with one subtle difference: the symbol on the door had changed. I turned to find myself facing the door with the two vertical lines on it. I smiled, took a few steps forward, and opened the door.

The door opened to another corridor, which extended to my left and to my right. Standing just to my left was another of the imp creatures. It regarded my face and then scampered down the passage to the left. I followed.

As I rounded the corner, I heard voices speaking in the distance. A series of torches lit the way to a door perhaps a hundred feet away. I continued down the hall until I came to the door. From the other side came voices and other faint, unrecognizable sounds. The imp opened the door and stepped aside for me to enter.

I walked into what appeared to be a vast laboratory, lighted by glowing orbs similar to—but much brighter than—those that had hung in the palace of Fold Alatt. The place was filled with wooden benches covered with flasks, mortars and pestles, phials, cannisters and other containers, as well as oil lamps, tongs, pliers, bellows, a dozen other sorts of tools and devices I couldn't identify, and many books and scraps of parchment. At the far end of the room was a great open oven. The place was buzzing with a score or more of the little imps. In the center of the room, engaged in an animated discussion, were three people: two men and a woman.

The room was warm and somewhat stuffy, and their clothing reflected this: the woman, who looked to be about sixty, wore a skirt and a blouse with no sleeves; the two men wore trousers and shirts with the sleeves rolled up. One of the men was very tall and thin, with a close-cropped white beard; the other was short and squat, with rosy cheeks. The thin man looked somewhat older than the woman, but the fat man seemed a bit younger. The imps, who were engaged in a variety of tasks—grinding dried pastes into powder, mixing various fluids together, heating pots over an open flame, blowing glass at the oven, and the like—were making so much noise that I couldn't make out much of the conversation. The three seemed to be the only ones talking; the imps appeared to be mute, or at least ill-disposed toward speaking.

As I approached, the tall man noticed me. He put his fingers to his lips and then gestured toward me.

"Konrad!" the woman said, turning to face me, and I knew immediately from her manner that she was Amira, who had come to me in the form of Beata. "It is good that you have come. We are running out of time. These are my comrades, Foli and Parello. Foli is the one who looks like he's eaten all of Parello's lunches. Have you had any success in your quest?"

The two men greeted me and I gave them each a cordial nod. So these were the so-called "Masters" of Sotetseg, who had sealed themselves off in a secret part of the keep when Bolond fled.

"Some," I said. "But there has been a complication."

Amira frowned. "What do you mean?"

"One of my party, a boy named Vili, has disappeared, taking the book with him. His parents were among those consumed by the wraiths of Romok. I believe he hopes to use the book to save them, or at least to see them relieved of their torment."

"This Vili is a sorcerer?" Foli asked.

"No, although I believe his mother may have been. It was she who told me how to defeat the wraiths, by trapping them in an infinite loop between Orszag and Veszedelem."

"What are his parents' names?" Amira asked.

"Arron and Haneen."

Amira shook her head. "I do not know them."

"How can he hope to use the book if he is not a sorcerer?" Parello asked.

"I do not know," I said. "Nor do I know how he could have learned that his parents were trapped in between the worlds with the souls of those who once escaped Elhalad."

"This is very troubling," Amira said. "Arnyek has been mobilizing his forces. We believe he plans to attack Sotetseg soon, and this time he may very well have the strength to defeat us. As you can see, we are hard at work on an artifact we hope to use to bind Arnyek, but the final steps are beyond our ken. We had hoped the Book of the Dead held the answers. Time moves much more quickly here, as you know. If you do not get the book back soon, Sotetseg is doomed. If Arnyek defeats us, he will be unstoppable. He will destroy Veszedelem and your world along with it."

"I realize this," I said. "Unfortunately, I am as much in the dark about Vili's plans as you are. If he were in contact with Eben or some other sorcerer, we would know it."

"Would you?" Amira asked. "When did Vili disappear?"

"This morning, before the rest of us awoke."

"And he showed no signs of disloyalty before this?"

"None."

The tall man, Parello, put his fingertips together. "This suggests something happened during the night to cause Vili's loyalties to waver." Amira nodded.

My heart sank. Of course. I was getting tired of always being one step behind. "You think Eben came to Vili in his dreams, as you did to me?"

"It is one possibility," Amira said. "If Vili's mother was a sorcerer, Vili may well have enough tvari in his blood to be able to receive a message while he dreams. If Eben knew you lied to Vili and decided to use that information to turn Vili against you...."

"I am a fool," I said. "I was so concerned with getting the book that I let my guard down against Eben. But... is he not still in Sotetseg? How is it that he can still plot freely while the three of you are here?" It was a question that had occurred to me often over the past few weeks.

"Our priority has been dealing with Arnyek," Amira said.

"In any case," Foli added sourly, "our influence is limited outside this enclave. A few imps outside still do our bidding, and we do our best to stay informed on Eben's activities, but you cannot expect us to know when he projects himself into a boy's dreams!"

"But if the threat from Arnyek is as great as you say," I said, "why does Eben not ally with you, at least temporarily? If Arnyek destroys Sotetseg, it will doom Eben's plan as well."

"We have made overtures to him," Amira said. "He does not respond."

"Does he think he and the demons in his employ can hold Sotetseg against Arnyek?"

"Doubtful," said Amira. "I can only assume he plans to leave Sotetseg before the attack."

"Leave and go where?"

"I do not know. There is nowhere in Veszedelem where he would be safe from the monsters that roam this world, and although I am certain he still plots to return somehow to your world, I assume that if he had the power to do so, he would have done it by now."

"Perhaps the book holds the secret," I said. "A way for Eben to return to Orszag."

"Perhaps," Foli said, "but Eben does not have the book. If he can speak to Vili at all, it would be in brief exchanges like the one you had with Amira. Vili could hardly communicate to him the contents of a book written in a language he cannot read."

"Even if Eben did find a way to leave Sotetseg, he would not be safe from Arnyek," Parello said. "With us out of the way, there will be nothing to stop Arnyek from laying waste to all of reality."

"Then Eben must be planning to face Arnyek at some later time, when he is more powerful."

"Or he has accepted that Arnyek will ultimately win," Foli said.

"I don't believe it," I said. "What Eben wants more than anything is power. But all his power means nothing if a bigger bully can come along and wipe the slate clean. Eben plans to take on Arnyek, but perhaps not yet."

"Whatever he is planning," Amira said, "it clearly involves the Book of the Dead. But the book is useless unless it is in the hands of someone who can make sense of it. Vili cannot bring the book to Eben. We are missing something. Did you look at the book?"

"Yes, but I could not read it either. There were sketches that appeared to be plans for the Temple of Romok, and others that suggested the temple may have been used for necromancy."

Amira nodded. "It is as we suspected, then. The secrets of necromancy hold the key to the binding of Arnyek. We must have the book to defeat him."

"Eben promised to use the book to bring my beloved, Beata, back from the dead," I said. "But the resurrection depicted in the book seemed to occur at the Temple of Romok. Is it possible that Eben intended to use the book to rebuild the temple?"

"Rebuild the temple?" Foli said. "Impossible. Even if Eben had the book and could interpret it correctly, and even if he commanded the hundreds of laborers it would require, the Cult of Turelem would never allow it. Their entire purpose is to rid Orszag of magic, and they are far stronger than when the temple was destroyed. We have heard of their victory over the Barbaroki, and that will only embolden them more."

An uneasy feeling came over me. "What if the Council was forced to choose between allowing the temple to be built and allowing the Cult to be destroyed?"

"The Cult destroyed?" Parello asked. "How?"

"I will explain," I said. "But first, I must ask you a question. Does the Cult itself employ magic while working to rid Orszag of sorcery?"

"Such rumors have plagued the Cult from the beginning," Amira said, "although they have been largely suppressed under the guise of persecuting blasphemy. Indeed, it sometimes seems the Cult works harder at protecting their reputation than at expunging sorcery. That said, we have never been able to determine for certain whether the Council secretly uses magic. If they do, it is of a type with which we are not familiar. And in the end, the question is somewhat semantic. Was that hailstorm sorcery or a miracle? It depends on your definitions of such things."

I nodded, expecting as much. "I have some reason to think the Cult has been deliberately obfuscating that distinction from the beginning. The subject of the necromantic ritual depicted in the book appeared to be Turelem herself."

The three exchanged glances as if I'd voiced something that they'd each secretly suspected but had never spoken of to the others.

"It is possible," Amira said. "But what of it? What does this have to do with Eben's plans?"

"Suppose Eben had Vili hide the book somewhere safe and then travel to Delivaros to approach the Council, threatening to reveal the truth of Turelem's resurrection."

"Blackmail," Foli said. "The Cult allows the temple to be rebuilt and Vili keeps their secret. Would your friend really do this?"

"I confess I find it hard to believe," I said. "I didn't think Vili had a devious bone in his body. He is, if anything, excessively loyal."

"But perhaps he is more loyal to his parents than to you," Amira said.

"In any case," Parello said, "the new Governor of Nagyvaros would never allow the temple to be rebuilt. It would undermine his authority in the city."

"I don't believe there is any reason the temple would have to be rebuilt in its original location," Amira said. "We have seen that it retained much of its power, even scattered across the floor the Maganyos Valley."

"There remains the problem of organizing a force of laborers to rebuild it," Foli said. "And wherever Vili's loyalties lie, he lacks the expertise to coordinate such a project, even if he were being advised by Eben."

"There is too much we do not know," I admitted. "But if there is anything to my suspicions, then Vili is probably already on his way to Delivaros. Perhaps we can catch him before it is too late."

"You must hurry," Amira said. "We believe Arnyek will begin his march across the plain within the next few months. That gives you only a day or two as time is reckoned in your world."

I nodded grimly. "I will do what I can."

CHAPTER TWELVE

We ate a quick breakfast and then headed to the stable with the intention of riding again toward Delivaros. My best guess was that Vili had gone there at Eben's bidding to blackmail the Reverend Mother into letting Eben rebuild the Temple of Romok. We didn't know when Vili had left, but he couldn't be far ahead of us. His pony was missing from the stable, lending credence to my suspicion about his plans.

Unfortunately, there was no traffic at the gate when we reached it, and we didn't have time to wait for a caravan to camouflage us. It isn't easy to remain unnoticed when one's face is covered by a black brand, and the Torzsek guards had obviously been instructed to be on the lookout for me. There were ten of them manning the gate, and while we might have fought our way out, I was loath to make an overt enemy of Nebjosa. If Eben intended to use Vili to exert influence over the Cult, we might very well need Nebjosa as an ally. I reluctantly ordered Rodric and Ilona to lower their weapons. We dismounted and allowed ourselves to be escorted to the Governor's palace. We were brought to a sitting room where Nebjosa waited for us.

"How did you get into the Palace yesterday?" Nebjosa asked. He had evidently figured out it was we who had slipped past him at the palace gate the previous evening.

"A sorcerer can be very persuasive," I said.

"You wish me to believe you persuaded my guards to let you in? For what purpose?"

"We were investigating a threat to Nagyvaros," I said, somewhat truthfully.

"What threat? Why did you deceive me as you left?"

"A warlock named Eben plots against the city. We believed there was someone in the dungeon with information that would allow us to defeat him, but we were mistaken. We concealed our identities as we left because we did not expect you to believe us."

"You speak the truth on the last point, at least," Nebjosa muttered. "I do not believe you. What I think is that you found an entrance into the tunnels below the city, intending to loot unexplored passages for treasures that rightly belong to me."

I shrugged. "I am not your enemy, Nebjosa. We have fought together against the evil that encroaches on this land, and we may very well need to do so again. If I do not tell you of all my plans, it is only because doing so would be to neither of our benefit."

"In that case, I suppose I should consider myself quite fortunate to have a powerful sorcerer such as you on my side. And yet, you allowed yourself to be brought to my palace by a handful of men armed only with spears and halberds, which leads me to believe that either you are not as powerful as you would like me to think, or that you need me at least as much as I need you. The fact is, Konrad, you are like a wild tiger roaming free within my territory. I cannot predict your next move, and you are as likely to harm me as you are my enemies. So tell me, why should I not have you thrown into the dungeon below the palace, so that I can at least keep my eyes on you?"

It was admittedly a good question. It's what I would have done if I were in Nebjosa's position. "You once offered me the post of court sorcerer," I said, "and while I am not ready to accept such a position at present, I would like to propose a partnership. You have many enemies, some of which you are not even aware. I can help you against them."

"The only enemy I have time to worry about right now are the Barbaroki."

"If you fear the Barbaroki, how much more do you fear those whom the Barbaroki fear?"

"The Barbaroki are superstitious fools, running from a hailstorm."

"That hailstorm was no coincidence. The Barbaroki were right to fear."

"You suggest the Council has the power to control the weather? Absurd."

"And yet, the Barbaroki are on the run, and Delivaros has been spared. It would be one thing if Delivaros were content with its status as an adjunct power to Nagyvaros, but they are now emboldened—both by their victory over the Barbaroki and by the disordered state in which Nagyvaros finds itself. I know you are doing the best you can under the circumstances, but your defenses are weak and your rule is tenuous."

"Delivaros would never attempt an attack on Nagyvaros."

"Not a direct assault, no. But they will try to undermine your power in other ways. Eben intends to rebuild the Temple of Romok, and when he does, neither you nor the Cult will be able to contain him."

"What evidence do you have of any of this?"

It was clear that Nebjosa was not going to let us go without some sign of goodwill. As my lie to Vili had gotten us into this situation, I decided to gamble on telling him the truth. "You asked what we were doing inside the palace," I said. "We were returning from an expedition under the city to retrieve an ancient tome called the Book of the Dead."

"Then you did lie to me."

"Yes, and I apologize. I did so because our mission is too important to be delayed by concerns over looted treasure. The book has little value except to those who can read it and have the power to make use of its teachings."

"Where is this book now?"

"One of my comrades, the boy, Vili, absconded with it. I believe he has been duped by the sorcerer, Eben."

"Your protégé has turned against you?"

"Vili's parents are being held captive in a place between our world and the shadow world. I believe Eben has convinced Vili that with the book he can free them."

"Where you found this book, were there other treasures?"

"I supposed it depends on what you consider a treasure, but it does not matter now. To reach the place where the book was hidden, we had to cross a vast chasm guarded by a terrible monster, much more powerful than even Voros Korom. We were able to cross the bridge only because we possessed an enchanted lyre that charmed the creature. The bridge is now gone and the lyre is lost. Whatever treasure may have been hidden along with the book, it is now out of our reach—and yours."

"Then how did you return?"

"By way of a pair of enchanted mirrors, one of which is in a treasury reachable via the collapsed passageway behind the kitchen. But the mirrors only work one direction. You cannot get to the ancient tunnels through the one in the treasury."

"How do you know of these things? Of this book and the way to reach it?"

"The important thing is that I know. It is your business to know the movements of the Barbaroki. It is mine to know the ways of sorcery."

Nebjosa waved his hand irritably. "If you had told me of your intention, I could have sent men to assist you."

"I could not risk the chance that you would forbid the expedition outright. In any case, your men would have been of no use and they would not have returned with any more treasure, assuming they returned at all."

"Why would this Eben rebuild the temple?"

"I do not know, precisely. It is part of some greater plan of his that is certain to include ruling Nagyvaros. You have seen the evil that lurked in the ruins of the temple. When it is rebuilt, I fear that evil will be increased a thousandfold."

"And how do you intend to stop this?"

"The temple cannot be rebuilt without the tacit blessing of Delivaros. I believe Vili has gone there on behalf of Eben to persuade the Reverend Mother to grant her blessing. My comrades and I would go there in an attempt to convince the Council that doing so would be shortsighted."

"How do I know that it is not you who is the true threat to my rule?"

"You do not. You know only that I have fought with you in the past and have never deceived you, save this one time, out of expediency and not malice."

"So you say," Nebjosa said tiredly. "Very well. Go to the Council and attempt to dissuade them of this foolishness. Tell them I am opposed to rebuilding Romok if it will do any good. When you are done, return here immediately and report back to me."

"That I will do, Governor," I said, with a slight bow. "Thank you."

"Fetch their horses," Nebjosa said to a nearby man-at-arms. "See that they are escorted to the southern gate."

CHAPTER THIRTEEN

Back in Nebjosa's good graces for the moment, we once again made our way south. We were now several hours behind Vili, and I doubted we would catch him. By the time we reached Delivaros, he would most likely already have met with the Reverend Mother. We would have to request an audience with her in the hopes that we could persuade her not to go along with Eben's plan, and possibly get some clue as to where Vili was headed next.

The journey took six days, and we had seen no sign of Vili by the time we reached the bridge leading to the northern gate of Delivaros. Fortunately, neither did we meet any Barbaroki. If they were on their way back to Nagyvaros, they were not taking this road. We asked several travelers that we passed along the way, but no one admitted to having seen a boy on a pony traveling toward Delivaros on his own. I began to wonder if I'd been wrong in my suspicions. But where else might Vili have gone? There was nothing to do but go to Regi Otthon and request an audience with the Reverend Mother.

We decided it would be better if I did not attempt to enter the city. As far as the Cult was concerned, I was Eben the Warlock, and although I'd been pardoned of the crime of sorcery, a lot had happened since I left Nincs Varazslat. It was quite probable word had reached the Council of some of my recent adventures. And if Vili really had turned against us, I couldn't dismiss the possibility that he would warn them of my coming. Ilona vouching for me might count for something, but she hadn't left Delivaros on the best terms, and I couldn't count on my nebulous association with Nebjosa to be of much help.

I made camp in a clearing in the woods a mile south of the bridge while Rodric and Ilona continued to across the bridge to the gate. It was just before noon on the third day of our journey from Nagyvaros. I ate some bread and cold meat and then sent my spirit to Veszedelem to see if I could contact Eben. Again, he did not respond to my attempts to summon him. I returned to the courtyard and called for Amira.

After a moment, the imp—or another one, perhaps; who could say?—appeared and escorted me again to the room with the painting. I noticed that the painting had been altered slightly, or perhaps replaced with another, almost identical painting: the two vertical marks on the door had now been replaced by a different symbol, two interlocking circles. It seemed an odd thing to do until I reflected on it a moment: I could not shift to the room on the other side of the wall without visualizing the room, and I could not visualize the room unless I knew which symbol was displayed on the painting in *this* room. It was a security measure preventing someone from memorizing the appearance of the hidden room and then transporting oneself there from somewhere else. So even if a sorcerer—Eben, for example—had been to the hidden room in the past, he could not shift there without first traveling to the room I was currently in. Not only that, but neither could he shift to this room, because he would have to know which symbol was displayed here as well. In other words, the only way into the secret part of the keep was through the front door, which was undoubtedly under observation from one or more of the imps, who would report any unauthorized intrusion to the Masters.

I did not know what would have happened if I had tried to transport myself to the hidden room using the wrong symbol. Perhaps I would simply have failed; perhaps I would have found myself lost forever in the in-between. The more I learned of sorcery, the more amazed I was that I had not yet gotten myself killed or trapped forever between worlds.

I focused on the room as depicted in the painting, sending my mind there. I opened my eyes to find myself in the room beyond the wall. Exiting into the hall, I was greeted by another imp and was taken to the laboratory to see Amira and the other Masters of Sotetseg. As before, they and their servants were busy with their project of stopping Arnyek, poring over ancient manuscripts and laboring over various potions and concoctions. They were very pleased to see me until I reported that I'd made no progress in retrieving the book, at which point they excused themselves and went back to work. I observed the work for some time, asking occasional questions, but the answers I received were curt and difficult to decipher. I knew only that they were working on a way of binding Arnyek.

Arnyek's plan, it seemed, was to bring about the destruction of Veszedelem and every other world with it. Somehow, even from within Sotetseg, the Masters were able to prevent him from bringing this project to fruition. To achieve his goal, Arnyek needed to penetrate Sotetseg and kill the Masters. Arnyek had been amassing his army for hundreds of years and was now almost ready to attack. The only way the Masters stood a chance against him was if they completed the talisman before the attack.

Several weeks had passed since my last visit, and time was growing short. Without the knowledge in the Book of the Dead, it was unlikely they would succeed in time. Arnyek's army had fully mobilized and might begin its march across the plain any day now.

I was about to leave when Amira, seeing my frustration, pulled me aside. "You must forgive us for our poor hospitality," she said. "We have at best a few weeks before Arnyek comes, and the most vital enchantment of the talisman remains a mystery to us."

"I understand," I said. "I wish I could be of more help, but although I've been told my brand carries great power, my knowledge of the arcane remains minimal."

"That is what I wished to speak to you about. If you intend to face Eben, you must deepen your knowledge. If our situation were less dire, I might train you myself, but there is something else I can offer that is perhaps nearly as good. Come."

She walked to a door in the far wall of the laboratory and I followed. Going through the door, we found ourselves in a smaller room lined with shelves on which rested hundreds of books. Many of them were so old they were practically falling apart.

"These volumes contain much of the arcane knowledge possessed by me and my fellows. You will not be able to read most of them, as they are written in long-dead languages, but there are several glosses and summaries on this shelf written in Eszeki that may be of use to you. You can read Eszeki, yes?"

"Indeed. And Prendish and Keleti as well," I said, examining some of the titles on the shelf Amira had indicated. "I studied a great deal of history and other topics while in the janissaries."

"Excellent. Then I will leave you to it. I gather you have some time while your friends are in Delivaros?" I had told Amira about Ilona and Rodric going to seek an audience with the Council.

I nodded. "They will be gone for several hours, at least. I may have a week or more, as time is reckoned here."

"Stay as long as you like, but beware that being in Veszedelem will drain your strength. If you spend more than a few hours here at a time, you may find yourself too weak to return. If that happens, your soul will become irrevocably separated from your body. Your physical form in Orszag will perish, and then your spirit will evaporate as well."

"What if I travel here physically?"

Amira stared at me. "You are capable of this?"

"I learned how by accident, while fighting the demon prince, Voros Korom. It's a matter of using tvari to pull my body through the opening between worlds. But you must have known this. How would I bring you the Book of the Dead if I were not able to bring physical matter to Veszedelem? Or would I be able to bring the book as I seem to bring my clothing with me, although I am not here physically?"

"We knew you possessed the power but assumed we would have to teach you how to use it. To answer your second question: your clothing is here as an extension of your spirit. It is not truly in Veszedelem any more than your body is. Have you noticed you are unable to take anything more substantial than garments with you?"

"I noticed my rapier and pack stayed behind, yes. But this was true even when I came here physically."

"The more substantial something is, the more difficult it is to carry it between worlds. It is possible to take the book from your world to ours, but doing so would require substantially more effort than bringing your clothing."

"I am sorry, I still do not understand. Could I not bring the 'spirit' of the book just as I bring the 'spirit' of my clothing?"

"You could, in theory, but a book—particularly a book like this one—has a substance all its own. A shirt is just a shirt, and if you look carefully you will notice that you have not in fact brought your shirt with you, but rather a sort of vague idea of that shirt."

Examining my clothing, I saw that it was true. My shirt in Orszag had a small patch on the elbow, where I'd had to repair it after our battle with Voros Korom at Magas Komaron, but this one had no patch. In fact, it was strangely lacking in features and texture, as if it had been constructed of some diaphanous material by someone who had only seen a crude drawing of the object.

"Now suppose you brought the Book of the Dead over in the same fashion," Amira said. "Unless you had spent many hours memorizing the form and contents of the book with great precision, you would find what you brought with you was not the Book of the Dead, but a shoddy representation of it, probably filled with blank pages or meaningless scribbles. You would have a vague idea of the book, but it would lack the book's substance."

"It is easier, then, to bring the book physically than spiritually?"

"For you, yes. For most sorcerers, the former would be impossible. Very few sorcerers have ever been capable of physically moving matter between worlds. Bolond is the only one I know of. Even Eben could do it only when he possessed the brand. It gives you great power."

"How is it, though, that it feels as if I were here physically, even when my body remains in Orszag? Why do I need a physical body in Orszag but not here?"

Amira sighed. "I wish I had time to explain all of this to you. What you must understand is that your world, Orszag, has more of what you might call *realness* than Veszedelem. As a result, something that seems completely solid in Veszedelem manifests itself in your world only as a specter."

"Like the wraiths of Romok."

"Yes. The wraiths traveled through a vortex between two worlds. At the end of the vortex touching Veszedelem, they appeared as flesh-and-blood beings, but in Orszag they were only ghostly apparitions. The converse of this is that a being that would be no more than a ghost in your world appears to be flesh-and-blood in ours. So when you come here in spirit, as you have now, you seem as real and solid as Foli, Parello or I. You could bring your body through as well, of course, but it is unnecessary. I can perceive that you are here only in spirit because I am attuned to such things, but for all practical purposes, you are 'here' either way. In a sense, you have an advantage over us. You can travel to our world, but we cannot travel to yours except in a very evanescent way. On the rare occasion that we do so, usually we cannot be seen, except by certain people, when their minds are amenable to it."

"As you came to me in my dream."

"Yes. Sometimes too we can use these individuals to observe what is happening in your world, to a very limited extent. With some effort, we can see through their eyes and hear through their ears, as it were. That is how we have some idea of the events in your world."

"Then there are more sorcerers? More people like me?"

"Very few sorcerers, and none like you. Most trained sorcerers learn early on to guard their minds against such intrusions. I am speaking of individuals who for some reason have greater-than-usual amounts of tvari in their blood. Usually not enough for them to become a sorcerer, even if they had the training. Most often they are not even aware of their own sensitivity. Perhaps one in ten thousand people has enough tvari that we can use them in this way. And we rarely do it, because it is quite taxing." She smiled. "Fortunately, time moves so slowly in your world that we don't miss much of importance."

"Then what of the dwellers of Fold Alatt? They seemed real enough. Are they not descendants of people from Veszedelem?"

"Indeed they are. Their ancestors, the original settlers of Elhalad, could not have survived in Orszag at all if it weren't for the dampening effect of the Temple of Romok. When the temple was destroyed, the people fled underground, and for centuries they were indeed little more than ghosts. Over many generations their descendants gradually took on more of the character of your world, so that they are now more similar to the natives of Orszag than their ancestors were. But they live like animals trapped in a cage, unable to venture aboveground for fear of the overwhelming realness of the sun and the elements.

"You can think of your own situation as the reverse of what happened to the settlers of Elhalad: the longer you stay here, the more realness you bleed away, until your substance is more akin to that of Veszedelem than Orszag. Whether you are here in spirit or in body, after a few hours you will have lost too much of your substance to return to your world. So to answer your original question: coming to Veszedelem physically will not allow you to spend more time here."

"What happens if I am stranded here? Will I die?"

"If you are here only in spirit? Your spirit can remain here indefinitely while your body lives. But the time differential will weigh on your spirit, and gradually you will lose your faculties and your will. It will essentially be an infinite regression toward dementia."

I shuddered, thinking of what had happened to Beata. Did Amira and the other Masters know what Eben had done to her? I wasn't certain I wanted to know.

"If you were here physically," Amira went on, "your body would slowly wither away, until all that remained was your spirit. But your being is both spirit and body; one cannot last long without the other. Without your body, your spirit would begin to dissipate as well. Your demise would be much quicker than if you were here only in spirit, but the result would be much the same. In the end, our two worlds are incompatible with each other: we cannot live in yours, and you cannot live in ours. So, as I say, stay as long as you like, but take care not to stay so long that you cannot return."

With that, she left the room, closing the door behind her.

I spent the next hour or so paging through several of the books, but they were difficult reading and I was distracted by Amira's warning. I had experienced the draining effect she had spoken of, but I had never stayed in Veszedelem long enough to know what my limits were. At last I gave up, returned to the laboratory, said goodbye to Amira and the others, and then sent my mind back to my body in Orszag. It required no great effort; evidently I had left in plenty of time.

I was tired but not exhausted. The sun had not moved; I had been gone for a little over a minute as time was reckoned in Orszag. I lay down on my bedroll and dozed for a while. When I had rested, I spent some time collecting wood, built a fire, and ate some food from my pack and drank some wine. Lulled into reverie by the fire and the wine, I lay down and slept.

When I awoke, it was full daylight. Apparently I had been more fatigued than I'd thought. Ilona and Rodric had not returned, but I wasn't going to allow myself to worry about that. In fact, there was reason to think the delay was good news: if their request for an audience with the Council had been summarily rejected, they'd have returned by now. In all likelihood, they were waiting to be summoned by the Council. Ilona had expected it to take at least a day or two to get an audience.

I had some breakfast, tended to Ember, and then sent my spirit back to the courtyard of Sotetseg. This time I did not seek Eben, but rather went straight for the laboratory. After greeting Amira and the others, I studied in the library for two hours, most of which was spent trying to get a general sense of the contents of the books and determine where I should focus my efforts to maximize my chances of besting Eben. By the time I felt I was getting a basic grasp on the scope of the material, I started to worry about getting back. With somewhat more effort than the last time, I returned to Orszag. Still Rodric and Ilona had not returned. I slept for a while and then went again to Sotetseg.

In all, I took three trips to Veszedelem that day, resting for an hour or two in between. Going back and forth between the two worlds is disconcerting, as it disrupts one's sense of time. My spirit had experienced the passage of several more hours than had actually passed in Orszag. Additionally, between each visit, several days passed in Sotetseg. On my third visit, it was apparently night in Sotetseg, as the Masters and most of the servants were not at work, although the sky seemed no darker to me than it was during the day. Fortunately, Arnyek's hordes had not yet come.

My understanding of tvari and the various schools of sorcery slowly grew, as well as my understanding of the history of Veszedelem and Bolond's ill-fated attempts to help the people of that world emigrate to Orszag. I still had barely scratched the surface of all the learning in the library, but each time I went it was more difficult to return. When the sun was still well above the horizon in Orszag, I decided I had better stop for the day. I ate another meal by myself and waited for Rodric and Ilona to return, but still there was no sign of them. By the time the sun set, I was already asleep.

I did learn one very practical lesson during my studies: it was not necessary for me to draw blood every time I traveled to Veszedelem or anywhere else via the in-between. I needed to exude some tvari, yes, but I did not have to do so by physically losing blood. Doing so had been a sort of crutch, compensating for my lack of facility in manipulating tvari. My skill had now advanced enough that I no longer needed to reopen an old wound every time I shifted, which was a relief.

By morning, Rodric and Ilona still had not returned. I waited until noon before packing up camp and mounting Ember. The danger to myself notwithstanding, I would have to go to Delivaros. If Rodric and Ilona had been captured by the Cult of Turelem, they needed my help.

At the bridge, I met a man who ran into the road, waving his arms at me and yelling at me to stop. I was on guard, but the man seemed to be unarmed. He had the lanky, filthy look of a beggar or bandit. "Sir!" he cried. "Sir, stop!" Ember was moving at a slow walk, but the man seemed desperate to stop me.

"Yes?" I said, impatiently. "What is it?"

"You're Konrad?"

"Who is asking?"

"My name is Yoder, sir," the man said. "But that isn't important. I was told to wait for a man with black markings on his face."

"Told by whom?"

"A Barbaroki, I think. Dressed like city folk, but he talked funny, like one o' them savages that attacked the city last week."

"What did he look like?"

The man shrugged. "Bigger'n me. Smaller'n you. Dark-ish."

"He didn't give you a name?"

"He did, sir, but not his own. Vili."

"What did he say about Vili?"

"Said he knows where Vili is. Gave me three ermes to wait for you here. Said you'd give me another three for giving you the message."

"What message? Where is Vili?"

"Sir, I'd like the ermes first, if it's not too much to ask."

I rummaged through my pockets until I found three ermes. It was most of the money I had left.

"Thank ye, sir," the man said. "The man said if you want to see Vili again, you should go to the Maganyos Valley."

"The Maganyos Valley? Why would Vili be there?"

"Don't know, sir. Never even heard of it myself. By your leave, sir?"

I waved the man away. He clearly knew nothing more of use. Someone—a Barbarok, evidently—had told him to wait for me here. Whoever the man was, he'd undoubtedly been doing the bidding of Eben the warlock.

I faced a decision: should I continue into Delivaros to find Rodric and Ilona, or should I make for the Maganyos Valley to go after Vili? Despite my worry about Rodric and Ilona, there was a good chance they were still waiting for an audience with the Reverend Mother. If I showed up now, my presence might sabotage their plans. And on the other hand, if they were being held in a dungeon somewhere in Delivaros, there was no great urgency in rescuing them immediately. The Cult were sticklers for protocol; they would not torture or execute prisoners without a trial. Vili, on the other hand, might be in immediate danger, and I'd already failed him once. No matter that I was undoubtedly being invited into a trap; I had little choice. I pulled on Ember's reins, directing her away from the bridge and toward the road that would take me to the Maganyos Valley.

CHAPTER FOURTEEN

It was a three-day ride to the Maganyos Valley. On the second night, while I was camped in a clearing just off the path, I dreamt that I was back at the janissary camp at Erod Patak. I had been informed that General Janos had summoned me to his tent, and I forced my way through the camp past men who had once considered me a brother-in-arms, but who now jeered and whispered to each other about the marks on my face. The camp seemed to take on preposterous dimensions, and I began to wonder if I would I would ever reach the general's tent. I muttered an angry incantation, and the soldiers around me began to fade, until they were no more than ghosts. The clouds overhead coalesced into a swirling black vortex, and the souls of everyone in the camp were sucked into it. I ignored their screams.

The general's tent was now directly ahead of me. I went inside to find not General Janos, but my own father sitting behind Janos's desk. His skin was deathly pale and gaunt.

"Father!" I cried. "Should you not be resting?"

"You summoned me here," my father said.

"Not I, Father. Please, lie down."

"I cannot rest as long as you carry that abomination on your face."

"It means nothing, Father. I am still your son, underneath."

"Then give up the brand."

"I cannot."

"You can, but you choose not to. It has corrupted you. Come to me, Konrad."

"I am here, Father." I went around the desk to him.

"Come to me, Konrad," he said again, his eyes affixed on the opening of the tent. "You must hurry."

"Father, I am right here. Can you not see me?" I put my hand gently on his shoulder.

"Hurry!" he shouted, still staring past me. "We haven't much time!"

Starting to get angry, I gripped my father by the shoulders and shook him. "Father!" I shouted. "Stop this! I'm right here!"

He opened his mouth as if to speak, and then his head rolled off his neck onto the desk. His shoulders came loose from his body, and he crumpled into a pile of bones. I let go and took a step back, screaming.

I awakened with a start. It was just a dream, I told myself, born of my guilt at failing to save Beata and lying to Vili. But something about it continued to vex me, beyond the obvious. Why had my father kept telling me to come when I was standing right next to him? The answer came to me almost immediately: it wasn't my father telling me to come.

I sent my consciousness to the courtyard of Sotetseg. I would have gone directly to the hidden section of the keep, but having only been there once, I was not confident I would be able to return there. Better to go to the courtyard and find my way back to the room with the painting. That was what I thought until I got there anyway.

Mayhem was all around me. Demons locked in combat shrieked and clawed at each other. Behind me, the gate had been smashed and scores of demons were pouring over the mist bridge. Sotetseg had fallen.

"Konrad!" cried a woman's voice. "This way!"

I could not see through the chaos, but I ran in the direction of the voice, dodging a great leathery beast with six legs as it fell, having been eviscerated by a creature with sharp bony spines protruding from its four elbows. I did not know which was the defender and which the attacker, but it did not much matter. Any of the demons would likely view me as an enemy; my only hope was that I didn't appear threatening enough to worry about. I circumvented a great bilious slug-like thing that was trying to consume four of the imps and then ducked under a razor-edged tentacle belonging to a squid-like creature engaged in battle with a pair of owlbears. It was only my spirit, not my body, that was in Veszedelem, but I was quite certain that the demons could kill me as easily as if I were there physically. I could of course return at any moment to Orszag, but then I would never find out why Amira had summoned me here.

Locating Amira at a doorway on the edge of the courtyard, I ran to her. She slammed the door behind us and said, "This way, quickly!" She turned and ran down the hall. I followed.

"Shouldn't we be out there fighting those things?" I called after her.

"There is no point," she shouted back. "Parello is already dead and Foli's wards have failed. This is only the first wave of attackers. Arnyek will soon be here, and if there is anyone left at that point, they will be unable to stand against him. In here."

She ducked into a side room and I followed. She closed the door behind me.

"What of Eben?" I asked.

"Some of his minions have joined the fight, but I have not seen him. Perhaps he hides in the passages below, thinking he will escape Arnyek's notice. But it does not matter. He will soon be dead along with the rest of us. Sotetseg is lost."

"Then why did you call me?"

"I must tell you something. When you were last here, you spoke of Vili's parents. I believe I know who they are. They were servants of the sorcerer Bolond. Until you spoke of them, I had thought they were all dead. But the names you spoke appear in a document I found in our archives…. The details do not matter. What is important is that if you can reach Vili's parents, you may be able to find Bolond."

"Bolond? I thought he was your enemy."

"He was. Perhaps is. But we are lost. Sotetseg has fallen. Our work here has failed. Finding Bolond is the only chance to stop Arnyek."

"Vili's parents are trapped between Orszag and Veszedelem, in an energy loop that is inaccessible from the outside. I have tried to reach it several times but failed. It is like trying to find a bubble in the ocean."

"They are in a place that is not truly a place. You cannot picture it in your mind because it has no form. But there is another way. You said that you met Vili's mother in Veszedelem?"

"Briefly, yes."

"If you can bring her to mind—not only her appearance, but an impression of her being—you may be able to go to her. It will require great concentration and will, but with the brand, you may be able to do it. I would not tell you of this if there was any other way, because it is very dangerous. If you fail, you may be trapped for eternity between the two worlds."

"And if I succeed? What do I do then?"

"Find out what you can about Bolond. Then open a conduit between the loop and Orszag. Those in the loop will be pulled into Orszag. The loop will collapse. Without Voros Korom to sustain them, the wraiths will dissipate."

"And Vili's parents will truly be at peace."

"Yes. And Konrad, there is one more thing."

"What is it?"

"If the Temple of Romok is rebuilt, it will only accelerate Arnyek's plans. Stop Eben if you can. And now you must go, before it is too late."

"I cannot leave you here to die!"

"You have no choice. We are not strong enough to stand against Arnyek. If it is any consolation, neither is Eben. Go. Find Bolond. Seek his—"

As she spoke, something crashed into the door, splintering it. We had just enough time to get out of the way before the thing struck again, smashing through the door and vaulting into the room. It was a foul, hairy beast, like a giant orangutan with long black claws and a head like that of an insect. Antennae flickered and a hundred eyes fixed upon us. Lacking time to coordinate with Amira, I cast one of the spells I had been practicing. The spell used tvari to drain all the heat from a given area. If I'd had more time, I could have frozen the creature solid, but I was in a hurry and my aim was poor: the thing howled as its left shoulder was suddenly encased in ice. The ice cracked and the creature's arm fell to the floor. Enraged, the beast launched itself at us. I had no time to do anything but put my body between it and Amira and throw my hands in front of my face.

I felt Amira's hand on my shoulder as the creature's claws swept toward me. And then I was back at my campsite again. Amira, Sotetseg, and the orangutan creature were gone.

"No!" I cried, trying to force my sprit back to the keep. But I had neither the strength nor the presence of mind to return. In any case, it was too late. During the few seconds I'd been back in Orszag, minutes had passed in Veszedelem. Amira was already dead. She had used her magic to send me back to Orszag rather than save herself. The Masters were dead and Arnyek would soon rule at Sotetseg. With the Masters out of the way, he would presumably be able to finally bring about the destruction of Veszedelem, although I did not know how he would do it or how long it would take. If Amira was to be believed, the destruction of Orszag would soon follow.

To have any chance of stopping that, I would have to find Bolond, and that meant going to see Vili's parents. But before I tried that, I needed to find Vili. If Eben were dead, then Vili would assume his parents were lost forever. And if he had been captured by the Barbaroki, it was my responsibility to rescue him. Saving the world would have to wait.

I reached the Maganyos Valley early in the afternoon on the following day. I was met by a pair of Barbarok sentries who seemed to be expecting me. One of them mounted his horse and instructed me to follow him. About two miles farther into the valley, I spotted the telltale animal hide tents of the Barbaroki. As the size of the camp became apparent, I realized that the entire Barbarok army had settled in the valley. Many were already at work on building more permanent structures, digging wells and other tasks. Some had begun excavation of the massive stones making up the ruins. So it was true: somehow Eben had recruited the Barbaroki to help him rebuild the Temple of Romok.

As we walked through the camp, I spotted Chief Csongor, conferring with two of his lieutenants, a stone's throw away. Csongor, the leader of the Barbaroki, had briefly imprisoned me and my friends in a cell under the palace after his army conquered Nagyvaros. I hadn't seen him since he and his men had deserted the city, leaving Nagyvaros to the Torzseki.

"Csongor!" I shouted.

Csongor turned to glare in my direction. He spotted me and scowled, but said nothing.

"Is this what you've been reduced to? Foreman of a construction project? You gave up the palace for this?"

Csongor turned away and resumed his conversation with the other two Barbaroki, pretending not to hear. I grinned. So my conjecture had been correct: if Csongor were in charge, he would not have tolerated such disrespect. I was being taken to the real authority in the valley.

The Barbarok sentry led me past the tents and workers through the valley to a wooden tower, about thirty feet high, that had been erected near the center of the camp. He dismounted at the foot of the tower and pointed me toward a ladder. I dismounted as well, and the Barbarok led Ember away. I put my hand on a rung and began to climb. Two Barbaroki climbed up after me. I felt terribly vulnerable, but I assured myself that if the Barbaroki meant me harm, I wouldn't have gotten this far without a fight.

As I climbed, I looked out over the valley. It seemed so long ago that Vili and I first faced the wraiths here together. The wraiths were now gone, having followed Voros Korom to their doom. The ruins remained, and now they were being dug up by the Barbaroki, who apparently intended to rebuild the Temple of Romok. But the Barbaroki knew nothing of the history of Nagyvaros or Romok; they would not undertake this project on their own. But how could Eben have coordinated such an effort from Veszedelem? And if he were dead, why did the work continue?

I saw the answer when I got to the top of the platform. I realized when I saw him, sitting on a chair overseeing the Barbaroki toiling away, that I had known the answer for some time. I just hadn't dared admit it to myself. Behind the chair, one on either side, stood two massive Barbarok warriors with axes. The two who had climbed after me stood to my rear.

"You are a monster," I said.

"That is no way to greet your old protégé," he said.

"You are not Vili," I said. You have stolen that body, as you once stole Beata's."

"Untrue," said Eben in the form of Vili. "This body was a gift, freely given. As was the Book of the Dead, which you so kindly retrieved from Fold Alatt."

"Then you lied to him to take it from him."

"No," said Eben, with a smile. "I do not lie unless I need to, as there are often undesirable consequences. Lying to protect someone's feelings, for example, has a tendency to cause greater problems down the road. I told Vili the truth: that with the Book of the Dead, I could bring his parents the peace they have been denied. But to do so, I would need to return to Orszag in physical form. For the past two years, as time is reckoned in Veszedelem, I have been working on a way to return here and finally succeeded. But I could not do it unless someone in Orszag willingly gave up their own life. Vili sacrificed himself so that his parents could be at peace."

"Then Vili is trapped in Veszedelem?"

"He is beneath Sotetseg, safe from harm."

"But Arnyek's hordes have taken Sotetseg."

"I made a deal with Arnyek. I would not resist his assault on Sotetseg, and in return, he would guarantee Vili's safety."

"Until Arnyek destroys Veszedelem."

"It will be time enough."

"You are a fool. If you'd allied with Amira and the others, we might have stopped Arnyek."

"I will deal with Arnyek in time. There are other matters I must attend to first."

"You mean rebuilding the Temple of Romok."

"That, and meeting my obligation to Vili. Something you would not understand."

"Then you really intend to put his parents to rest?"

"I do. It will be a trivial matter for one such as I—once I have retaken the Brand."

"So that is why you summoned me here. You still lust after the power you gave me."

"If you spent less time worrying about me and more time living up to your promises, Vili and his family would not be in this situation. I can bring his parents peace. You cannot. If you have any loyalty to Vili, you will give me the brand."

"Even if I trusted you to do it, I suspect that is not the true reason you want the brand."

"It is true that I will also need it to complete the rebuilding of the temple. You will give it to me willingly or I will take it from you. Understand, Konrad, that you cannot stop me. I will rebuild the temple with or without your help. The best you can hope for is to delay me for a little while. The brand is powerful, but there are other ways of channeling the power I need."

"Why do you wish to rebuild the temple?"

"I intend to reopen the gateway between Orszag and Veszedelem. When I control passage between the two worlds, I will rule both of them. Then I will deal with Arnyek. I am the only one who can stop him."

"Perhaps it would be better to allow Arnyek to destroy the world rather than let you rule it."

"You do not believe that," Eben said with a smile that seemed out of place on Vili's face. "You are the naïve sort who thinks it's always better to survive, to keep fighting, no matter what. You would choose a life of slavery over annihilation because some part of you will always believe that someday you will be free."

"Then you have your answer. I will never willingly give you the brand."

Eben sighed. "Fair enough," he said. "I see that I will have to take it." He waved his hand, and the two men behind me seized my arms. They were both exceptionally large, and I struggled in vain as they dragged me toward Eben. Eben drew a silver dagger from a sheath at his side as one of the men tore my shirt open almost to the waist. Eben flicked his wrist, and I winced as a shallow gash opened on my chest. He sheathed the blade and then put his hand on the wound, warm blood oozing around his fingertips. I renewed my struggle, but could not break free. Eben began to murmur an incantation.

I felt tendrils of energy tugging at me, trying to separate the power from my body. Faint lines began to appear on Vili's face, a shadow of the brand I carried. I had been ready for this; Eben had tried this once before, when he was in the form of Beata. Since then, I had learned a great deal about how tvari worked, and while I was no match for Eben in a sorcerer's duel, I thought I could repel his efforts to take the brand.

I let my body go slack, focusing all my strength into resisting Eben's pull. Vili's face revealed surprise as he sensed the level of my resistance. Then determination took over as he redoubled his efforts. I gasped audibly as I felt the pull of his will like an icy wind. The power began to leave me, and as it did, so did my ability to resist. I had not counted on this: if Eben could drain even a little of the power from me, it would weaken me enough that I'd be unable to hold onto the brand. Stopping him would require more than brute resistance.

I let part of my mind drift to the in-between, where I dipped into the flow of tvari. Rather than holding onto it or taking it into myself, this time I let it flow past me, toward Eben. As the surge of energy hit him, I felt elation come over him. But then he grew angry as he realized what was happening. He could not take the brand from me without pulling more tvari into himself than he could possibly hold. Eben was a powerful warlock, but even he had his limits.

I felt him trying to close off the conduit I had opened, but now his attention was divided, and I was able to wrest control of the brand from him. I cannot say for how many seconds or minutes we struggled, but at some point Eben managed to construct what seemed to be a mental barrier between me and the in-between, preventing me from drawing more. I thought I could break through the barrier, but not while holding onto the brand. We were at an impasse.

Again Eben redoubled his efforts to pull the brand from me. I could tell he was weakening, but so was I. Eben was more practiced at manipulating tvari than I; I simply could not beat him in a fair fight.

I fought against him with all my will. Sweat poured from his forehead as the effort drained him. By this time I was barely aware of my own body; I hung limp, supported by the Barbaroki on either side of me. Every ounce of my strength was focused on holding onto the brand. I was failing. I put up a tremendous fight, but ever-so-slowly the power slipped away from me. As I grew weaker and Eben grew stronger, I felt the power drain more quickly. There had been a time when I would have done almost anything to rid myself of that brand, but I had accepted the fact that the brand was the only weapon I had against Eben. I would not let him have it, even if it cost me my own life.

I tensed my legs underneath me and sprang backwards, breaking contact with Eben's hand. The Barbaroki were unprepared for this sudden movement, and I easily slipped from their grasp. I felt the power of the brand hanging in the air between me and Eben, an undulating dark mass of energy swirling in nothingness, and for a moment I thought I had waited too long. But then the power surged back into me and I felt a burning on my face as the brand returned. Eben stared at me, pale and shaking, the fingertips of his right hand covered with my blood.

There was nowhere to go. The edge of the platform was two paces behind me, and there was no time to climb back down the ladder. The two Barbaroki moved to seize me again.

I spun around, took a step, and then leaped off the platform.

I had just enough strength and presence of mind to summon a small kovet, which appeared under me about three feet off the ground. It did not stop me, but it gave way enough to break my fall. The kovet vanished and I tumbled to the ground.

Dazed but unhurt, I got to my feet and started running. It didn't matter which way I went: Barbaroki were all around me. Shouts went out from atop the platform to seize me. I had no weapon and didn't dare attempt to use magic again for fear that I would not have the strength to escape. Already I was weak and trembling from my battle with Eben.

By some miracle, I managed to get away from the main group of tents near the foot of the ravine that served as the northern boundary of the valley. From the shouts behind me, I knew the Barbaroki were not far away. If I followed the contour of the ravine to the east or west, the Barbaroki would surely catch me, so I did the only thing I could do: I started to climb.

I only made it as far as I did because Eben wanted me alive; the Barbaroki did not fire arrows or throw spears because Eben could not take the brand from a dead man. I was halfway up the ravine before a strong hand grabbed my right ankle and pulled me down. Soon half a dozen men were on top of me. My hands were bound behind my back and I was marched, soiled, bruised and bleeding, back to Eben, who now stood near the base of the tower. I smiled as I saw that he was leaning heavily on one of the Barbaroki: our battle had taken nearly as much out of him as it did me.

"I can see," Eben said, unable to hide the quaver in his voice, "that we are going to have to do this a different way."

CHAPTER FIFTEEN

I was gagged and dragged inside an empty tent. While a heavy wooden stake was pounded into the ground in the center of the tent, I looked out the opening to see someone walking around the tent, pouring something from a bucket onto the ground. I realized, as my hands were being tied to the stake, that the bucket was full of salt. So there was something to that old myth after all. Eben was doing everything he could to prevent me from using magic to escape. I was strangely flattered by the precautions. A sack was thrown over my head and tied around my neck, and then I was alone.

Sitting awkwardly with my hands tied to the stake behind my back, I could do nothing but listen to the bustle of the Barbarok camp and reflect on all the ways I'd failed the people I cared about. Beata was dead. Vili's spirit was imprisoned in Sotetseg, which was now ruled by the demon lord Arnyek. Vili's parents were still trapped between worlds. Rodric and Ilona were probably incarcerated by the Cult of Turelem. I could do nothing to help any of them. Undoubtedly Eben was even now preparing some ritual that would strip me of the brand, giving him the power he needed to rebuild the Temple of Romok. And then? He would either defeat Arnyek to become the ruler of both Orszag and Veszedelem or Arnyek would destroy all of reality. I wasn't sure which was worse.

The salt was unnecessary. I was too exhausted to use magic, and even if I could summon enough tvari to break my bonds, I'd still be in the center of the Barbarok camp, with nowhere to go.

There were probably a dozen men standing guard. Eben wouldn't take any chances.

The light filtering through the tent diminished as the sun dipped below the rim of the valley. After another hour, activity in the camp began to die down. My thoughts went from self-recrimination to escape fantasies to preoccupation with my overwhelming thirst. Eventually I nodded off, but my thirst and general discomfort kept me from getting any real rest. I began to wish for the coming of dawn just to get the ritual over with.

Some time after dark, a man entered the tent, his massive form silhouetted for a moment by the dim torchlight outside. Had Eben sent someone for me already?

"Hello, Konrad," said a familiar voice. "I did not have the opportunity to welcome you to my camp earlier."

I swallowed hard. "What do you want, Csongor?"

"As I said, to welcome you. You embarrassed me in front of two of my captains earlier."

"Well, perhaps if you hadn't agreed to be Eben's lapdog…"

He hit me hard enough that I was too addled to really mind the next twenty blows.

At some point the beating must have stopped. The next thing I was aware of was a cold knife blade rubbing against my palm. A moment later, my hands came free. Rubbing my wrists, I looked up stupidly at the dark figures inside the tent. The hood had been removed and someone was cutting the rope around my ankles. A strong hand seized my arm.

"Konrad, can you walk?" a man whispered.

I nodded, although I was not at all certain I could. Another hand seized my left arm and I was hauled to my feet. I managed to put one foot in front of the other and we exited the tent into the cold air of night. By the moonlight, I saw the bodies of several men lying in the grass. The Barbarok guards, no doubt. My rescuers seemed to number five. Very stealthy and deadly men, to have penetrated to the center of the Barbarok camp and taken out the guards so quickly and quietly. They were Torzseki, I realized.

"Davor Sabas?" I whispered to the man on my left. I recognized Nebjosa's right-hand man as the moonlight hit his face.

He gave me a curt nod. "This way. Hurry."

I half-walked, half-stumbled across an open yard the Barbaroki had been using for combat practice, Davor Sabas and the other Torzsek supporting me on either side. We reached a series of closely-grouped tents.

"We'll have to move single-file from here," Davor Sabas said. "Can you walk on your own?"

"I think so," I said. Blood was now circulating in my legs again.

Without a word, Davor Sabas slipped away into the shadows, and I followed as best I could. He moved quickly, darting from shadow to shadow, until we reached the edge of the camp. We had seen no one else moving; the Torzseki had evidently taken out the guards, and the rest of the Barbaroki were asleep. We had nearly reached the foot of the ravine when a shout went up from somewhere behind us. I turned back to see a man standing just outside his tent, thirty or so paces away. One of the Torzseki loosed an arrow, but the man ducked under it. He ran toward the center of the camp, still shouting.

"Move!" Davor Sabas urged, pulling me forward. We began to climb the slope of the ravine. Behind me I heard more shouts as men exited their tents. I struggled to make my sluggish legs obey as Davor Sabas continued to pull on my arm. I didn't see how we were going to escape. Even if I were at full strength, the Barbaroki would catch us eventually—assuming Eben the warlock did not catch us first.

"Slow them down," Davor Sabas barked to the other Torzseki. "I'll get Konrad to safety." The men complied without hesitation. They turned and moved back down the slope toward a group of Barbaroki converging on our location. The Torzseki had the high ground but they were already outnumbered, and more would soon be coming. Davor Sabas's men were going to die.

There was nothing I could do about it. I was almost certainly going to die myself in short order. I continued to stumble-climb up the range, Davor Sabas dragging me like a sack of beets, which is about how useful I felt at the moment.

The battle raged below us as Davor Sabas and I reached the crest of the ravine. We ran to where a group of horses waited. A pang of sadness struck me as I remembered that Ember was still in the Barbarok camp. It was probably just as well, though: the Barbaroki treated horses well, and if I'd been able to take her, she'd probably be killed along with me. Davor Sabas mounted one of the horses and I climbed onto another. He dug his heels into his mount and we shot off across the plain, the riderless horses following.

We traveled at a full gallop for about three miles. There was no sign of the Barbaroki, so we stopped just long enough to gulp some water and switch horses and then continued for another mile or so. By this time, all of the horses were fatigued and could no longer maintain a gallop. We could only hope the Barbarok mounts had no more endurance than ours. As the first light of the dawn appeared in the east, we slowed to a walk, watching behind us for any sign of the Barbaroki. When the sun was above the horizon, we still had not seen them. Davor Sabas's men must have put up quite a fight. We stopped again to allow the horses to rest and drink some water, and then kept moving.

"Why did you come for me?" I asked.

"There were reports of the Barbaroki moving into the Maganyos Valley, so Governor Nebjosa sent us to investigate. We observed your capture."

"You could have left me there."

"The Governor believes you may yet prove to be a valuable ally against his enemies, all appearances to the contrary."

"You do not share his opinion."

"I thought the Governor would not approve of leaving you in the hands of the Barbaroki, but I did not expect to lose five men in the rescue. If I had it to do over, I would not."

"Well, I thank you in any case. Your men must have fought fiercely, or we would not have made it this far."

"They died on your account."

"I am very sorry, Davor Sabas."

He ignored me. "Why did Eben not kill you when he had the chance?"

"He needs the power signified by the brand on my face to complete the reconstruction of the temple."

"Sorcery," Davor Sabas said, with a grimace. "And if he completes the temple?"

"It will give him great power," I said. "He will be a threat to Nagyvaros and the rest of Orszag. But we have, at the very least, delayed his plans."

"You will have to brief the Governor."

"I am sorry, I cannot. There is little more to tell in any case, and I have another urgent matter to attend to."

"More sorcerer's business? Do not tell me; I do not wish to know. It is probably better that you do not come to Nagyvaros anyway. If Eben needs you so badly, he will look for you there. The city's defenses are still weak, and if Eben knows you are there, he will not hesitate to throw the entire Barbarok force at us."

"Agreed," I said.

"You will need a horse, I suppose?"

"I will take some rations if you can spare them, but I do not need a horse. Where I am going, a horse will be of no use."

Davor Sabas grunted his assent. We traveled together until sundown to be sure that we were well away from the Barbaroki. We tended to the horses, ate a cold supper, and then bedded down for the night. The next morning, Davor Sabas set off for Nagyvaros, taking the horses with him.

I remained at the camp, where I spent several hours reflecting on my meeting with Vili's mother, Haneen. I had met her in a particularly dismal area of Veszedelem, where the analog of the Temple of Romok had served as the anchor for one end of the conduit in which the wraiths were trapped. I had disconnected the conduit from Veszedelem, turning it back on itself to form an infinite loop floating in nothingness. It was possible that Haneen was still in Veszedelem, but I thought it more likely that she had been sucked into the vortex along with everyone else in the vicinity. If that were the case, and if Amira were right, I could transport myself into the vortex by focusing on Haneen.

I had spoken to Haneen only briefly, but my visual memory was finely honed from six years of practice in Nincs Varazslat. I held a picture of her in my mind, going over every blemish, every dimple, every hair. I thought of how her body moved, how her tattered clothing hung on her, and how her voice sounded as she pleaded with me to help Vili and explained how to vanquish the wraiths and kill Voros Korom. At last, when I could practically feel her presence with me there in the clearing, I sent my spirit out to the in-between, seeking her.

I had expected the process to be similar to traveling to a physical place, but it was not. The essence of a person is fundamentally different than that of a place; the spirit exists in a way that is both more ephemeral and yet somehow less transient than matter. A physical place exists in relation to other places, even in Veszedelem; to find any given place, one needs only to get one's bearings in relation to some other point in the same world. But spirits exist in a realm of pure being, without any spatial relation to each other.

The mind, however, cannot make sense of such a realm, so it interprets it as a sort of space. What I experienced was like moving slowly through a murky sea populated by gray, shadowy creatures that moved toward me or away from me, or simply hovered just beyond my ability to discern their features. The creatures were human-like, and as some came close, I saw that they all looked vaguely like Haneen.

As I continued to move through the murk, I realized there were hundreds, perhaps thousands, of them, and I nearly despaired of ever finding Haneen. I realized, though, that my own thoughts were determining which faces I saw. Were these beings real? Were they products of my own imagination? Or were they something else—perhaps demons using my own thoughts to camouflage themselves? I got the distinct sense, as the women beckoned silently to me, that there was something sinister motivating them. These were not harmless apparitions, but manifestations of some malevolent force that wished to keep me from reaching Vili's mother. I pushed past them, forcing myself to focus on my image of Haneen.

As I moved, the apparitions gradually began to resemble Haneen more and more, and at last I found her, looking exactly as she had when I'd last seen her. I moved toward her, and she extended her arms to embrace me.

"Konrad!" cried a voice from behind me. It sounded like Haneen. I turned back to see only a hundred indistinct figures beckoning to me. *Another trick*, I thought. *Do not let yourself be distracted.* But as I looked again at the figure I had taken to be Haneen, I realized something was wrong. She was too perfect— not perfectly beautiful, but too perfectly aligned with my idea of Haneen. This was not Haneen, but Haneen exactly as I had expected to find her. I did not know how time had passed where Haneen was, but she would surely not be identical to my image of her.

I hesitated, just out of the apparition's reach, and suddenly the thing's face was twisted with rage. A tortured hiss escaped its throat and its fingers turned to claws as it tried to take me into its arms.

CHAPTER SIXTEEN

I recoiled in horror.

"Konrad! I am here!" cried the voice again. All around me, the apparitions were shrieking and hissing at me, but I heard that one clear voice over them all. I moved toward it. I had no choice. If the voice did not belong to the true Haneen, I was lost anyway. I could not possibly tell the real thing from the thousands of impostors.

The shrieking intensified, and the apparitions clawed at me as I passed, but the voice penetrated through the clamor. As it grew louder, the apparitions nearby began to mimic it like demented mockingbirds.

"Konrad!" cried the voice.

"Konrad, Konrad, Konrad!" shrieked a thousand apparitions.

"I am here! Come to me!" cried the voice.

"I am here come to me, I am here come to me, I am here come to me!" shrieked the apparitions.

"Haneen!" I shouted. "Where are you?"

"Here, Konrad! This way!"

But her voice was lost among a thousand others crying "Konrad! Here! This way!"

"Please hurry!" the voice called. "They are coming! I am Haneen, Vili's mother. My husband is Arron. I spoke to you in Veszedelem. Told you how to defeat Voros Korom...."

Her voice was fading, but I had found her, a figure almost indistinguishable from all the others, but somehow more substantial. Her arms were extended toward me and I pushed past the clawing hands to her. For a moment I was enclosed in her embrace, and then—

I was lying on top of her on the stone floor of a dimly lit, cylindrical tunnel that was perhaps fifty feet in diameter. The tunnel extended as far as I could see in both directions. The bottom of the tunnel was filled with slimy green liquid.

"Get up!" shouted a man's voice. I rolled onto my back to see a man standing a few feet away with his back toward us. I got to me feet and helped Haneen up. We were both covered in the green muck. I heard voices echoing down the corridor: the tortured souls that had once been the wraiths of Romok.

"We have to keep moving," the man said again, turning toward us. "This way." He strode past us, sparing me only a quick glance. He was like a somewhat taller, more muscular version of Vili. As with Haneen, it was difficult to determine his age; time spent in Veszedelem and in the vortex between worlds had drained them of vitality in ways that were difficult to pinpoint. Their clothing was tattered and filthy.

"Can they kill us?" I asked.

"They can separate your spirit from your body," Haneen said. "Then you will be like us, a soul trapped between worlds. Arron and I cannot die in this place. We have been torn apart by the ghouls a thousand times, but we always find ourselves back here again. The energy of our souls has nowhere to go. True death would be a mercy. You have returned to free us?"

"Yes. I think I can cause the loop to collapse. If I do, you will die."

"All we want is to be at rest," Arron said, "Away from this place... and those things." He gestured vaguely behind us. "How is Vili?"

I was tempted to lie to spare their feelings, as I had to Vili, but I did not. "Vili is imprisoned in Sotetseg," I said.

"What?" Arron growled, stopping in his tracks and turning to face me. "How could this have happened?"

"He was trying to save you," I said. "I am sorry. He found out that you were still trapped here and he made a deal with Eben in an attempt to save you."

"You fool!" Arron shouted. "This is your fault!"

"No, Arron," Haneen said, putting her hand on his shoulder. "It is mine. I told Konrad to lie to Vili. I thought it better that he not know what became of us."

"I swear I will do everything I can to see that Vili is freed," I said. "But first I must ask you something."

Arron snorted. "I thought as much." He turned and continued walking. The voices behind us were getting closer. We followed him.

"A demon called Arnyek threatens to destroy our worlds—both Veszedelem and Orszag, and whatever other worlds there are."

"We know of Arnyek," Haneen said. "What do you expect us to do about him?"

"I know that you were once servants of Bolond," I said. "He is the only one who can stop Arnyek. If you know where he is, you must tell me."

"You ask us to betray Bolond?" Arron asked.

"I ask only that you tell me where he is, so that I can appeal to him for help against Arnyek."

"Bolond will not help you."

"Why not?"

Haneen replied, "He has gone mad."

"In that case," I said, "there is little reason for you to follow his dictates."

"His present mental state notwithstanding," Arron said, "we swore to keep our knowledge of him secret."

"If you do not tell me," I said, "our world will be destroyed."

"And we will be at peace," Arron replied. "Along with Vili."

"Is that all you wish?" I snapped. "Oblivion? If that is the case, why did you not do us all a favor and kill yourselves before Vili was born? It would have saved me a lot of trouble."

"You bastard!" Arron snarled, turning to face me again. "How dare you invoke my son's name, after what you have done?"

"Ah, so he does care about something other than ending his own suffering!" I said. "Has it occurred to you that there are thousands of other fathers who care just as much about their children, who would like to see them grow up and perhaps have families of their own? Do you speak for those men as well, or only for yourself? You would condemn them to oblivion because your own family suffers?"

"I'll not hear another word of this," Arron growled, launching himself at me. I slipped aside and he flew headlong into the muck. The voices down the tunnel continued to grow louder. Arron got to his feet. "I will kill you!"

"Kill me?" I said. "No, I think not. You are too enervated by your stay in this accursed place to be any threat to me. If you do not help me, I will simply return to my own world and leave you to rot."

"You cannot stop Arnyek on your own," Haneen said.

"Perhaps not. But I will try. And I will save Vili, not to help you, but because he deserves better than the fate we have sentenced him to. And if I do somehow manage to stop Arnyek, I will leave you both trapped here forever, to suffer for your sins!"

Arron lunged at me again, but again I easily dodged the attack. I could now see shapes moving toward us in the distance.

"Stop this!" Haneen cried. "We have to move!"

"It is too late," I said, turning away from the creatures slogging toward us. "Look." I pointed at the figures moving toward us from the other end of the tunnel. We had run as far as we could. The tunnel was a circle, and the ghouls were coming at us from both ends. "I must go," I said. "If you will not help me, I must try to find Bolond on my own." I closed my eyes and thought of the place where I had waited for Ilona and Rodric, just outside of Delivaros. Perhaps they would be there, waiting for me. If not, I would go into the city and try to find them. After that, I did not know.

"Wait!" cried Haneen. "I think I can help you." I opened my eyes. The ghouls were now less than forty paces away on either side, shuffling slowly toward us.

"Haneen, do not do this," Arron said.

"It is not a betrayal, Arron," Haneen said. She turned to me. "We do not know where Bolond is. We were looking for him when the wraiths at Romok took us. But I have a suspicion."

"Haneen!"

"Quiet, Arron!" Haneen snapped. "We followed Bolond because we thought he knew a way to repair the two worlds, but he is lost. I think perhaps he lost his way many years ago, and we did not see it. Now he is truly mad. He has come to me a few times, trying to communicate, but his thoughts are jumbled, and each time he has no memory of his previous attempts."

"That is how he was when he spoke to me in Nincs Varazslat," I said. The ghouls were now less than twenty paces off.

"Yes. You said he came to you one day and then disappeared not long after. I do not know how the acolytes caught him, but they did something to him that drove him mad. If he had his faculties about him, they would not have been able to keep him in Nincs Varazslat. And when you said that he disappeared, I assumed he had escaped. But what if he did not? What if they moved him to another prison, specifically designed to hold him?"

"Does such a place exist?"

"If it does, it would need to be augmented by something more powerful than salt and rock."

"You speak of magic."

"Yes. Powerful magic. The sort used to protect Regi Otthon at Delivaros."

"You think Bolond is imprisoned in Regi Otthon?"

"It is the best guess I have," Haneen said. "Now please, go help Vili."

"Thank you," I said. "I will do what I can."

The ghouls were nearly upon us. Arron advanced toward the closest one, gripping it by the arm and shoving the ghoul backwards into the others. Several fell, but behind them dozens more pressed onward. They had lost even more of their human form than when I had seen them last; they were now featureless, vaguely humanoid shapes. They were weak and moved slowly, but there was an endless procession of them extending away from us in both directions.

On my other side, Haneen faced the other horde. She grabbed the nearest ghoul by its wrist, pulling it off balance so that it fell, causing several others to stumble. Another advanced to her right, and she fended it off with a kick to the stomach, sending it staggering into those behind it. But the ghouls continued to close ranks and press forward. There were simply too many to fight.

I closed my eyes and reached for the flow of tvari, pulling it toward me and redirecting it toward the stone wall in front of me. From what I had learned in my studies, a kovet would not work here. The tunnel was not a real place, but merely a shared delusion we had created to represent the metaphysical loop between the two worlds. To break out of it, I needed to channel enough tvari to reconnect it to Orszag. That had been the purpose of the Temple of Romok: to tear an opening in the substance of reality, allowing beings to travel through from Veszedelem. It had taken thousands of men several years to build that temple. I was going to have to do it on my own, in a matter of seconds.

The rift only needed to remain open for a moment, but even so, I was not certain I had the strength to do it. Despite not being "real," the stone wall stubbornly resisted my efforts to break through. The tvari, manifesting as a stream of glowing purple energy, flowed from my fingertips and splattered against the wall in an impressive shower of sparks. The stone, however, remained undamaged.

Haneen and Arron crowded toward me as the ghouls pressed closer. There was no longer enough room for them to fight in earnest, but they continued to do their best to push the ghouls back. The ghouls avoided the stream of tvari, and I suspected I could effectively repel the ghouls by directing some of the energy toward them. But then what? I could not kill them, and eventually I would weaken. Then I would be trapped forever along with Haneen and Arron. No, we had only one chance to get out of this place.

I redoubled my efforts, allowing the tvari to completely consume me, until I existed only as a living conduit of energy. In the past I had been careful to moderate the flow of tvari, knowing that to lose control would be disastrous, resulting in my death—or worse. But now I had nothing to lose. If I didn't open the rift, the three of us were doomed.

To my amazement, as I surrendered to the overwhelming power of the tvari, my capacity to channel and direct it only grew.

I had been wasting much of my effort fighting the flow, but that was unnecessary. The tvari was powerful, but it was mere potential. It had no will. In essence, I had been fighting against myself.

I heard Haneen scream as the ghouls began to tear at her flesh. Arron tried to get to her, but the ghouls seized him as well. They overwhelmed him, pulling him to the ground. I felt claws dig into my shoulder. A hand grasped my ankle. Cracks began to form in the wall. I ignored the ghouls and sent the flow toward the cracks.

The cracks spiderwebbed across the stone. Mortar crumbled. One of the blocks began to slide away from the tunnel. Then another, and another. A dozen ghouls were grasping at me. The wall gave way, a man-sized hole appearing as stone and mortar exploded away from me into the void. A blast of wind struck me and I was sucked through the hole.

CHAPTER SEVENTEEN

I lay on the cold ground, unsure where I was. Pale apparitions whirled around me, screaming. For a moment, Haneen stood before me, a grateful smile on her face. And then they were gone—Haneen and Arron and the ghouls. I had done it. Vili's parents and what was left of the tortured souls who had been trapped between Orszag and Veszedelem were finally at peace. I fell asleep.

I awoke, teeth chattering, under a clear starry sky. Realizing I was back at my camp, I found my bedroll and wrapped it around me, huddling with my knees to my chest. My fingers and toes were numb. Eventually I warmed up enough to fall asleep again. I woke some time later, still cold but no longer feeling like I was freezing to death. I got up, stomped around for a while to get my blood moving, and then made a fire. When it was blazing nicely, I lay down and fell asleep once again.

When I woke, it was mid-morning. The fire had nearly died out but the air had warmed somewhat. I made myself some breakfast and thought about what to do next.

If Bolond really was being held in Regi Otthon, I needed to go there. But Regi Otthon was vast, and Bolond's cell would be hidden and guarded. I thought I could remember the storage room well enough to shift there, but it would do me no good to wander aimlessly through the corridors in the hopes of finding him. I needed to consult with Ilona. I closed my eyes and thought of the clearing where I'd waited for Ilona and Rodric outside of Delivaros. A moment later, I was there.

Ilona screamed, and Rodric seized his bow and nocked an arrow. They had been eating lunch in front of a fire when I had suddenly materialized before them.

"Easy, friend," I said, and Rodric lowered his bow. I staggered forward, the effort of shifting through the in-between having drained me. Rodric caught me and helped me to sit on a log near the fire.

"I may need to start drinking again if you plan to continue traveling this way," Rodric said. "You look awful."

"Where have you been?" Ilona asked. "We've been waiting here for a day and a half."

"I am sorry," I said. "It has been... an eventful few days." Ilona tended to my wounds while I proceeded to tell them about my capture and escape from Eben and the Barbaroki in the Maganyos Valley, and about saving Vili's parents from the ghouls in the in-between.

"Then you made good on your promise to Vili," Rodric said.

"Yes, but it was too late to help Vili. He is imprisoned in Sotetseg, where Arnyek now rules, and Eben has taken Vili's body. He has persuaded the Barbaroki to help him rebuild Romok."

"Eben has taken Vili's form, the same way you said he took the form of Beata?"

"I am afraid so," I said.

"He is pure evil," Rodric said.

"Agreed."

"Why does he wish to rebuild the temple?" Ilona asked.

"I think he believes it will give him the power to defeat Arnyek and conquer Orszag."

"Can we not just let Eben and Arnyek fight it out?" Rodric asked. "It is demoralizing to vanquish one enemy only to find you are doing the work of another."

"I do not think you want to see what Orszag will become under Eben's rule. But at this point, the greater threat is from Arnyek. He plots even now to destroy reality itself."

"That would seem undesirable," Rodric said.

"Aye," I replied. "In any case, I do not have the option of remaining neutral. As long as I carry this brand, Eben will hunt me. But what of your mission to Delivaros? Were you able to get an audience with the Reverend Mother?"

"We were, but little came of it," Ilona said. "The Reverend Mother would not admit to knowing anything about the reconstruction of the temple. She insisted that the Cult officially disapproved of any such project."

"Is that exactly what she said?" I asked.

"Yes," Ilona said. "It was strange. It was as if she wanted to help us but could not."

"Then Eben has gotten to her," I said.

"But how?" Rodric asked. "You said Vili—that is, Eben in the form of Vili—was in the Maganyos Valley, overseeing the unearthing of the ruins. It would be impossible for him to get from Nagyvaros to Delivaros and then to the Maganyos Valley in the time that he was gone."

"There is another possibility," I said. "Amira was able to come to me in my dreams because of the tvari in my blood. If the Cult secretly uses magic, perhaps the Reverend Mother herself is able to receive such messages."

"So you are now accusing the Reverend Mother of being a sorcerer?" Ilona asked.

"Far be it from me to make any accusations. I suspect that if the Cult uses magic, it does so in a somewhat different way than Radovan or Eben. But it seems reasonable to think that Eben could communicate with the Reverend Mother or perhaps one of the other Council members this way. Did you mention Eben to her?"

"Yes," Ilona said. "We told her Eben intended to rebuild the temple. She told us that was impossible, as Eben was still imprisoned in Nincs Varazslat."

"She was testing you," I said. "Trying to find out how much you know."

"That was my thought as well. We told her that the man they'd sentenced to Nincs Varazslat was not Eben, and that in any case, he'd been released. She denied both claims, but did not seem surprised. She ended the meeting shortly after that. It was how the meeting ended, in fact, that convinced me for certain that she knew more than she was letting on."

"How is that?" I asked.

"They let us walk out of there," Rodric said.

Ilona nodded. "I am an acolyte who violated her vows, and we as much as admitted to consorting with a sorcerer. By all rights, we should ourselves be imprisoned in Delivaros. The Reverend Mother let us go, for what reason I do not know."

"The Council certainly does not want to see the Temple of Romok rebuilt," I said. "But the secrets in the Book of the Dead could be even more damaging to them if they came out. And of course they cannot be seen conspiring with me. We cannot hope for any help from the Reverend Mother—not publicly, anyway."

"Then what do we do?" Rodric asked.

"I must try to get to Bolond. If he is being held by the Cult, he must be somewhere in those passageways under Regi Otthon. We were probably a stone's throw from him when we were looking for the lyre. I think I can shift myself to that room. Ilona, can you sketch out as much as you know of the layout of those passages?"

Ilona nodded. She and Rodric cleared the leaves and twigs from a patch of ground near the fire and then Ilona proceeded to draw as much as she remembered of the passageways. There wasn't much more than what I'd already seen.

"That's it?" I asked.

"I'm sure there are more passages," she said, "but I never saw them. If there's some kind of secret prison down there, it would probably be behind this door." She tapped a door she had marked with a small piece of twig. "It's under constant guard."

"Very good," I said. "Then that's where I will go."

*****

I spent the remainder of the day resting while Rodric and Ilona tended to the fire and the horses. There was little more I could do to prepare for my infiltration of Regi Otthon, and I was still exhausted from traveling through the in-between earlier that day. I would need all my strength if I was going to have a chance of getting to Bolond, much less get him out. I fell asleep before dark and slept until well after sunrise.

After breakfast the next morning, I sat by the fire while Rodric and Ilona went to gather firewood. I closed my eyes and tried to envision the storage room below Regi Otthon, but my thoughts kept wandering. I realized there was something else I needed to do first.

I sent my consciousness to the courtyard of Sotetseg and made way downstairs toward the place where Szarvas Gyerek had kept Beata. In all likelihood, If Eben had made a deal with Arnyek to preserve Vili's soul, Vili was now probably imprisoned in the same place. As I had learned when Beata was imprisoned, it would be futile to try to break him out, but I might at least be able to talk to him.

The chaos of the battle had died down; indeed, Sotetseg seemed deserted. I reminded myself that several months had passed here since my last meeting with Amira. I supposed the keep had little value to Arnyek; he had attacked it only to eliminate the Masters.

I met no one on my way to the chamber where the red lantern glowed. As I suspected, Vili was there. He lay on the floor, apparently asleep. I went to him and put my hand on his shoulder.

He awakened with a start and sat up. "Konrad? Have you come to get me out of here?"

"I am sorry, Vili. Doing so is beyond my abilities."

Vili nodded sadly. "Thank you for telling me the truth."

"I am sorry I did not do so before."

"It is all right, Konrad. I was angry before, but... Konrad, I think I have made a terrible mistake."

I chuckled grimly. "I have made a few myself. But I do have some good news. I have freed your parents from their prison."

"You swear it?"

"I swear it. Their souls are at peace."

"That is a great relief, but now I feel even more the fool for making a bargain with Eben. Konrad, is there any way I can leave this place?"

"I do not know. I hope to find a way, but... Vili, there are forces at work more powerful than I can comprehend."

Vili nodded. "It is all right. I expected to be here for a long time. It's just... well, it's worse than I thought it would be. I feel like I'm fading. Like part of my mind is going. It would be all right if I could just let it go, but I can feel it slipping away. I worry about it all the time, even when I can't remember what I'm worried about. I think eventually all that will be left of me is the worry. What I mean to say is that I think I would rather it just end than go on this way forever."

"I understand, Vili. I am sorry I failed you. I will not do it again."

I heard footsteps approaching.

"I must go now, Vili," I said. "I will return when I can."

Vili nodded sadly and lay down again. I wondered if he would even remember me being here. I let my consciousness return to Orszag.

I stood up and took a short walk to clear my head. Then I sat down again and closed my eyes. I envisioned the storage room as vividly as possible. A moment later, I was there. Physically transporting my body required a lot more effort than sending my consciousness to Veszedelem, but the process did not seem as draining this time—whether because I was traveling a much shorter distance or because I was getting better at it, I did not know.

The room was dark, but the door I had forced open was still missing and dim light penetrated from a torch in the next room. I walked quietly across the room, being careful not to upset any of the crates or artifacts lying around. As I reached the doorway, I saw that there was a single guard standing just on the other side, to my right. He was facing the entrance opposite him, having no reason to think an intruder would be coming from behind. I reached out and touched his cheek with my fingertips, then caught him as he crumpled to the floor, unconscious. The spell cost me minimal effort; I was definitely becoming more skilled. For the first time, I allowed myself to believe that I was more than a fraud: I was becoming an actual sorcerer.

I moved through the passageways toward the door that Ilona had marked. I encountered no one until I reached the passage that led to the mysterious door, which was guarded by two men. There was no way to sneak up on them, but I pulled the air from their lungs before they could raise an alarm. While they lay on the floor, gasping and writhing, I touched each of them on the forehead, rendering them unconscious. I located the key and opened the door. Beyond was another passageway, perhaps thirty feet long, at the end of which was a doorway, through which a dim, flickering light penetrated. I dragged the guards one by one through the door and then closed it behind me.

If I hadn't been in a hurry to reach Bolond before the guards regained consciousness, I might have spotted the trap. When I was halfway across the hall, the floor gave way, the stone surface suddenly pivoting sharply under my weight. There being nothing to grab onto, I braced for impact. I fell perhaps eight feet, landing hard on my right shoulder. Pain shot through my body, and I lost consciousness for a moment.

When I came to, I saw that I was lying in the center of a square chamber perhaps thirty feet on a side. By the light of torches in sconces, I saw a score of men lining the walls around me. They wore chain mail and helmets, and had longbows trained on me.

"Do you intend to resist?" asked a woman's voice behind me.

I sat up slowly and turned toward the sound. The woman was small, with a deeply hunched back. She wore a crimson robe with three silver stripes on the right shoulder: the accoutrement of the Reverend Mother herself.

When I didn't reply, she went on, "I suspect you've spent most of your energy getting in here, and the salt will inhibit your power. It is unlikely you will escape, but I will understand if you feel the need to try."

Looking around, I saw that I was inside a ring of salt that took up most of the room. I could of course step over it, but I suspected that doing so would be an invitation for the archers to riddle me with arrows.

"Where is Bolond?" I asked. My shoulder throbbed, and intense pain gripped me when I tried to move it. I had either broken something or dislocated it.

"Ah, so it is as I suspected. You seek Bolond. For what purpose?"

"I have sworn to stop Eben the sorcerer, who intends to rebuild the Temple of Romok with the help of the Barbaroki."

The Reverend Mother nodded. "Then it was your friends who came to me three days ago. I suspected you might pay me a visit next."

"You know who I am?"

"I have long known who you are, Konrad. I have been receiving reports on your activities since you were released from Nincs Varazslat."

"But then… you knew I was not Eben, even while I was in that dungeon?"

"The Council knew, yes. We thought it better, for a number of reasons, to maintain the façade that Eben the warlock had been apprehended."

Rage surged through me. If it weren't for my shoulder causing me agony with every movement, I might have thrown myself at her. "You let me rot in Nincs Varazslat for six years, knowing that I was innocent?"

"Knowing that you were not Eben. You had taken his brand, and we did not understand how. We still do not. Given the power of the brand and the uncertainty of how you were able to take it, we thought it best to keep you imprisoned."

"I was innocent!" I growled. "I knew nothing of sorcery. You threw me in a dungeon because I looked like an enemy of yours!"

"Not because you looked like him, but because you hold his power. You were too dangerous to be allowed to go free."

"You say you considered me dangerous. But when I was freed, you did not send your minions to find me."

"It was clear by that time that you were being used as a pawn in a game played by more powerful sorcerers. We decided not to interfere, and that decision has proved wise. Radovan is dead, and Eben was rendered powerless, at least for a time."

"But now he has returned, and he is more dangerous than ever."

"That is why we are speaking now."

"You are hypocrites, all of you," I seethed. "You claim to oppose magic, but you were quite willing to use me against Radovan and Eben. You have no qualms about using magic to summon a hailstorm to protect your temple. Why, your entire faith is built on a lie. The goddess you revere was resurrected only through—"

"Enough!" shouted the Reverend Mother. "Speak not another word, or I will give the order to shoot. Now, I will ask you again: do you intend to resist?"

I shook my head wearily. I was trembling with anger and exhaustion. I had no fight left in me.

"Good. Can you walk?"

I nodded.

"Come with me. Archers, lower your bows. You are dismissed."

To my surprise, the men immediately complied, leaving the Reverend Mother defenseless. Did she somehow know I was telling the truth? Or did she simply sense how weak I was? She turned and walked to a door behind her, and I managed to pull myself to my feet and follow. I stepped over the salt barrier. Nothing happened.

I followed the Reverend Mother down a hall to a small room furnished with two chairs. She closed the door behind me and bade me to sit down. As far as I could tell, we were completely alone. I could have reached out with my good arm and strangled her if I wanted to, but somehow she knew I would not.

I sat, and the Reverend Mother approached me. She reached out a bony hand and touched my shoulder, murmuring a prayer to Turelem. A strange warmth flowed through me, and the pain lessened. The Reverend Mother smiled and sat down across from me.

"More magic?" I said, moving my arm cautiously. My shoulder was still sore, but much of the damage seemed to have healed.

"That is not the word we use," the Reverend Mother said disinterestedly.

"What word do you use to describe the resurrection of Turelem?"

"Then you have read the book."

"I could not read it, but I saw enough to get the gist."

"And what is that?"

"The Book of the Dead is Bolond's notes on the building of the Temple of Romok. He used the temple to—among other things—raise Turelem from the dead. He put her on the path to starting the Cult."

The Reverend Mother smiled. "Why would Bolond, a sorcerer, start a movement to stamp out sorcery?"

"Perhaps he was trying to eliminate the competition," I said.

"Is that what you believe?"

"No," I said, after a moment. "I think Bolond had a change of heart. I think he realized that the spread of arcane knowledge throughout Orszag was only making things worse. I think he decided sorcery itself needed to be wiped out."

"But you also believe that the Cult uses sorcery to that end. This is a contradiction, as you have pointed out."

"That's right. You are hypocrites, using magic while decrying the use of magic. Bolond was evidently a hypocrite as well, of course, as the resurrection of Turelem indicates, but I think that perhaps he really did believe in a goal other than amassing power for himself. Unlike you."

The Reverend Mother smiled again. "You have it backwards, I'm afraid. I will not pretend that the Cult has always been pure in either intent or action, but it has always been our overarching goal to eliminate the use of magic in Orszag. Bolond, on the other hand, is… inconsistent."

"You mean he is mad."

"He is mad now, yes, but even before that, he was unstable. A factor we could not control. When it seemed that he had begun to work against us, we were forced to take action."

"You mean you imprisoned him. First in Nincs Varazslat, and now here."

"That is correct."

"I assume you intend the same fate for me?"

"Not necessarily," the Reverend Mother said. "You have been quite helpful to our cause since you were released. And we hope that you will help us deal with Eben."

"You want to me be your errand boy after what you did to me?"

"You will continue to act of your own volition, as you always have. As I said, we have been watching you. If we had wanted to exercise power over you, we would have apprehended your friends and held them for leverage. You have shown a curious tendency to look after those closest to you, even at the expense of your own efforts at seeking vengeance upon those who have wronged you. I think you know that Eben is a greater threat to those you care about than we are, and that you will work with us against him, even as you worked with him against Voros Korom."

"I have not forsworn my vengeance against you any more than I have against Eben," I said. "If anything, I hold you more responsible, because Eben was at least acting out of self-preservation. You knew I was innocent and threw me in Nincs Varazslat anyway, because it was convenient for you."

"I do not blame you for such sentiments. It is likely we deserve your approbation. But there will be time for your vendetta against us after Eben is dealt with."

"If you are so eager to stop Eben from rebuilding the temple, why did you send my friends away when they sought your help?"

"We could not be certain they were not spies working for Eben. We had heard you were traveling with an archer and a young acolyte, but it could have been a trick. We assumed that if we turned them away, you would come to us next, one way or another."

"Then take me to Bolond. He is the only one who can stop Eben."

"I do not believe Bolond can help you."

"Why? What have you done to him?"

The Reverend Mother sighed. "As I say, he has always been... unstable. But something happened to him when we apprehended him six years ago. It was not intentional, you understand, but magic is a dangerous thing. For you to truly understand, I must start at the beginning."

CHAPTER EIGHTEEN

"Thousands of years ago," the Reverend Mother began, "men in Orszag discovered the secrets of sorcery. Over time, their knowledge and power grew, and they began to document the workings of the energy called tvari and pass this knowledge down to other students. In the beginning, these men were little more than soothsayers and primitive physicians, but after many centuries they had gathered enough knowledge that the word *sorcerer* provoked fear rather than drawing jeers.

"The greatest of these sorcerers was a young man named Bolond, who dazzled the rulers of the land with his tricks, becoming wealthy and famous. Tiring of frivolous entertainments as he grew older, Bolond set his mind to a new project: traveling from Orszag to one of the many other worlds that sorcerers had long believed existed but had never been to. After many years, Bolond succeeded in traveling to a place called Veszedelem. Veszedelem was a rich and beautiful world, similar in many ways to Orszag, and Bolond greatly impressed the rulers of the kingdoms there, as the people of Veszedelem had no knowledge of sorcery.

"Bolond returned to Orszag with tales of this new world, but to his annoyance he was greeted with skepticism. He was unable to carry any artifacts from Veszedelem to Orszag, and many whispered that he had invented the place to cover his failure. Bolond determined to provide proof by finding a way to allow others to travel between the two worlds. For years, Bolond worked on this project, perfecting methods of focusing more and more tvari in order to increase his power. At last he mastered a spell that would allow him to transport others between worlds. He went to Veszedelem intending to use the spell to bring someone back with him.

"When he arrived in Veszedelem, though, he found that world strangely different. The sun seemed less bright, the colors of the flowers not as vibrant, the food less flavorful. The change was so subtle that the people in Veszedelem, who had experienced the degradation over the course of several years, could not point to anything specific that was wrong. They knew only that life was no longer as enjoyable as it once was.

"Bolond, who had hoped someday to open a channel of communications and trade between two vibrant, prosperous worlds, was disheartened at the change. Having discovered that tvari was the substance underlying all reality, he suspected that something was draining tvari from Veszedelem. He set up a laboratory in Veszedelem where he hoped to find a solution to the problem.

"It is said that Bolond made two important discoveries in the years that followed: the first was the secret to immortality, which he found almost by accident. This is Bolond's most closely guarded secret; as far as we know, he has never told anyone how he is able to use tvari to extend his own life. His secrecy on this matter is explained by his second discovery: Bolond found that it was his own sorcery that was draining Veszedelem of its vitality."

I interrupted her. "This sounds like more Cult propaganda," I said. "It is convenient to blame sorcery for the degradation of Veszedelem because it gives you an excuse to oppose the use of sorcery outside the Cult."

"Disbelieve if you wish," the Reverend Mother said, "but by now you have learned enough about sorcery to know I tell you the truth. The energy used by sorcery has to come from somewhere. For whatever reason, tvari flows readily from Veszedelem to other worlds, such as Orszag, but not vice versa. Some say this is because Veszedelem was the one true world, and that all the other worlds are mere shadows of it. The sorcerers of

Orszag had unknowingly been sucking the life out of Veszedelem, and the greatest culprit among them was Bolond. Not only that, but the degradation would continue to accelerate as arcane knowledge was disseminated to more and more sorcerers in Orszag—and perhaps even in other worlds. Bolond became convinced it was his responsibility to repair the damage.

"Upon returning to Orszag, Bolond discovered another consequence of the draining of tvari: time now passed more quickly in Veszedelem than in Orszag. He had been in Veszedelem for several years, but less than a year had passed in Orszag. He realized that this differential too would increase as the degradation of Veszedelem continued.

"Bolond traveled across Orszag, recruiting sorcerers with the ostensible goal of finding a solution to the problem plaguing Veszedelem. A cynic might think he intended primarily to slow the degradation of Veszedelem by gathering all the sorcerers in one place and putting them to work on a project that would allow them little chance to share their knowledge with others. In any case, he brought them to Veszedelem using his magic, where he built an outpost far out on a plain where they could work in peace. After a few years, many of the sorcerers became convinced the task was futile. Veszedelem continued to deteriorate, and the sorcerers lived sad, solitary lives in the outpost on the gray plain. Some threatened to leave, but Bolond bribed them with the gift of immortality.

"The sorcerers realized too late that Bolond had tricked them. While he was careful to return to Orszag periodically, the sorcerers toiling away in Veszedelem had remained there for years. Their bodies had begun to be drained of their vitality, and they found that they could no longer return to Orszag. Most of them lacked the power to return to Orszag on their own in any case, but even those who had mastered traveling between worlds could no longer do it.

"By this time, Veszedelem had devolved into a state of constant war between rival kingdoms. Additionally, people there began to suspect what Bolond had already ascertained: that sorcerers were to blame for what was happening to Veszedelem. Fearful that the people would turn against him, Bolond made his outpost into an impenetrable fortress, the keep called Sotetseg.

Those who worked there were essentially prisoners, unable to
return to their homeland but hated and feared by the natives of
Veszedelem. Seeing no alternative, they continued to work at the
task of restoring Veszedelem, all the while fearing that their
efforts were only making things worse.

"The population of Veszedelem dwindled over the next
several centuries, as fertility decreased, babies were stillborn, and
war, famine and pestilence spread across the land. Many of the
children who survived carried strange deformations. The most
monstrous of these were killed or left to die. The deformations
grew worse with each succeeding generation, until many were no
longer recognizably human. Bands of hideous monsters roamed
across Veszedelem. The most powerful of these monsters was
Arnyek, who wished to destroy all of reality to end the suffering
of Veszedelem.

"The sorcerers working at Sotetseg did have one success: they
managed to create a protective aura around the keep that repelled
the monsters and inhibited the worst of the mutagenic effects. It
wasn't enough to make the sorcerers beloved among the
population, but as word spread of the protective aura, hundreds
of people came to settle on the plain around Sotetseg.

"Bolond and the sorcerers in Sotetseg were the only ones
who could stop Arnyek from destroying Veszedelem and all the
other worlds along with it. Knowing this, Arnyek raised an army
of monsters to wipe out humanity and destroy the keep. He
might never have gotten through their defenses—"

"But Bolond was betrayed by a sorcerer named Lorenz," I
interjected, "who let Arnyek's hordes into the keep. I'm
beginning to understand why he did so."

The Reverend Mother nodded. "Bolond was not well-loved
in Sotetseg, and many of the sorcerers plotted against him. As far
as I know, only Lorenz went so far as to ally himself with Arnyek.
He believed the efforts to save Veszedelem were hopeless, and
that Arnyek's solution was preferable to continuing the charade.

"The attackers were repelled, but only Bolond and three
other sorcerers remained alive after the assault. The three
sorcerers, sometimes called the Masters, sealed themselves in the
upper levels of a tower where Bolond could not reach them.

"Realizing he had failed, Bolond turned his efforts to saving the few human beings left alive in the villages on the plain. At this time, the Plain of Savlos was mostly unpopulated, so he thought it safe to lead the refugees there. To allow the natives of Veszedelem to travel to Orszag, though, Bolond would need a permanent gateway between the worlds. He commissioned the building of two identical structures to act as portals, one in Orszag, at the current location of Nagyvaros, and one in a remote location in Veszedelem. He needed to keep both locations secret for fear that his plans would be disrupted. In Veszedelem, this was not a problem, as there were now many areas of unpopulated wasteland where his builders could work in peace, but in Orszag he encountered resistance from a group of nearby settlers presided over by a woman named Turelem."

"I know the story," I said. "Bolond met with Turelem, explaining his intention to build a gateway between the two worlds. Turelem refused his request. Bolond appealed to the settlers directly, persuading them that their lives would be improved by the union of the two worlds. Turelem was thrown into the river Zold and drowned. Bolond had the locals build the gateway. Refugees came pouring through, but they could not tolerate the realness of our world. So Bolond expanded the gateway into a temple that was designed to absorb tvari, to make the area around it more like the shadow world the refugees had left. Around this time, Turelem returned from the dead and founded the Cult that bears her name.

"But Orszag was still too real for the people of Veszedelem, so they dug tunnels underground to escape the sun. The locals were also displeased, because the temple had turned the area into a strange, dismal place. Fearing that the locals would appeal to one of the kingdoms of Orszag for help, Bolond made a preemptive alliance with one of them. The alliance was formalized by the marriage of the king's daughter to a man from Veszedelem, whom Bolond had set up as king at Elhalad. Their child was Voros Korom, the demon prince."

"Correct so far as that goes," the Reverend Mother said. "But Voros Korom was not their only child."

"What are you saying? There was another heir to the throne of Elhalad?"

"Indeed. Voros Korom's younger brother, the more monstrous of the two. His name is Eben."

"You are joking. Eben is Voros Korom's brother?"

"He is. Although he does not share Voros Korom's monstrous appearance, Eben was, in his way, just as powerful. He had a preternatural gift for sorcery; as far as I know, he is the only sorcerer other than Bolond to have found the secret to immortality—although he must continually swap bodies to keep his spirit alive."

"That explains the rivalry between the two. Each of them wanted to rule Nagyvaros."

"More precisely, they each claimed the legacy of Elhalad."

I nodded but said no more. Was the Reverend Mother speaking only of the Book of the Dead or something else? Did she know about Fold Alatt?

The Reverend Mother went on, "Eben aspired to the throne and plotted against Voros Korom but could not defeat him. Finally Eben conspired with Elhalad's enemies against the city. There was no clear victor in the battle that followed. Voros Korom was nearly killed and was forced to flee to Veszedelem. In the chaos after the attack, Bolond and Eben were forced to flee as well.

"The invaders tore down the gateway and the temple and dragged the stone slabs to the Maganyos Valley. Many of the city's residents, desperate to escape, attempted to flee through the gate back to Veszedelem. Those who did not make it were trapped between worlds as the gateway was torn down.

"I suppose you know the rest. The blight remained for several hundred years, but eventually the history of Elhalad was forgotten. The Szaszok people began to build settlements on the plain and founded the city of Nagyvaros. The Cult of Turelem grew along with the population of the region. The Cult did what it could to apprehend the sorcerers who remained in Orszag and to secure any artifacts left behind by Bolond and his followers.

"We had nearly wiped out sorcery completely when Varastis discovered the Book of the Dead in the tunnels under Nagyvaros and began to spread the knowledge contained in that book. Our efforts to destroy his school culminated in the Purge, after which only Eben, Radovan, Varastis and a few others at Magas Komaron remained alive. Thanks to you, Radovan is dead, and I gather from Ilona's report that no one is left alive at Magas Komaron. Only Eben remains."

"Eben and I," I said.

"Yes," the Reverend Mother said with a smile. "And for now at least, Eben is the greater threat. So great that when we learned he was looking for the Book of the Dead under Nagyvaros, we sent an acolyte to the Governor to warn him. She was torn apart by creatures summoned by Eben."

I nodded, having deduced as much. "You fear the truth getting out."

"The Cult exists to promulgate the truth."

"The Cult is built on a lie."

"Not a lie, a concealment of part of the truth. The truth guides us, but not all truths are fit for all people."

"Listen to me, Reverend Mother. I will work with you to stop Eben, but I will not keep your secret. When this is over, I will see that everyone knows what is in that book."

"I am counting on it," the Reverend Mother said.

I was taken aback. "You do not intend to stop me?"

"Once Eben has been defeated, the Cult's battle against sorcery will be finished. If the Cult is to survive after that, it must be in a different form. The current regime will fall, and we will have to hope that our message is strong enough to survive the defeat of our enemies."

"Forgive me if I am skeptical of your willingness to give up power."

"You are right to be so. I am in the minority in the Council. We are in agreement that you are our best hope against Eben, but I may not be able to keep the Cult from turning its efforts against you after Eben has been dealt with."

"What does the Council expect me to do against Eben?" I asked. "He is a far more powerful sorcerer than I. Do they intend to use their magic to help me?"

The Reverend Mother shook her head. "Our 'magic,' as you call it, does not work that way. We have only the power to request aid from Turelem, and only in very specific and prescribed ways."

"Then how did you heal my shoulder?"

"Higher level acolytes have access to what you might call a pool of healing energy. The pool is constantly being replenished by appeals to Turelem. But it can be used only to heal, not to harm."

"And the hailstorm?"

"In extreme situations, the energy can be redirected to defend Regi Otthon or its acolytes. The most effective way of doing this is to manipulate natural conditions, such as the weather. We have only had to do it three times in the history of the Cult, and each time it has completely depleted the energy pool. If the Barbaroki had pressed their attack, we would have been slaughtered. It has taken two weeks of constant appeals by hundreds of acolytes to get the pool back to the level where I can perform a simple healing touch. The point is, our 'magic' is unlikely to be of any use in preventing Eben from rebuilding the Temple of Romok."

"Then I fail to see how I am to defeat him."

"You possess the brand. It holds most of his power."

"So I've been told," I said, "but it does me no good if I do not know how to use it. The Masters are dead and I can't very well go to Eben for tutoring any longer. Unless I can learn to fully harness the power of the brand, I cannot defeat Eben."

The Reverend Mother regarded me silently for a moment. "That is unfortunate," she said at last. "The Council was hoping you had learned enough to be a match for Eben. If you are not, you are a liability."

"You mean the Cult will kill me to prevent Eben from taking the brand back."

"No one has spoken the words aloud, but I believe they would not hesitate if they thought that was the only way to defeat Eben."

"You cannot stop them?"

"I am only one vote among seven. I would not betray you, but I am not confident I could carry the day, and my resistance might cost me my leadership position. Then the Cult would be free to hunt you down. We have many allies; you would not live long."

"Then you must allow me to see Bolond."

"Impossible."

"Why?"

"As I've said, he will not help you. He is not in possession of his faculties, and if he were, I do not think he would be inclined to aid us. Furthermore, even allowing you to communicate with him would pose great danger to us."

"Do you not hold him in a specially constructed prison?"

"My opinion is that the prison is largely theater. Our barriers may inhibit the flow of tvari somewhat, but not enough to stop a sorcerer as powerful as Bolond. Bolond remains in his cell because it has not occurred to him to try to escape."

"What if he does escape? How could that be any worse than Eben seizing control of both Orszag and Veszedelem? How could it be worse than Arnyek destroying both worlds, which seems likely to happen whether or not we stop Eben?"

The Reverend Mother sighed. "No, I will not loose another evil on the world simply because we cannot contain the evils already here."

"I am not asking you to," I said. "I am merely asking you to give me a fighting chance. Put whatever restrictions on my visits you wish, but at least let me speak to the man. I've learned a great deal from Bolond already, even though I don't think he ever intended to teach me. Perhaps I can learn something from him even in his madness."

The Reverend Mother sat quietly for some time. "All right," she said wearily. "I will arrange for you to see Bolond. Return here tonight, one hour before sundown. I will leave word with the guard at the side entrance that you are to be allowed to pass. Come directly to this chamber. If anyone else sees you, you are in danger. The rest of the Council will not approve of me allowing you to meet Bolond. If you are apprehended, I will not help you."

"I understand, Reverend Mother," I said. "Thank you."

CHAPTER NINETEEN

I left Regi Otthon and spent the afternoon in the darkest corner of a nearby tavern, hoping not to be spotted by any agents of the Cult. Delivaros is not the place to be walking around with a warlock's brand on one's face. Fortunately, acolytes tended not to frequent taverns, and their other agents apparently had better things to do. I was unmolested.

Just before sundown, I returned to Regi Otthon, finding my way to the door the Reverend Mother had told me about. The guard greeted me with a nod and let me inside. The halls were deserted; I suspected the Reverend Mother had selected this time because the acolytes would be at supper. I made my way to her door and knocked. The Reverend Mother exited and gestured for me to walk alongside her.

"Before I take you to Bolond," she said as we walked, "I must tell you how we came to capture him, because that is the reason for his current state."

"Please do," I said.

"Since the fall of Elhalad over a thousand years ago, Bolond has remained mostly aloof from the struggles between the Cult and the sorcerers of Orszag. Some of our kind believe he continued to work at undoing the damage he had done to Veszedelem, while others believed he was working on other tasks. Some thought he had sworn off sorcery entirely and lived as a simple hermit in some remote location.

"After the Purge, however, Bolond reappeared. He founded a new school of sorcery at Yenoom Nivek, about a hundred miles west of here, with the apparent purpose of destroying the Cult. It seemed that with the near-total eradication of sorcery in Orszag, Bolond feared that the Cult was becoming too powerful—and for good reason, as you suggested. Bolond had always hoped the Cult and the sorcerers would cancel each other out, but now it appeared that the Cult would survive, unopposed. Bolond might have succeeded in his aim of destroying the cult, but Yenoom Nivek was wiped out by the Torzseki, who claimed the settlement was on their territory. Bolond was not present during the attack, but his students were slaughtered."

"A hundred miles to the west of Delivaros? That would put it on the other side of the Zold, well outside Torzsek territory. And I've never heard of the Torzseki engaging in wholesale slaughter." In my experience the Torzseki tended to be shrewd and pragmatic in their raids, which was one of the main reasons they had lost so much territory to the more vicious and fanatical Barbaroki over the years. Even if there had been a territorial dispute with the settlers of Yenoom Nivek, I couldn't see the Torzseki slaughtering non-combatants.

"It was unexpected, that is for certain," the Reverend Mother said. "The Council had considered approaching the Torzseki to form an alliance against Yenoom Nivek, but nothing came of it. So I was surprised to learn the Torzseki had obliterated Yenoom Nivek on their own."

"Perhaps some of the others on the Council decided to proceed in secret?"

"It is possible, but unlikely. They would have needed my support to make any sort of significant offer to the Torzseki. Stranger still, Nebjosa denies the Torzseki had anything to do with the attack."

"Nebjosa is usually honest to a fault," I said.

"That is my experience as well. But one of our acolytes claimed to have seen a Torzsek war party heading toward Yenoom Nivek shortly before the attack. It was led by the man who is now Nebjosa's right hand."

"Davor Sabas?"

"That is the one."

"How long ago did this happen?"

"About four years ago."

"Just before Bolond was imprisoned in Nincs Varazslat."

"Yes. After the destruction of Yenoom Nivek, Bolond was desperate to stop the Cult. Perhaps he suspected we had something to do with the Torzseki attack. He went to the Governor of Nagyvaros and told him of his concerns. The Governor, Nandor, was sympathetic and instituted a policy of eliminating agents of the Cult from his government. The Council reacted by having Nandor assassinated."

"Then it's true," I said. "I had thought that was just a rumor started by anti-Cult partisans."

"I voted against the plot, for what it's worth, but I was overruled. Governor Nandor was poisoned and replaced with a puppet of Delivaros."

"Why not just kill Bolond?"

"Bolond was too powerful and too wary for us to attack directly. We already had agents in place in the Governor's Palace. Killing him was relatively easy."

"It seems your organization will do just about anything to retain its power," I observed.

"Moreso even than you think," the Reverend Mother replied. "For the purpose of the assassination was not merely to replace the Governor. It was to test a theory, and hopefully catch Bolond in the process. You see, some on the Council believed that Bolond had become fascinated by the way time passed more quickly in Veszedelem than in Orszag, and that since the fall of Elhalad one of his goals had been to master time itself. We believed this partly because of rumors we had heard about Bolond's activities, and partly because our own work on the subject suggested that mastery of time was possible."

"The Cult can control the passage of time?" I asked, dubiously.

"Not in so many words. But we can sometimes... exert influence over events in the past. Our ability to do so is very limited, and requires a great deal of power and preparation, but we knew enough to suspect that Bolond was trying to manipulate the flow of time to undo what he had done to Veszedelem."

"So you set a trap for him."

"Precisely. We suspected that if Nandor were killed, Bolond would attempt to undo the assassination by somehow going backwards in time and warning him. We were right. Bolond tried it. What he didn't realize was that we were waiting for him. In order to shift backwards through time, Bolond had to first go to the place between worlds, where time does not exist. We caught him there and brought him back to Orszag. At the time there was no better place to keep him than Nincs Varazslat, so he was taken there."

"That is where I met him," I said. "Rather, that is where I heard his voice coming to me through a hole in the wall. I was not entirely certain he was there at all. He did not seem to know where he was."

"Being apprehended in the in-between caused Bolond's mind to become confused. He had been attempting to move a day backward in time, and now he is stuck reliving the same day over and over. Every day he awakes with no memory of the day before. It was probably only his confused mental state that prevented him from escaping Nincs Varazslat. When the prison we constructed for him here was finished, we had him moved. Even now, he thinks he is in an antechamber in the palace, awaiting his meeting with the Governor."

"Then he has not changed since I last spoke with him."

"It would appear not."

"You think he is faking?"

"No. I mean to say only that not all is as it seems." We had reached a door at the end of a long hallway. Two men in full armor and bearing halberds stood, one on either side. They saluted as the Reverend Mother approached.

"This man needs to speak with the prisoner," she said.

"Your Holiness?" the man on the right said uncertainly, looking at my face.

"Were my words unclear? The prisoner is to be interrogated."

"Yes, Your Holiness. It's just… is this man not a sorcerer himself?"

"This man is in my employ, and I need him to interrogate the prisoner. Open the door and step aside."

The guard looked to his comrade, who shrugged. "Yes, Your Holiness," said the first man after a moment. He took a key from his belt, unlocked the door and opened it, standing aside to let me pass.

"Be quick about it," the Reverend Mother said, and I gave her a nod. She turned and walked back down the hall. I went through the door, and the guard followed. We were in a narrow, curved hallway that was dimly lit by a flickering light somewhere out of sight to my right. The wall in front of me was made of blocks of some pale gray mineral. To my left was a blank wall of ordinary stone blocks. The guard closed the door and began walking down the hall to the right. I followed him, and we made our way around the curve to the left.

As I walked, I allowed my fingers to rub against the left wall. Pulling them away, I found my fingertips coated with white residue. Tasting it confirmed my suspicion: salt.

We followed the hall until we had walked a half circle with a diameter of about forty feet. At this point, the guard reached another blank wall and turned sharply left to enter another, more tightly curved hallway, nestled inside of the one we had just traversed. When we'd again walked a half circle, we came to another blank wall. In the right-hand wall was a heavy wooden door. The guard opened an eye-level slot in the door, barked an order to stand back, and then opened the door. He held it open long enough for me to slip inside and then closed it behind him.

Bolond's cell was a circular room about twelve feet in diameter, with a domed ceiling. The walls and ceiling were made of blocks of salt into which had been carved hundreds of protective wards that had then been filled in with silver. Even the door was coated with salt and inscribed with the same silver glyphs, so that when it was closed, the pattern was unbroken. Having a basic understanding of how tvari flowed and how salt impeded its movement, I could appreciate the design of the prison: two concentric walls of salt blocks, separated by an open passage, would make it nearly impossible for the occupant to draw tvari from outside the cell. Whether the glyphs augmented the effect in some way I did not know. The room was lit by a single lamp far overhead; it seemed to be supplied by oil from somewhere outside. The room was furnished only with a bed and the rug. Bolond sat cross-legged on the far end of a tattered oval rug.

I had never actually seen Bolond before, but he looked about as I expected. He was small, not much over five feet in height and compactly built, with short, greyish-white hair. He looked to be about forty years old, though of course he was much, much older. He greeted me with an air of expectation that immediately turned to disappointment when he realized I was not going to be taking him to the Governor.

"Hello, Bolond," I said. "My name is Konrad."

"I do not care who you are," Bolond said. "I am here to see the Governor. There is an urgent matter I need to discuss with him. Take me to him or leave."

"I cannot take you to the Governor," I said. "We are in a cell below Regi Otthon, the temple of the Cult of Turelem. You intended to warn the Governor of his impending assassination, but you failed. That Governor is long-dead, and a new Governor reigns in his place."

"If you intend to keep speaking foolishness," Bolond said irritably, "you may do it elsewhere."

The Reverend Mother had warned me that telling Bolond the truth would only annoy him, but I did not see the point in lying. I'd never been able to get any information out of Bolond while I was in Nincs Varazslat except by way of his songs, no matter what story I told him, so I thought I might as well start with the truth.

"Do you remember me, Bolond?" I asked, taking a seat across from him on the rug. "We spoke with each other many times while we were incarcerated in Nincs Varazslat."

"I have never been to that place."

"Forgive me for my brusqueness, Bolond, but you are mistaken. About four years ago, you attempted to go back in time to warn the Governor, but you were apprehended by the acolytes. Since then, you have been reliving that day, over and over. They threw you in Nincs Varazslat, where I was being held for the crime of sorcery. After a time, they brought you here, where you have remained since then. Every day you awake with no memory of the day before, convinced that you are awaiting a meeting with the Governor."

"Foolishness!" Bolond shouted, getting to his feet. "Attendant, I insist you remove this man! And take me to the Governor, immediately!"

I got to my feet as well, towering over the little man. "Sit down!" I barked, surprising myself with my own belligerence.

Bolond jumped and then looked at my face as if seeing me for the first time. "The brand…."

"I am a sorcerer," I said. "I took this brand from Eben the warlock."

He nodded thoughtfully.

"Please, sit down."

Bolond sat down again, and I did the same.

"You defeated Eben?" Bolond asked.

"No. I exiled him to Veszedelem, but he has returned. He intends to rebuild the Temple of Romok. Do you understand what that means?"

Bolond nodded slowly. "I thought Eben was dead. If he is not…."

"If he is not, then Eben is a greater threat to Orszag than the Cult of Turelem. I need your help to stop him."

"Stop him," Bolond echoed, straining to follow my train of thought. "But first, we must warn the Governor."

"The Governor is dead," I said. "You tried to warn him of the attempt on his life, but you failed. That was over three years ago. We must focus on stopping Eben."

Bolond shook his head. "Eben is dead."

It was pointless. I had nearly broken through, but there just wasn't enough of his mind left to grasp how much had changed since he had begun his mission to save the Governor. I opted for a different tack.

"Bolond, it may be several hours before the Governor is able to see you. While we are waiting, would you teach me some of what you know about manipulating tvari?"

Bolond shook his head furiously. "No, no! Who are you?"

"It is I, Konrad. One of your followers, along with Arron and Haneen. You intended to teach us in order to help you defeat the Cult of Turelem."

"No, no. Attendant! This man is vexing me. Please have him removed. And take me to the Governor!"

I sighed. The problem was not only that Bolond was stuck reliving the same day; his mental capacity had been reduced to the point where he could no longer entertain a new thought. If I learned anything from him, it would only be inadvertently on his part, the way I had learned from his songs at Nincs Varazslat.

What had happened to Bolond's mind? Was it gone for good? If so, where had it gone? I thought of the Reverend Mother's words: *not all is as it seems.*

Bolond had been captured in between worlds. I had learned that it was possible for a being to exist in two worlds at once. But was it possible for a person's spirit to be split between two worlds? Or between our world and the place in between?

I decided to try once more. "Bolond, while we are waiting for the Governor, would you sing me a song?"

Bolond seemed puzzled by the request. "A song?"

"There is a song I heard once, years ago. I have been trying to remember the words, but I cannot. Perhaps you know it. It goes like this." I cleared my throat and began to sing.

No one knows what Varastis found
buried so deep under the ground
He left that night without a sound
for Magas Komaron

Setting out early on Nyarkozep
he led his disciples 'cross the wind-blasted steppe

I broke off, humming the rest of the stanza. As I'd hoped, Bolond resumed the song:

to the path of Polgar his company kept
toward Magas Komaron

Turelem's eyes watched the plain and the heath
and all of the gaps in Galibar's Teeth
so clever Varastis took the way underneath

to Magas Komaron

While Bolond sang, I closed my eyes and sent my spirit to the in-between. It required somewhat more effort than previous attempts, probably owing to the salt barrier interfering with the flow of tvari, but the prison was no real impediment to the power of the brand. I supposed that Bolond had access to at least as much power, in some other way. The Reverend Mother was right: it was only Bolond's compromised mental state that was keeping him here.

Once in the in-between, I listened for the song, and after some amount of time that was no time at all, I heard:

The door that goes nowhere can still be a key
if opened when ogres are having their tea
and the throat choked with poison will soon breathe free
toward Magas Komaron

A wizard can't tell the wind not to blow
but there are places where not even the wind can go
and there in the dark the glimmer did show
of Magas Komaron

Whatever it is that Varastis knows
it led him to the place where the beacon now glows
and he gazes down upon his helpless foes
from Magas Komaron

I stood on the crest of a grassy hill overlooking a well-kept vineyard. An orange sun blazed pleasantly in the afternoon sky. A man stood not far off, regarding the vines, which hung low with ripe grapes. This was, I realized, another shared delusion, like the tunnel where I'd found Arron and Haneen, though a much more agreeable one. The man turned toward me, smiling. It was Bolond.

Hello, Konrad," he said.

CHAPTER TWENTY

"Bolond," I said, taking a step toward him. "You recognize me?"

"In this place, yes. That thing you were talking to in the cell below Regi Otthon was little more than a shell. My physical form, animated only by a basic awareness of its surroundings and a few residual thoughts. It is similar in some ways to a kovet, possessing material form and a rudimentary will but no real intelligence. Some would call it a homunculus."

"Then you are not truly insane."

"I am in full possession of my faculties, for all the good it does me. While my body is locked in that cell, I cannot escape."

"It is a more pleasant prison, at least. You remember speaking with me in Nincs Varazslat?"

"Yes, I am able to make use of my senses, although I cannot speak or act through the homunculus."

"Then when you sang to me in Nincs Varazslat, it was not truly you at all. Just a mindless simulacrum of you, repeating sounds the way a mockingbird does."

Bolond smiled. "Yes, but the homunculus is not entirely outside of my control. I have learned I can teach it simple things, the way you can teach a young child through repetition."

"Songs," I said.

"Yes. Little more than nursery rhymes, but containing deeper truths. Truths I suspected you might have need of."

"Then you did intend to instruct me. Why?"

"To be honest, I did it partly to amuse myself. But knowing that you possessed the brand, I also thought you might prove a valuable foil against Radovan and Eben if you ever got out. In this, I gather I was correct."

"Then you are aware of developments in Orszag?"

"Whenever something important happens in Orszag, the Council sends an acolyte into my prison to interrogate my homunculus. By virtue of sheer persistence, sometimes they are able to get some answers from it. Fragments of memory lodged in the homunculus's brain. Lately they've been interrogating it for several hours every day. Often I am able to deduce what has happened from the line of questioning. On rare occasions, I am able to direct the homunculus to prompt them for more information."

"How is that possible, if you have no direct control over it?"

Bolond smiled. "You must understand, Konrad, that time does not exist here. If I wished, I could spend a hundred years training the homunculus to answer questions in a particular way."

"And have you done this?"

He laughed. "No. It is a terribly slow and imprecise process, like training a dog to play chess. I might train it to answer a question in a particular way, but I have no way of knowing for certain what question will follow, and the more complicated the training gets, the more likely the homunculus is to revert to rote behavior. If I were to try to guide the homunculus through an hour of interrogation, I would truly go mad. No, the best I can do is to occasionally get the homunculus to utter a word or phrase that might provoke the questioner to reveal some additional information."

"And they get information from you as well."

"Some, yes. Since I have been here, they have been able to fill in most of the gaps in their understanding of the history of Veszedelem and Orszag."

"Then it's true, what the Reverend Mother told me. That you used the power of the Temple of Romok to bring Turelem back from the dead."

"Yes. I manipulated Turelem and her followers into starting the Cult, over a thousand years ago. I intended for the Cult to be a check on the spread of sorcery. I suppose it's fitting that I'm now imprisoned by them myself."

"You know of Eben's plotting?"

"I know that Radovan and Voros Korom are dead, and that Eben has been banished to Veszedelem."

"Eben has returned," I said. "He has taken the body of one of my comrades, a young man named Vili."

Bolond nodded. "That explains the Cult's renewed interest in the Temple of Romok. I assume Eben has the book?"

"Yes. He is using the Barbaroki to rebuild the temple in the Maganyos Valley."

"What of Sotetseg?"

"It has fallen to Arnyek."

Bolond sighed. "Then Orszag is doomed."

"It seems that way," I said. "Either Eben will rule Orszag or Arnyek will destroy it."

Bolond shook his head. "Eben cannot stand against Arnyek, even if he manages to rebuild the temple. With me in prison, Sotetseg was our only defense. As long as it stood, Arnyek could not bring his plan to fruition. If Eben had joined forces with the Masters, they could have held him at bay indefinitely."

"Apparently Eben was too ambitious for that," I said. "What is it that you want, Bolond? Ever since Nincs Varazslat, I have been trying to figure out what side you are on. The Reverend Mother told me you intended to repair the damage done to Veszedelem by the use of sorcery. Is that true?"

"That has long been my goal, yes. If Sotetseg has fallen, though, we are beyond that. Arnyek must be stopped at all costs."

"Meaning what?"

"We cannot allow the Temple of Romok to be rebuilt. The only way to save Orszag is to cut it off entirely from Veszedelem. Veszedelem then must be destroyed, along with Arnyek and everyone else in it."

"Is that possible?"

"I believe so. But not as long as I am imprisoned."

"What of the innocents in Veszedelem? You would destroy them too?"

"There are no innocents left in Veszedelem. There are only monsters."

"Vili's soul is there," I said. "And until recently, two of your followers, Arron and Haneen, were there as well. There are almost certainly others who still struggle against Arnyek and his demons."

"You know of Arron and Haneen?"

"Evidently they survived the massacre at Yenoom Nivek. They were seeking you in the Maganyos Valley when they were killed by the wraiths that haunted that place. Their souls were exiled to Veszedelem, where they had to constantly fight against being pulled into the vortex that connected Orszag and Veszedelem. When I defeated Voros Korom, they became trapped in a loop between the two worlds. It was only yesterday that I was finally able to destroy the loop and bring peace to them and the other poor souls trapped there."

"That is all I want for everyone in Veszedelem," Bolond said. "To end their suffering."

"But is that your decision to make?" I asked. "Some may wish to be freed of their suffering, but what if some want to continue to fight?"

"Did you ask every soul trapped in that loop whether they wanted a chance to keep fighting?" Bolond asked.

"It isn't the same," I said. "They weren't even human anymore."

"And you think the other creatures in Veszedelem are? Anything that has survived until now in that place is more monster than human."

"In any case," I said, "our priority at this point must be preventing the rebuilding of the Temple of Romok."

"We are agreed on that. You understand that it will be very difficult for Eben to complete the reconstruction without the brand?"

"What are you suggesting?"

"You are the true threat to Orszag, Konrad."

"I am also the only one who has a chance to stop Eben. Or Arnyek, for that matter."

"Only as long as I remain imprisoned here."

"In any case," I said, "Eben claimed he could complete the reconstruction even without the brand."

"That is true, I'm afraid. But eliminating the brand will at least buy me some time."

"Buy *you* some time? How do you expect to stop Eben while you are stuck in between worlds?"

"The cell allows me only tenuous contact with my physical form. If my body were removed from the cell, however, I believe I could rejoin it."

"That is not going to happen," I said. "The Cult will not allow it, and even if I wished to, I do not think I could break you out."

"You have little choice if you wish to stop Arnyek—or even Eben."

"I do not accept that," I said. "I killed Radovan. I defeated Voros Korom. I sent Eben to Veszedelem. I think I can beat him again. I only need you to help me learn how to use the power of the brand."

Bolond shook his head. "There is no time."

"Don't try that on me," I snapped. "You said yourself time does not exist here. I could spend the equivalent of a thousand years training to defeat Eben and then go to face him tomorrow."

"Impossible," Bolond said. "This place will not drain you in the same way that Veszedelem does, but you will still tire. You will need to return to your body periodically to rest, and time will pass while you are there. It will take Eben at most a few months to rebuild the temple, even without the brand. To learn what you must to defeat Eben would take years. Furthermore, I cannot teach you what you need to know in the in-between."

"Why not? I thought you were the greatest sorcerer who has ever lived."

"That I am, but one cannot learn to use tvari in the in-between. It would be like trying to learn to swim in the desert. I can teach you theory and concepts, but you will truly learn only by practicing, and you can only practice in Orszag."

"There must be another teacher, then. Are there perhaps others like Haneen and Arron? Sorcerers who escaped the Torzsek massacre at Yenoom Nivek? Or students of yours elsewhere?"

Bolond shook his head. "Yenoom Nivek was a failed experiment. I had tried for centuries to find a way to channel tvari that would not worsen the deterioration of Veszedelem. In theory, there should be many sources of tvari, but I had learned only one. It occurred to me several years ago that perhaps my early education had biased me against other ways of using tvari, and that centuries of practice in my own way had blinded me to the others. I thought perhaps if I trained a group of students from an early age in the possibilities of magic without constraining their methods, some of them might learn to pull tvari from a place other than Veszedelem. An unpopulated world, perhaps, or a place with so much tvari that the drain would not even be noticed."

"But you failed."

"Yes. Most of the students quit in frustration, despite the fact that I'd specifically selected them for their innate ability. The few who succeeded in harnessing tvari ended up doing it the same way I did. They somehow found their way to Veszedelem without me telling them. Haneen and Arron were my best students, but I could not continue to train them without worsening the problem I had set out to solve. Meanwhile, most of the remaining sorcerers were killed or forced to flee during the Purge, and I became convinced that the balance of power had swung too far toward the Cult of Turelem. I left Yenoom Nivek and refocused my efforts on weakening the Cult's hold on Nagyvaros. Not long after, the Governor was assassinated. I made the mistake of transgressing the Cult's turf by attempting to go a day backwards in time to warn him, which is how I ended up here."

"Then you must teach me what you can. If I can learn the theory, I can practice on my own. If you help me defeat Eben, I promise I will do what I can to persuade the Cult to release you."

"Very well," Bolond said. "Listen closely, because although we may have unlimited time, I am not fond of repeating myself."

*****

Bolond spent what seemed like several hours explaining to me the workings of tvari. Occasionally I would ask questions to clarify some matter, but most of the time I was silent and simply listened. At first Bolond seemed reticent and perhaps a bit resentful at having to explain basic concepts to me, but I have always been a fast learner, and between my own studies and Eben's instruction, I knew enough that I possessed a basic framework on which to hang the specific points Bolond made. As the lesson progressed, I flattered myself that Bolond was beginning to enjoy himself, having found a pupil who was perhaps as apt as Haneen or Arron. Bolond was certainly a better teacher than Eben had been, and he made free use of our surroundings to illustrate various concepts. The orchard and everything else around us were products of Bolond's imagination, and it was no trouble for him to cause diagrams to come into being on the ground in front of us or to reconfigure the clouds into a moving illustration.

The downside of such a teaching environment was, as Bolond had indicated, that tvari does not work there the same way as it does in a physical place like Orszag. The power of tvari comes from the interplay of spirit and substance; in the in-between, nothing is truly real, so working miracles there is a trivial matter. Bolond had likened it to learning to swim in the desert, but it was more like learning to balance on a high wire while standing on the ground: success was assured, and there was no penalty for failure. I could go through the motions of casting a spell, but I would have no idea whether I was doing it correctly until I returned to Orszag and tried it there.

Another matter on which I was unable to get a definite answer was whether I could kill Eben without killing Vili as well. "You must give up on the idea of rescuing your protégé," Eben said. "By the time you face Eben, he will have been in Veszedelem so long that it is unlikely his mind will be capable of returning to his body, even if Eben could be enticed to leave it."

"Then it is possible to cast Eben's spirit out?"

"Possible, but even more difficult than killing him. You would have better luck trying to convince Eben to leave voluntarily, as he did when he transferred his spirit to Beata."

"Is it possible for him to switch bodies again?"

"Of course. To return to Orszag from Veszedelem, he needed a willing vessel. But to move from Vili's body to another is much simpler. It is still a draining transition, and Eben loses a little of himself with each transfer, so he will not make the decision lightly. But this is foolishness. You will have no leeway for such niceties. You must be prepared to kill Eben without hesitation. Your friend is lost."

The sky reddened as the sun sank toward the hills in the distance, and Bolond told me it was time for me to go. On some level I realized that the sun here was just another product of Bolond's imagination—and mine, to the extent that I participated in creating the illusion—but it was convincing nevertheless. I had begun to grow tired; the lesson was more taxing than I had realized. Still I pleaded with him to teach me more. I felt that I was finally beginning to understand how sorcery worked, and I did not want to stop now.

"No, you must go," Bolond said. "Your mind is growing dull, and you will find that you are still more fatigued when you return to your body. Rest and return when you can."

"I do not know when that will be," I said. "The Reverend Mother arranged for me to come to your cell in secret. There are others on the Council who would not approve."

"Be that as it may, I can teach you no more today. Get some rest and practice what you have learned. If you are able to return, that is good. If not… perhaps we will meet again when I am out of this place."

"You are quite confident you will get out."

"I have learned patience over the past thousand years. Even the Cult of Turelem will not last forever. If nothing else, they will see when Arnyek comes that I am their only hope."

"Unless I am able to defeat him."

Bolond smiled indulgently. "Yes. But in that case, you will have become so powerful that I am no longer any threat to you, and perhaps you will free me out of pity."

I saw he meant it as a joke, but I did not laugh. "We will see, Bolond. We will see." With that, I forced my consciousness back to the cell.

"—not going to take me to the Governor," Bolond's homunculus was saying, "I suggest you cease vexing me and depart!"

"Very well," I said, getting to my feet.

"You intend to tell the Governor I am here?"

"Indeed. Wait right here." I turned to leave.

As I did, the door to the cell opened and a young woman rushed inside. She wore the close-cropped hair and habit of an acolyte. She approached me, waited for the door to close behind her, and then whispered, "Konrad, you are in danger!"

CHAPTER TWENTY-ONE

"What do you mean?" I asked. "Who are you?"

"My name is Szofi. I am the Reverend Mother's personal aide. She asked me to watch to see if either of the guards at the door left their post. One of them left a little while ago, and I fear he has gone to warn the Council that you are here."

"How did you get inside?"

"The Reverend Mother has sent me to ask questions of Bolond many times in the past; the guards know to let me in. But if the guards learn that the Reverend Mother let you in here without their approval, they will try to detain you. If you leave now, you may yet escape."

As she spoke, I heard the muffled ringing of bells.

"Hurry!" Szofi cried. "That is the alarm! Every guard in Regi Otthon will be looking for you!"

I moved to the door and tried to open it, but of course it was locked. "Guard!" I shouted. "Let me out!" But the only answer was the shuffling of boots in the distance.

"Who is coming?" the homunculus said. "Is the Governor coming?"

I ignored him. "It's too late," I said. "We're trapped in here."

"What do we do?" asked Szofi.

I thought for a moment. There wasn't much we *could* do. I had no weapons, and I doubted I could draw enough tvari inside the cell to summon a kovet or cast any other type of offensive spell.

"Hold the door as best you can, in case they try to get in. I need a moment." As Szofi went to the door, I closed my eyes and sought out Bolond again. This time it was even more difficult than the last time, but I managed to find him.

"It seems the Cult has forced your hand," Bolond said, standing in the middle of the vineyard where I'd left him.

"You have to help me find a way out."

"Impossible," Bolond said. "You just used the last of the tvari in the cell coming here."

My heart sank as I realized he was telling the truth. Although the salt walls comprised a nearly perfect barrier to the flow of tvari, some residual tvari had remained in the air of the cell. That was why, despite, the barrier, I had been able to send my consciousness to the in-between. But now all that tvari was gone. My only consolation was that there probably hadn't been enough to do anything about the guards in any case—affecting a physical change in Orszag was much more taxing than sending my consciousness to the in-between.

"There must be some way," I said, forcing myself to remain calm. Time didn't exist here, so I had an unlimited amount of time to solve the problem—or at least until my mind gave out from exhaustion. But it seemed pretty clear there was no solution. If there was no tvari in the cell, there was no way to use magic. I would have to face the guards the old-fashioned way.

It occurred to me that I'd been assuming the guards intended to remove me from the cell to prevent me from helping Bolond escape. But faced with two sorcerers, the smart move would be to leave us both inside. Once again, I was imprisoned with Bolond.

The cell was not a perfect barrier to tvari, though. I had learned that such a thing was impossible. Over time, tvari would leak into it from outside, the way the sun will eventually warm even the innermost rooms of a house. All we had to do is wait.

"How long will it take the room to fill with tvari again?" I asked.

Bolond shook his head. "Weeks. Months, perhaps. It is a well-designed prison."

"Too long," I said. By the time we could escape, Eben would have completed construction of the temple, even without the brand.

"There is one possibility," Bolond said.

"What is it? Tell me!"

"Every human being has a store of tvari. It is what makes up the akarat, the thing that ties the body to the soul. You could pull enough tvari out of a person to cast a single, simple spell. The subject would perish, of course."

"You are suggesting I kill you to save myself?"

Bolond laughed. "You forget, we are not alone in the cell."

He was right: even now, the acolyte, Szofi, braced herself against the door, frozen in time. It would be a simple matter to drain her of tvari. It would be enough to smash through the door so I could escape the inner ring of the prison. From there, I thought I could summon enough tvari to fight off the guards.

"No," I said.

"It is the only way."

"I could kill you instead."

"You could, but then you would be unable to defeat Eben. If we escape together, I could train you. Together we could destroy Eben."

"I will not do it," I said. "She is innocent."

"She is an acolyte of the Cult that imprisoned you in a dungeon for six years! She is as guilty as the rest of them!"

"I don't care. I will not kill her."

"Then you will die."

I tore my consciousness away from Bolond, returning to the cell. Bolond's homunculus still sat on his rug, looking vaguely annoyed. The acolyte stood staring at me fearfully, her back pressed against the door. I heard murmurs and the shuffling of boots outside.

"Come here," I said.

The acolyte continued to stare at me in terror.

"It's all right," I said. "Come here."

She walked toward me. I put my hand on her shoulder. "You're going to get out of here," I said. "But you have to trust me, all right?"

She nodded.

I gripped her by the shoulder, spun her around, and pulled her against me, wrapping my arm around her neck. "I've got an acolyte in here," I shouted. "Open the door to the cell or I snap her neck!"

More murmurs outside.

"I mean you no harm," I said. "I only wanted to talk to Bolond. If you let me walk out of here, I will leave him in his cell and I will not harm the girl. But do it quickly! I have little patience for games!"

The slot in the door slid open, and for a moment a pair of eyes regarded me. "Step away from the door," said a woman's voice.

I stepped backwards, pulling the girl with me toward the homunculus. The door opened and two guards stepped inside. They moved aside to allow a woman to walk in. She was tall and angular, with a terse, cruel face. She wore the robe of a member of the High Council of the Cult of Turelem.

"So you are the elusive Konrad," said the woman. "I am Myra, a Priestess of Turelem. I knew that the Reverend Mother met with you, but I did not think she would be foolish enough to allow you to converse with Bolond. She will pay for her betrayal of the Cult."

"The Reverend Mother was acting under duress," I said. "This is the only way of stopping Eben."

"If the Cult is facilitating meetings between sorcerers, then it has truly lost its way."

"I would argue you had already lost your way when you started sentencing innocent men to die in a dungeon."

"Our mission is bigger than any one man. In any case, it seems we were right to be concerned about you. If I had my way, you would have been hunted down after you were released from Nincs Varazslat."

"I've committed no offense against the Cult."

"You are a sorcerer. That is offense enough. Release the acolyte and we will discuss your fate."

"No. You will let me walk out of here or she dies."

Myra let out a snort. "If I was willing to throw you in a dungeon merely for possessing that mark on your face, how much do you think I care for the life of a single acolyte? I did not come into this cell to save her, but only to tell you face to face that you will surrender or you will die. Break her neck if you have the courage."

I hesitated, and the priestess laughed. "I thought as much." She turned to the guard on her right. "Take the girl. If he resists, kill him." The two men moved toward me.

"Wait," I said. She held up her hand, and the men stopped.

"Don't drag this out, Konrad. We both know you don't have it in you to kill an innocent. You swear oaths of vengeance but then you are distracted by trivialities. Oh, yes, we know much about you and your planned vengeance upon Eben. But you are weak, and you will fail. Defeating Eben will take greater will than you possess. With the Reverend Mother out of the way, I will take command of the Cult, and I will see Eben destroyed."

"I'm afraid you've misread the situation, Your Holiness," I answered. "I do not hesitate because I lack will, but because I wish to make something clear to you first. I do not take lightly what I am about to do, but you have forced my hand. Until now, I have restrained my animosity toward the acolytes, believing my true enemy to be Eben. But now I see that the Cult is as evil as he is. Even if I thought you could defeat him, I would not allow it. I will make the Cult my enemy as well. And I will see you, Priestess, dead at my feet."

As I said this, I removed my arm from the acolyte's neck and thrust her toward the guard on the right. She screamed and stumbled into him, and he fell backwards, lowering his sword to catch her. The second guard rushed me, but I ducked under his blade and caught him around the hips, hoisting him into the air. I released him and the momentum caused him to somersault over my shoulder, landing with a hard thud on the salt-coated floor. I turned and for a second stood face to face with Myra, who stared at me in shock. "This is a better death than you deserve," I said, reaching out to touch her cheek, "but I am in a hurry." As the tvari flowed into me, her face turned as pale as the salt walls. She slumped to the floor, dead.

The guard holding Szofi shoved her aside and moved toward me, sword at the ready. His comrade was getting to his feet.

Boots rushed toward us down the hall. I held just enough tvari for one small spell. Not enough to incapacitate them all.

I closed my eyes and forced myself to forget the men advancing toward me. I summoned a kovet, no larger than a mouse, and imbued it with a single, overpowering motivation: *get out.*

I loosed the thing and it shot upwards, punching a hole in the domed ceiling above. The guard lunged at me and I fell backwards, barely avoiding his blade. His comrade advanced toward me. The kovet kept going, through I-don't-know-how-many layers of wood and stone, until a thin shaft of sunlight penetrated the cell from somewhere high above. Tvari poured into me. I rolled aside as the second man's blade came down, hacking a deep gouge in the salt floor. Szofi had gotten to her feet and was nearly to the door when men began pouring in. One of them raised his sword toward her. She screamed and stepped back. I rushed forward and tackled her as the sword sliced through the air over our heads. As we skidded across the floor, kicking up the powdery dust, I continued to pull tvari into me until I could hold no more. Then I let it go.

More precisely, I transmuted it into a wave of pure kinetic energy, which shot outward from around my body. If there were screams, they were lost in the deafening boom of that wave. Walls of salt and walls of stone shattered in all directions. For some time I lay there, my ears ringing and my eyes blinded by tears and salt. Szofi lay in my arms beneath me, unmoving. I was certain she was dead until I felt her body spasming underneath me. "Are you all right?" I shouted, but I couldn't even hear my own voice, much less any response. I realized, as the spasms continued, that she was only coughing: she'd undoubtedly inhaled some of the salt dust. When the dust began to clear and the tears had left my eyes, I saw that she was dazed but unhurt. I got to my feet and helped her up.

We were surrounded by dust and rubble; above us was a clear blue sky. I had destroyed a large section of Regi Otthon, along with anyone in the vicinity. Body parts lay strewn about the debris; I consoled myself that they all seemed to belong to guards who'd had every intention of killing me. It was unlikely that there were any acolytes or other civilians in this part of the temple at this time of night. Bolond was nowhere to be found; I had to assume he'd been torn apart by the blast.

Shaking with exhaustion, I became aware of men's voices shouting in the distance, but I could not see anyone. For now, the rubble seemed to have blocked off access to this part of Regi Otthon. That meant the guards couldn't get to me, but it also meant the only way out was up, through the hole in the roof.

I would like to report that I stayed to make sure Szofi was all right, but the truth is that I was in no shape to give her aid or to carry her out of the temple. I could only hope someone found her. What they would do with her I would not speculate. She had been acting on orders from the Reverend Mother, who had defied the Council by allowing me to meet Bolond. Myra had seemed confident she could depose the Reverend Mother, but now Myra was dead, and I did not know enough about the disposition of the rest of the Council to know which side would come out on top. I left Szofi there, still dumb with shock, and climbed toward the light.

CHAPTER TWENTY-TWO

In the chaos, I managed to climb out of the rubble onto the roof of Regi Otthon and then lower myself into an alley. I stumbled half-blindly away through a maze of narrow streets and alleys until I found an abandoned haycart. I climbed into it and promptly fell asleep. When I awoke, it was nearly dawn. I was ravenous and still fatigued, but I was able to summon enough tvari to shift myself back to the camp, where Rodric and Ilona waited for me. I gave them an abbreviated, probably half-delirious account of what had happened, ate some of the pheasant that Rodric had shot and roasted, and then fell asleep for another six hours.

When I woke again, I was more lucid. Rodric had shot a rabbit, and the three of us sat around the fire discussing what to do next.

"So now we have made an enemy of the Cult as well," Rodric said.

"Maybe," I replied. "With Myra dead, I don't know which faction will take charge. But even if the Reverend Mother retains her position, I don't think we can count on any help from them. The Council is united in not taking a stand against Eben, for fear that the truth about Turelem's resurrection will come out."

"The Reverend Mother told you Bolond brought Turelem back from the dead?" Ilona asked.

"She as much as admitted it, yes," I said. "I'm sorry, Ilona. I know you hoped it wasn't true."

Ilona shrugged wearily. "I've pretty well lost my faith in the Cult of Turelem at this point. Perhaps that is what my father wanted me to learn. They claim to oppose sorcery, but they've given tacit approval to Eben to rebuild the Temple of Romok. I should have gone to Kijarat when Mother Lara suggested it."

"Kijarat?" I asked. It was the first time I'd heard her say the name.

"A settlement in the woods east of Delivaros. About five years ago, a group of disillusioned acolytes left Regi Otthon to start a new movement, free of the corruption infecting the Cult. Mother Lara was sympathetic to them, although she did not leave, thinking it better to work for change within Regi Otthon. When I confessed my doubts to her, she told me how to get to the place, which she called Kijarat. I sought the truth about my parents instead."

"It does no good to dwell on the past," Rodric said. "Our choices have brought us here, and it is not an enviable position. I must say, though, that I am not unhappy to hear that Bolond is dead. I did not like the idea of having to rely on a sorcerer. No offense intended, Konrad."

"I am not certain he is dead," I said. "I did not see his body, although of course it may have been unrecognizable. There wasn't much left of the guards in the vicinity."

"In any case," Rodric said, "we will have to proceed under the assumption that we will not be getting any help from Bolond either. Where does that leave us?"

"In a rather poor state, I'm afraid," I replied. "We could appeal to Nebjosa for help, but the Torzseki are preoccupied with securing their control of Nagyvaros. Even if Nebjosa was willing to send some men to the Maganyos Valley, his forces would be vastly outnumbered by the Barbaroki. Eben alone is probably worth a thousand fighting men, and I am no match for him."

"And there are no other sorcerers left alive in Orszag," Rodric said.

"There may be a few," I said. "The Reverend Mother told me of a settlement Bolond founded about a hundred miles west of here. A place called Yenoom Nivek. It was centered around a school of sorcery. According to the Reverend Mother, it was destroyed by the Torzseki, and all the inhabitants were killed. But I know that at least two escaped: Vili's parents, Haneen and Arron."

"But they are dead," Ilona said.

"Yes, but if they escaped, maybe there are others."

"It seems a faint hope," Rodric said.

"Indeed," I said, "but it is all we have. If any of Bolond's students survived, they may be able to help us defeat Eben."

"Assuming they share our antipathy toward him."

"Yes."

"Very well," said Rodric. "Are you able to travel? You can ride Hamu."

"That won't be necessary," I said. "Head northwest along the Zold. I will meet you in three days at the inn in Hatar."

"And if you are not there?"

"Then I suppose you may as well start drinking again."

I closed my eyes and brought my horse, Ember, to mind. I had spent so much time clinging to her back or sleeping next to her that it required little effort to locate her. A moment later, I was standing next to her. Another horse, somewhere behind me, gave a startled whinny, and I moved aside just in time to avoid a powerful kick. I was in an open corral somewhere near the southern edge of the Barbaroki camp. Several other horses whinnied in response. It turns out that horses do not think highly of people appearing out of thin air. Ember greeted my return with stoic approval.

I stood close to her and cooed gently in her ear for a minute, more to convince the other horses that I was not a threat than to soothe any anxiety Ember might have had. When the other horses grew bored with my presence, I led Ember to the fence, climbed over it, and retrieved a saddle, harness and a bag of oats from a nearby tent. Several Barbaroki were busy building fortifications nearby, but none of them noticed me. I saddled Ember, led her to the gate, unlatched it, and then mounted her. I was halfway up the southern ravine when I heard someone shout that the horses had gotten loose. No one seemed to have seen me. We reached the top of the ravine and turned west toward the Zold.

It was after dark by the time I reached the river. I doubled back once to be sure I wasn't being followed, but I saw no sign of pursuit. If word reached Eben that my horse was gone, he might have realized I'd been in the camp, but I doubted the Barbaroki would bother him with such a mundane concern. Most likely they would assume someone accidentally left the gate open and Ember had taken advantage of the situation to run away. I suppose retrieving Ember was an unnecessary risk, but I couldn't leave her with the Barbaroki. She had risked her life for me on several occasions, and she deserved better than to be the mount of some Barbaroki captain.

We followed the river south until we reached some shallows where we could drink and bathe. Then we followed a hunting trail into the woods until we got to a secluded clearing, where I made camp. I gave Ember some oats and ate some cold pheasant and then fell asleep.

The next morning, we set off for Hatar, a small town about a day's travel south of Nagyvaros. It would take Rodric and Ilona a couple of days to catch up, and I was still worn out from efforts at sorcery, so I traveled at a leisurely pace, reaching Hatar just after nightfall. I left Ember in the stable and spent the night in the common room of the inn. I got some suspicious looks from other patrons on account of my appearance, but no one bothered me.

The next day I left town on foot and walked a couple of miles into the woods, where I spent the rest of the day attempting to put into practice what I had learned from Bolond. Converting tvari to kinetic energy, as I had done in Regi Otthon, made for a devastating attack, but it would be of limited use against the Barbaroki. I might kill a hundred of them, but that would hardly put a dent in their numbers—and unless I intended to take on the entire tribe by myself, I would be as likely to take out allies as enemies. Most importantly, though, I doubted Eben would permit such an obvious attack. I would never defeat Eben with raw power: he would sense what I was doing, neutralize my attack, and then counterattack with something even more devastating. A duel between sorcerers, Bolond had told me, was much like a duel between swordsmen. Channeling raw tvari was like lunging at one's opponent with no regard for one's own defense: it might work if your opponent is inexperienced or off guard, but you're in for a lot of trouble if it doesn't.

So I practiced more subtle, and more carefully targeted attacks, on trees, boulders, and a few unlucky squirrels. When I was confident in my ability, I worked on negating the spell before it took effect. Not having a sparring partner, this was the closest I could come to practicing defensive magic. It was unlikely to do much good against Eben, but it was all I had. By the time the sun began to sink toward the horizon, I was thoroughly exhausted. I returned to the inn and slept until Rodric and Ilona arrived the next day. We ate lunch together and then mounted up and headed toward the bridge that would carry us across the Zold.

In most places the Zold is so deep and so wide that very few permanent bridges cross it. Near Hatar, however, there are numerous small, rocky islands that made it possible to construct a segmented bridge. One of these segments is a drawbridge, and the tolls collected from boats traveling north and south on the river, as well as foot traffic across the bridge, are the primary source of income for the town of Hatar. Hatar is surrounded by territory claimed by the Torzseki, but it has remained an independent municipality for nearly two hundred years primarily because the town has no other wealth. The soil of the area is poor and there are no other resources to speak of. Most of the people living in the town are employed in the upkeep or defense of the bridge. The crossing is a potential chokepoint for trade, and several past Governors of Nagyvaros had tried to rally support for seizing the town, but given the more pressing threat from the Barbaroki, nothing ever came of it.

We paid the bridge toll and then another, smaller toll to the Lealtoki party camped on the far side. Although the Lealtoki had no permanent settlements in this area, they claimed the area west of the Zold. The toll was a nominal one, meant to remind people of this fact. As long as they didn't get greedy, the guardians of the bridge didn't contest their right to it.

We asked the Lealtoki for directions to Yenoom Nivek, and after several attempts at dissuading us from going there, they finally relented in exchange for another donation. We were told to follow the Zold south until we reached a place where the remnants of an abandoned boat dock protruded from the water and then head due west. Following these instructions, we found a trail through the woods that eventually brought us to a large clearing where we found the charred rubble of a dozen or so buildings. Nearby were the remnants of wooden fences, a plow and a few other implements hinting that this had once been a self-sustaining farming community. It had obviously been years since anyone had lived here; the ruins had nearly been consumed by weeds.

"So this is what is left of Yenoom Nivek," Ilona said. "The Torzseki were thorough."

Rodric shook his head. "It makes no sense. This land is claimed by the Lealtoki, but even they have made no use of it. If the Torzseki did this, someone put them up to it."

"At this point, I wouldn't put it past the Cult," Ilona said. "They would certainly disapprove of a school of sorcery so close to Delivaros."

"The Reverend Mother denied the Cult had anything to do with it," I said. "That doesn't prove anything, of course, but I don't see what she'd gain by lying."

"Whatever happened here," Rodric said, "it is clear that no other sorcerers remain in Orszag. We will have to face Eben alone."

"No," said a voice from the ruins, somewhere behind Rodric. "There is one other." I knew who it was before I saw him. There was only one other man in Orszag who could materialize out of thin air.

"So you survived after all," I said.

"No thanks to you," Bolond said with a grin. "Although I do have you to thank for punching a hole in that prison. I had just enough time to find my way back to my body and shift out of there before you wrecked the place. Are you going to introduce me to your companions?"

"Bolond, this is Rodric and Ilona. Rodric and Ilona, Bolond. What are you doing here?"

"Looking for you, of course. I thought you might come here, after what I told you. I could have saved you the trip. Davor Sabas left no one alive."

"Except Arron and Haneen. And you."

"None of us were at Yenoom Nivek at the time of the attack. If we had been, we might have been able to stop them. And if there were any other survivors, they would be unlikely to return here."

"Why did Davor Sabas destroy this place?" Ilona asked. "Were they doing the bidding of the Cult?"

"I do not know," Bolond said. "I chose this place specifically because it was out of the way and unlikely to draw attention. We kept to ourselves and were very guarded about the true purpose of the settlement. As far as I was aware, the Council knew nothing of Yenoom Nivek. The Lealtoki knew of our presence, of course, but not of our purpose. Why the Torzseki would venture into their territory with the apparent purpose of destroying Yenoom Nivek is a mystery to me."

"The good news, I suppose," Rodric said, "is that we now have two sorcerers to face Eben."

"Indeed," Bolond said. "Ilona, you are an acolyte of Turelem?"

"Former acolyte," Ilona said. "It seems I have made my peace with sorcery. At least until the threat of Eben has been dealt with. Do you really intend to help us?"

"Of course. Eben is a powerful warlock, but he is also a short-sighted fool. He intends to rule Orszag, but rebuilding the Temple of Romok will only pave the way for Arnyek the Destroyer. We cannot allow the temple to be rebuilt. Eben must be stopped."

"In that we are agreed," Rodric said. "But although two of our number are sorcerers, we are only four altogether. How can we hope to vanquish the Barbaroki?"

"We have more allies than you realize," Bolond said. "While you were on your way here, I have engaged in some diplomacy with Governor Nebjosa. He has agreed to send two thousand men to the Maganyos Valley to oust Eben and the Barbaroki. They left Nagyvaros yesterday. If we hurry, we can meet them at Kalyiba."

"Two thousand men?" I said. "Even after their defeat at Delivaros, the Barbaroki have four times that number."

"Yes, but we have two sorcerers, and they only have one. With my protection, the Torzseki will be able to occupy the bulk of the Barbaroki force while you penetrate the camp and kill Eben. It doesn't matter how many Barbaroki are left standing at the end of the battle as long as Eben is dead. Without him, they will be unable to complete the reconstruction of the temple and will be forced to move on. Unless that plan is not to your liking?"

"Any plan where I get to kill Eben is fine with me," I said.

"When you say you are going to kill Eben," Ilona said, "you mean that you are going to kill Vili as well."

"Vili is already gone," Bolond said. "Killing Eben now would be a mercy. Vili's spirit would be freed from his prison."

Rodric and Ilona did not seem convinced, but they did not protest further.

I continued, "If I am to have a chance against Eben, though, I will have to get close to him without wasting any tvari on Barbaroki."

"Ilona and I will go with you," Rodric said. "If there is anybody who can get you past the Barbaroki defenses, it is we. You can save your strength for defeating Eben."

"Thank you, friends," I said. "Perhaps if we work together, we will have a chance. But I have another concern. Is Nebjosa leading the Torzseki force?"

Bolond shook his head. "Nebjosa has his hands full in Nagyvaros. There has been unrest in the past few days, and he daren't leave the city. I'm sure you realize what this means."

I nodded, smiling grimly. "Davor Sabas."

"Yes."

"Can we trust him?" Ilona asked.

"I would be lying if I said I knew for certain," Bolond replied. "But as far as I know, he is loyal to Nebjosa, and Nebjosa wants the Barbaroki out of the valley. In any case, we have little choice but to trust him, at least until Eben is dead."

CHAPTER TWENTY-THREE

There being nothing for us at Yenoom Nivek, we returned to the river and headed north. We crossed the bridge—paying the two tolls again—and then continued toward Kalyiba, where we planned to meet Davor Sabas. Bolond had no horse, but he insisted on traveling with us rather than shifting through the in-between because he wanted to make use of the time to give me more instruction in using tvari. To facilitate this instruction, Bolond and I walked ahead while Rodric and Ilona rode on horseback and Ember carried all of our packs.

Now that he was free, Bolond seemed much more amenable to the idea of training me in sorcery. His previous reluctance, I think, had been due in part to his belief that the less I needed him, the less likely I would be to help him escape. In any case, he now seemed fully committed to training me in how to defeat Eben. He made it clear, though, that there was no way he could get me anywhere close to Eben's level with a few days of training. Our strategy would rely heavily on the element of surprise and keeping Eben off his footing. If I could get close to Eben, attack quickly and not let up, I might be able to take him down. Bolond and the Torzseki would keep the Barbaroki occupied.

We arrived at Kalyiba three days later, about two hours before Davor Sabas and his two thousand Torzseki warriors on horseback. While the Torzseki set up camp for the night just outside of town, we met with Davor Sabas and his senior officers in an upper room of the inn. Nebjosa had apparently advised Davor Sabas to expect us; I judged it to be an inopportune time to ask him about the massacre at Yenoom Nivek. Bolond was a model of restraint, considering that Davor Sabas had allegedly been responsible for the murder of his students. We were in no position to be picky about our allies. Our business was confined to the matter of defeating Eben and the Barbaroki.

We came up with a plan that was as audacious as it was simple. I gave it about a fifty-fifty chance of succeeding, assuming everyone did exactly what they were supposed to do. The only people in the room I trusted, though, were Rodric and Ilona.

We moved out at first light. The entire Torzsek force was mounted, and they carried minimal supplies, so we moved quickly. Sentries had been posted on the road the previous night to ensure that no spies could get word to the Barbaroki before we arrived. For good measure, when we were a few leagues from the valley Bolond employed a trick he had borrowed from Eben's assault on Elhalad nearly a thousand years earlier: he cast a spell to camouflage our entire force, causing us to be nearly invisible from a distance of more than a few hundred feet. The Barbaroki would not see us until we were nearly on them. Eben might be able to sense the use of tvari, but Bolond was counting on him being distracted with the building of the temple. He thought it unlikely Eben would expect a Torzsek attack, given Nebjosa's tenuous hold on Nagyvaros.

When we were within a mile of the northern edge of the ravine, Davor Sabas ordered the force to be split into two groups. Half of the men would remain on the plain north of the ravine, hunkered down and unmoving to avoid being seen, while Bolond would escort the rest, employing his camouflage spell, along the Zold to the southern edge of the valley. At sunset, scouts would eliminate the sentries on both sided of the valley. Then the two contingents would fan out along the edges of the ravine. When the southern group was in place, an archer would fire a single fiery arrow over the valley. On that signal, the men on both sides would mount up and charge down the sides of the valley toward the Barbarok camp.

Even with full surprise and Bolond fighting along with the Torzseki, I didn't give them much of a chance at defeating the much larger Barbarok force. The best we could hope for was a few minutes of chaos while the Barbaroki rallied their defense. That would be all the time I would have to kill Eben.

Rodric, Ilona and I broke off from the main group at the same time as Bolond's contingent, but we headed east rather than west, leaving our horses with the Torzseki. Both the Torzseki and the Barbaroki were experts in fighting on horseback, but horses would be of little use in this fight. The horses would balk at being ridden down the steep slopes of the valley at night, and the ruins and other debris on the valley floor would make maneuvering a horse difficult. The battle would be fought on foot, on both sides.

By the time the sun touched the horizon, we were well past the eastern edge of the Barbarok camp. Confident we would not be seen in the dying light, we made our way down the slope of the ravine. Our goal was to get as close to Eben as we could before the signal went up. I hadn't had a chance to do any real reconnaissance, but I had a rough sense for the layout of the camp from my previous visits. I knew Eben's tent would be near the observation platform where I'd confronted him, so I made that my goal. We crept from boulder to boulder, slowly nearing the edge of the camp. We had perhaps a quarter of an hour until the southern contingent was in position.

Soon we found ourselves faced with a difficult choice: most of the valley floor was flat and easy to traverse, but there were places where boulders blocked passage except along a stretch of ground less than fifty feet across. A hundred yards or so from the eastern edge of the camp, we came across one of these places, lit by a torch on a vertical pole. Two Barbaroki, armed with spears, stood watch nearby. There was no way we could sneak past them. We might sneak around them by climbing over the boulders on one side or the other, but I wasn't sure we would have time before the signal went up.

Ilona volunteered to approach them, deeming this to be our best chance to take them by surprise and prevent them from raising an alarm. I didn't like it but couldn't think of an alternative. I didn't want to waste tvari on sentries before I even got near Eben. I could draw more tvari from my surroundings, as I'd done in Bolond's cell, but the process was draining. Fatigue was as big a liability as a lack of tvari.

Rodric and I crept as close as we dared while Ilona walked toward the sentries, looking for all the world as if she were out for a casual evening stroll. As the torchlight hit her, one of the sentries barked at her to stop, but he did not raise an alarm. She kept walking, and he shouted at her again. There was still enough activity going on in the camp that I doubt anyone heard him.

Ilona stopped a few paces in front of the sentries. I heard her say something but could not make out the words. The sentry on the left replied. The one on the right shifted nervously on his feet, peering into the darkness beyond the torchlight. Ilona took a step closer to the man on the left, blocking our view of the one on the right. Ilona had left her fighting stick behind, but I knew she had the training to incapacitate a man with a well-aimed strike. She was now close enough to hit the man in front of her, but his comrade, looking increasingly nervous, had moved toward her. Rodric swore under his breath.

"I can't get a clean shot," he whispered.

"Ilona knows what to do," I replied. "She'll give you your shot."

"Her head is blocking his throat. If I'm going to put him down before he raises an alarm, I need to hit him in the throat." The Barbaroki wore leather armor that covered their vitals, leaving only their faces and throats exposed.

"Be patient, Rodric. You'll have your shot." I wished I was as confident as I sounded. I trusted Ilona to do her part, but the signal to attack could come at any moment. If we weren't inside the camp by then, we'd have to fight our way through a hundred men to get to Eben.

"Konrad, I know you think I've never missed a shot, but I'm not certain I can do this. If I'm an inch off...."

"Rodric, enough. You and I both know you can make the shot. It's not a matter of your skill with the bow. You need to trust Ilona. She will give you your shot."

"Aye, Captain."

The exchange between Ilona and the sentries had grown more animated. The man on the right kept glancing back toward the camp, as if he intended to call for help. If that happened, we were all dead.

Suddenly Ilona's fist shot forward, striking the man on the left in the windpipe. His eyes went wide and he stumbled backwards, clutching at his throat. There was a sharp snap as Rodric loosed his arrow.

Ilona threw herself backwards and the arrow shot past her. It missed her nose by an inch and lodging itself in the man's throat. Ilona tumbled to the ground as the two sentries fell to their knees. I ran to them, reaching the one Ilona had struck just as he got his breath back. I slit his throat with a knife I'd borrowed from a Torzseki—having made a habit of traveling via the in-between, I had a hard time holding onto metal weapons. Rodric finished the other man. Ilona removed his cape and threw it over the torch. So far there was no indication that anyone had seen us, but at any moment someone might glance over and see the commotion. Better for them to think the torch had gone out than see us dragging two dead sentries behind the rocks.

Once we'd dealt with the corpses, we pressed on toward the camp. A row of torches had been erected on the perimeter, but there were enough Barbaroki bustling about on the edge of the camp that it was easy to slip between them unnoticed. No doubt someone would soon go to investigate the doused torch, but hopefully by then we'd be well inside the camp.

Once past the row of torches, we kept to the shadows as well as we could but walked boldly so as not to attract suspicion. Besides the tents and other semi-permanent structures, there were the massive ruins of the temple to provide us with cover. As long as no one looked too closely, we could pass for two Barbaroki warriors and a slave girl.

We soon spotted the torches of the observation tower in the distance. Peering around a slab of granite, I saw a throng of Barbaroki gathering around the tower. My gut tightened as I recognized the slender figure of the young man climbing the ladder to the top of the tower: Vili.

"What do you see, Konrad?" Ilona whispered from behind me.

"This is going to be tricky," I said. "Looks like Eben is going to give a speech. Half the camp has assembled around the tower. I'm not sure we can get any closer without being seen." In truth it was only the men who had assembled; the Barbaroki women were presumably in the tents, cooking, caring for children, and attending to other domestic chores.

"Then we wait for the signal," Rodric said. "When the attack comes, they'll clear out quickly."

I nodded. There wasn't much we could do but wait in the shadow of the slab and hope nobody came close enough to see us. The crowd continued to grow, until the latecomers were only a few paces from the other side of the slab we were hiding behind. Then the murmurs of the crowd fell silent and I heard a familiar voice speaking. The voice was Vili's, but the words were those of Eben the warlock.

"Fearless Barbaroki!" Eben shouted. "You have achieved a great victory. Nagyvaros stood for a thousand years, protected by the greatest army in the land. The wisest men in Orszag said that Nagyvaros would never fall. Those men did not know the fury of the Barbaroki!"

A roar of exultation went up from the throng.

"You sacked Nagyvaros. You took its finest treasures and its most beautiful women. The city's defenders have been crushed. If we had wished to, we could have ruled Nagyvaros for the next thousand years. But I tell you, the Barbaroki are destined for even greater things!"

The throng cheered again.

"We left the city to the Torzseki, because there was nothing left of its treasure but scraps fit for dogs. Some of you have been grumbling that we should not have let Nebjosa proclaim himself Governor. You say that your chief, Csongor, should have been crowned in his place."

More cheers.

"But I tell you that the throne of Nagyvaros is not yet ready for one as great as Csongor. Let the Torzseki fight over scraps. Let them become comfortable in that hollowed out shell of a city. The time of the Barbaroki has not yet come. We have a still greater victory to win. What we do here will assure Barbarok hegemony not for a thousand years, but for ten thousand!

"You have seen the power of my magic. With my illusions, I was able to draw the janissaries away from Kozepes Pass so that your army could march across the plain unhindered. But you have not yet seen the true power of sorcery. You have been told that we are rebuilding an ancient temple. Some of you have grumbled that this is work for slaves, not for fighting men. And you would be right if this were any ordinary temple. But I tell you that this temple will allow us to harness unimaginable power, and every man giving his sweat to this project will share in that power. Slaves will have their reward as well, yes, but I would not consign the power of this place to the hands of slaves. The Barbaroki will be gods, and whoever toils the hardest will be the greatest among them!"

"With this temple we will open a doorway to other worlds—worlds of untold wealth and beauty. We will conquer those worlds and take their treasure. We will make their women our own, and press their men into our army. We will have an army so vast that each man here will command a regiment. That army will travel from world to world, conquering each in turn. And when we have sated ourselves on blood and treasure, we will return to Orszag and conquer it as well. We will take Nagyvaros from the Torzsek dogs, and build there a greater city than even the famed Builders could dream of. Csongor will sit upon the throne there, and I will be at his side. But he will not be a mere governor, nor even a king, but an emperor commanding entire worlds!"

The crowd again erupted in cheers. Peering around the slab, I saw that Chief Csongor stood at the center of the crowd, on a small platform only about two feet above ground level. He was shaking his spear in the air and generally doing his best to seem imposing, but surely I was not the only one who thought he looked a little ridiculous, standing at the foot of the tower while Eben presided over the throng from far above. No doubt this was intentional: despite his words, Eben wanted there to be no question about who was really in charge. Csongor must have fully bought into Eben's narrative to allow himself to be subjected to such degradation.

So this was Eben's plan, I thought: he intended to use the rebuilt temple to travel not only to Veszedelem, but many other worlds as well. He would seek out the weaker kingdoms, conquer them, steal their wealth and enslave the men to make his army stronger. Eben intended to rule not only Orszag and Veszedelem, but every other world too. I wondered if he had also come up with a way of stopping Arnyek.

Eben's mention of Csongor ascending to the throne of Nagyvaros must have been the chief's cue to begin his own speech, because when the cheers died down this time, Csongor addressed the throng. I was straining to make out the words when I heard a gruff voice from behind me.

"You three, what are you doing there?"

A Barbarok sentry stood some ten paces away, holding a torch. In the dim light, he must not have been able to tell that we were not Barbaroki. I spoke Barbaroki with reasonable fluency, but my accent would surely give me away. I remained silent. Cheers went up in response to something Csongor said.

The sentry took a few steps toward us and then stopped short. We were hidden from the throng by the slab, but several other sentries stood watch not far away. Rodric probably had an arrow trained on the man, but if the sentry suddenly fell, there was a good chance one of the others would see. We would have better odds of remaining unnoticed if we could coax the man a little closer.

"Friend is drunk," I mumbled, doing my best to hide my accent. I leaned over Ilona, who was sitting next to me with her back against the slab.

"If you're not on watch, you need to be at the gathering." He peered into the shadows, holding the torch aloft in an attempt to discern what we were doing.

"Need some help," I said.

"Is that a woman? Where are you from?" the sentry demanded.

I didn't answer. Glancing to my right, I saw that Rodric was holding his bow flat on the ground, an arrow nocked.

"Hey!" cried the sentry. "Drop that before I—"

There was another shout in the distance, from the direction we'd come. Somebody had found the sentries we'd killed. More shouts sounded, from closer by. I heard the *thwick* of an arrow being loosed, followed by hoarse screams from the sentry. He fell to the ground, an arrow shaft protruding from his throat.

A horn blew. Csongor ordered the men to defend the camp. Rodric, Ilona and I remained perfectly still. We could only hope that in the chaos, we would remain unseen.

Ilona tapped my shoulder. She pointed up, and I saw a fiery arrow darting overhead. Whether the Torzseki were in position or the signal was prompted by the Barbarok alarm, I did not know. Men would soon begin to pour down the ravine toward the camp. Hopefully they would reach it before the Barbarok defenses were fully manned.

Men ran past the slab on both sides of us, shouting war cries, fanning out toward the edges of the camp. We remained dead still, our bodies pressed against the cold granite. After the bulk of the Barbaroki had passed, I began to have hope that we would remain unseen. But a straggler noticed the sentry's torch, still fizzling on the ground a few steps from us.

"Hey, Armad," the man said to his compatriot, coming up behind him. "What's this?" The dead man had fallen face-down, the arrow snapping off underneath him, so it looked like he had merely fallen asleep. While the first man nudged the dead man's ribs with his boot, Armad turned toward us.

"Hey, you three," he growled. "Get up! Didn't you hear the alarm?"

It seemed we'd had the good fortune to be spotted by the two dimmest Barbaroki in the camp. Any moment, though, they were going to realize what had happened.

"We'll take care of these two," Ilona whispered to me. "Go after Eben."

I nodded and the three of us got to our feet. "Hey!" the Barbarok shouted again, as I slipped around the granite slab. There was the sound of an arrow flying followed by a grunt. Ilona gave a battle cry as she launched herself toward one of the men. I ran toward the tower, not looking back.

The assembly area had been cleared except for a small group of men near the base of the tower. I suppose it had been too much to hope that every last man would rush to the camp's defense. By the light of the torches lining the northern and southern edges of the camp, I saw hundreds of men pushing past each other to meet the as-yet-unseen attackers. There was no order to their movements, and captains barked orders to little effect. The Barbaroki had clearly been overconfident, relying on their superior numbers to deter any attack. In many places there were wood fences and other partially constructed defensive fortifications, but the bulk of the Barbarok effort had been directed toward digging up the ruins of the temple. They were unprepared for a surprise attack.

As I closed within fifty yards of the tower, I saw a man halfway up the ladder, climbing toward the platform where Eben still stood, peering out over the valley floor. Although I could see the man on the ladder only in dim silhouette, I recognized him from his size and clothing: Chief Csongor. Undoubtedly he was hoping to get an idea of the sort of attack he was facing. The six men at the foot of the tower were his personal guard.

To my right, I spotted another man running toward the tower: a Barbarok sentry bringing word of the attackers, I assumed. He had not seen me. I veered to my right, closing with him. About twenty paces from the tower, he spotted me, but it was too late. I locked my forearms together and slammed into him from the side, knocking him off his feet. He tumbled to the ground, dazed. I leaped on him, slicing his throat, and then grabbed his short sword from its sheath. If I was going to face six men without exhausting my supply of tvari, I needed a better weapon than a six-inch hunting knife.

I got to my feet and continued to advance toward the tower. The men around the tower had spotted me, and they closed ranks, brandishing their axes. I strode toward them, undeterred. One of the men broke ranks to take a step toward me.

"Wait," said Csongor from the ladder. "This one is mine." He climbed a few rungs down and then jumped the last six feet to the ground, landing in a crouch. Csongor was a good ten years older than I, but he moved like a much younger man. He got to his feet and strode past the others toward me, pulling a double-edged war axe from behind his back.

"Step aside, Csongor," I said. "I have no quarrel with you."

"This valley is mine, Konrad. You disrespect me by skulking into my camp." He strode toward me. By this time, most of the Barbaroki had disappeared into the darkness beyond the torches.

They jostled and shouted at each other. Farther away, I heard Torzsek battle cries.

"Surely you can forgive the transgression, given how I was treated upon my last visit."

"Your last visit should have taught you to stay away. It seems you are a slow learner."

"Csongor, drop this ruse. Do you think you are fooling anyone? You are not in charge here. You've sold the Barbaroki out to that coward hiding up there." I pointed to the figure of Eben, staring down at us. I was well aware that Eben could kill me with a snap of his fingers, but I was betting that his vanity would not allow it. I could not defend myself against his magic while remaining on guard against Csongor.

In the distance, I heard more shouts and the clash of metal against metal. The battle for Maganyos Valley had begun.

"Enough talk!" Csongor growled. "Now you will die!" Csongor launched himself toward me, axe raised.

Parrying the huge axe with the little short sword would be nearly impossible; my best bet was to dodge and try to get inside his guard. He was stronger and had a heavier weapon, but I was quicker.

That was what I thought, anyway, until the axe came down like lightning, nearly severing my right arm at the shoulder. I was able to move aside quickly enough that the blade slid down my upper arm, tearing open my shirt. It continued downward, slicing open a deep laceration in my forearm. A flap of skin and muscle peeled away from the wound, dangling off my arm, and blood poured down my wrist and fingers. I gave an involuntary yelp and fell back.

CHAPTER TWENTY-FOUR

Csongor hefted his axe again, and his Barbarok guard, who had gathered around us, cheered. The gash on my arm looked bad, but as long as I didn't bleed too much, it wouldn't hamper my fighting significantly. I've always been ambidextrous; I prefer to shoot a bow right-handed, but tend to use a sword with my left. I tore the rest of the sleeve off, folded the flesh back into place, and then tied the fabric in a clumsy knot. As the sounds of battle continued in the darkness all around us, Csongor moved slowly toward me.

When I'd tightened my makeshift bandage, Csongor came at me again. This time he swung sideways toward my left side. I got inside the swing and the handle struck my left hip, not hard enough to do any real damage. I stabbed at Csongor, but the blade slid across the left side of his cuirass, slicing into the thick leather but failing to penetrate to flesh. I pulled back and stabbed again, but by this time he had moved back out of range. He brought the axe down again, and I dived to my right, landing hard on gravel. Pain shot through the wound on my forearm.

I knew I could beat Csongor in a fair fight, and in any other circumstance, I might have given it a go. But I was tired and bleeding, and when I was finished with Csongor, I had a much tougher opponent to face. The battle raged in the darkness north of us; at any moment the tide might turn against the Torzseki. It was, in fact, only my impatience with this fight that had given Csongor the edge so far. I had wanted to finish him quickly, without tapping into my reserve of tvari, and so I had gotten sloppy. All the tvari in all the worlds wouldn't do me any good if I didn't have the strength to use it. So I took the obvious course of action: I cheated.

Casting the first offensive spell I had learned, I pulled all the air from Csongor's lungs. He made a sort of whooshing sigh as he dropped his axe and fell to his knees, clutching his throat. The spell wouldn't kill him, but it was a quick way to end a fight.

Unfortunately, Csongor and I were not alone—and the Barbaroki don't look kindly on cheating. While one of the men tended to the chief, the other five circled around me, axes in hand. I might have taken on one or two of them, but I could not face five Barbaroki at once with only a short sword. I had no choice but to use magic again. I had already wasted some of my power; if I incapacitated five more men, I wouldn't have a chance of defeating Eben.

I looked up to see the silhouette of Vili still watching from above. In this light, without Eben's megalomaniacal rhetoric coming from his mouth, it was easy to imagine this was the same brave young lad I'd first encountered a stone's throw from this very place. Did I have it in me to kill him? I put the question out of my mind. I had no choice.

"Eben!" I shouted, as the Barbaroki drew closer. "Is this how it is to be? You hide up there while the Barbaroki do your dirty work for you?"

Eben did not reply. The Barbaroki moved still closer. Several were now within striking range; the only question was which of them would attack first. Csongor, having gotten his wind back, moved toward the circle. Looking up, I saw that Eben was gone. So this was how I would die. In the end, I wasn't even enough of a sorcerer for Eben to bother with. He was going to let the savages finish me. I readied my sword, hoping to at least take one or two of the Barbaroki with me before their axes cleaved me to pieces.

Then suddenly the men were gone, thrown backwards as if by some repulsive force. They flew some thirty feet through the air and landed on the ground. None of them moved. In the dim light of flickering torches, they looked more like bags of rotten vegetables than men, as if their very bones had been turned to

mush. Until a moment ago, these men had been Eben's allies, and
he had thrown them away like garbage.

"Does this suit you better, Konrad?" Vili's voice asked from
behind me. I turned to see him standing not ten feet away. Eben
the warlock, wearing Vili's body like a costume. Oh, how I hated
him.

"I won't be happy until you're dead," I said. In the distance,
the battle seemed to be reaching a crescendo. The fighting was all
around us now; the Torzseki were attacking from all sides.

"And not even then, I would imagine," Eben said, raising his
voice to be heard over the clamor. He spread his hands in a
supplicatory gesture. "Listen, Konrad. This is all unnecessary.
Let's you and I retreat to the tower and watch the battle unfold
like civilized men. We can make a friendly wager on the outcome,
if you like. My money is on the Barbaroki, but it doesn't really
matter, does it? These savages are just pawns. Both Barbaroki and
Torzseki make fine laborers."

"You think the Torzseki will work for you after they've
defeated your army?"

"In the unlikely event that that happens? Of course they will.
I will make them the same offer I made the Barbaroki. Fame,
glory, wealth, adventure. Men are all the same, Konrad. Who can
offer them anything better? Nebjosa? The Cult of Turelem?"

"The Torzseki have honor," I said. "Nebjosa has pledged me
his support. As long as I defy you, they will fight."

"I doubt that," Eben said, "but I will admit that things would
go more smoothly if you willingly allied yourself with me. I will
even let you keep the brand."

"Quite generous of you, considering that removing it would
kill me."

"I've come to the conclusion that you may be more valuable
to me alive than dead. Come, Konrad. Join me and I will teach
you how to use the power of the brand."

"Even if I trusted you, I would not do it."

"Then let's make this as painless as possible. Let me take the
brand."

"No."

Eben sighed. "Very well, then. Goodbye, Konrad." As he
spoke, the blade of the sword in my hand shattered. I threw away

the useless hilt. Eben raised his hand, and a bolt of purple energy shot from his palm toward me. Fortunately, Bolond had warned me to expect such an attack and told me how to defend against it.

What Eben had done was simply to convert a small amount of tvari into some form of energy that could manifest itself in the physical world. All I had to do is turn it back into tvari. I did a poor job of it, losing much of the tvari in the process, but the attack left me unscathed—and Eben had inadvertently increased my pool of tvari.

Realizing what I had done, Eben cursed under his breath. I smiled, enjoying the recalibration of his expectations, but I suspected the next attack would not be so easy to counter. I was right.

Eben next tried the inverse of what he had just done, pulling tvari out of me. There were two possible defenses against this: one was to use his attack against him, trying to overwhelm him with more tvari than he could handle. Because of the brand, I held more tvari than Eben, but he was far more skilled than I. There were ways of getting rid of excess tvari, and I had little doubt Eben could execute an attack at the same time as he pulled tvari from me. Further, if my attempt to overwhelm him failed, I would be completely powerless, having expended all of my own tvari.

The safer option was to put up a block, preventing the flow of tvari. The efficacy of this method depended on my skill relative to Eben's, but the balance was tilted in favor of the defender. Eben would have to expend some of his own tvari to drain mine, which meant that even if my block was not completely successful, he might well lose tvari faster than I did. This is what I did.

It was a shoddy block, but it was enough. After a few seconds, Eben realized that it was going to take too long to defeat me this way. The battle continued to rage in the distance, and the longer it dragged on, the fewer laborers Eben would have, regardless of who won. Eben no doubt also saw the flashes of what looked like lightning toward the northeast and deduced that the Torzseki had a sorcerer with them. He wanted to finish this duel quickly, and I could use his haste against him.

Eben switched tactics again, this time trying something much simpler: stopping my heart. Tvari is incredibly powerful, and killing a human being requires a trifling amount of energy if it is applied appropriately. Causing my heart to stop beating would take less effort than knocking a glass of water off a table. If a competent sorcerer wants to kill you, you're as good as dead.

Fortunately, I'd anticipated this as well. Eben would have preferred to incapacitate me rather than kill me so that he could take the brand, but he was in a hurry to get the duel over with. Stopping my heart was the quickest and easiest way to do that. As soon as I felt the pull on my tvari weaken, I wrapped a shield of it around me to prevent Eben from manipulating the matter inside my body. He could break through the shield by channeling more tvari, but I would react by strengthening the shield, and again we'd be deadlocked.

Eben broke off the attack. I could see that he was frustrated, not having expected such resistance. My training had been mostly theoretical, as I'd had little opportunity to put into practice what Bolond had taught me, but so far my implementation had been adequate if not exemplary. I suspected Eben's next attack would be aimed at exploiting my inexperience. I decided not to wait for it.

I used tvari to pick up an axe from one of the dead men behind Eben and threw it at him. He smiled, sensing the attack, and stepped aside. The axe shot past his left ear and kept going. Feeling a fool, I dived to the ground to avoid my own attack. The axe flew over my head and landed on the ground behind me. Determined not to give Eben a chance to take advantage of my mistake, I pressed the attack. I hurled three more axes at him, but all three halted in mid-air a few feet from him and fell to the ground. I kept up the attack as I got to my feet, hoping to at least keep Eben occupied while I thought of a more effective line of attack. I threw rocks, helmets, knives, spears and torches at him. None of them even got close. A ring of debris began to form on the ground around him. Eben seemed unconcerned, but he did not counterattack.

I knew I was missing something, but I couldn't figure out what. Eben wasn't throwing anything at me or draining tvari from me, but I doubted repelling my attacks was taking all his attention. He was up to something.

Then I realized I was shivering. Somehow, despite all my exertion, I had gotten very cold. While I'd been futilely throwing objects at him, he'd drawn all the heat out of the air around me, converting it to tvari and then pulling it into himself. It was a terribly inefficient way of gathering tvari, but it was highly effective at making me freeze to death. It was such a subtle attack that I didn't notice until my fingers had nearly gone numb. The cold would slow my movement—and if he kept it up, it would kill me.

I could convert tvari to heat, but Eben would just drain it faster. Instead, I blocked his attack and moved toward him, leaning down to pick up one of the fallen axes. I didn't have the training to execute offensive and defensive spells simultaneously, but I could block Eben's cold attack while attacking him physically. The exertion would also, I hoped, get my blood flowing again.

My hands were so stiff I could barely hold onto the axe, but I brought it back over my shoulder and advanced toward Eben. As I approached him, though, I became aware of a massive shadow moving toward us from somewhere behind him. For a moment, I thought it was a kovet, larger than any I'd ever seen, and I despaired of fighting it off. If Eben could summon a kovet of that size while fending off my feeble attacks and freezing me nearly to death, this battle was hopeless.

As the thing continued to loom larger, I realized it was not a kovet but the guard tower. Eben had given it a push, sending it falling toward us, timbers groaning as it fell. The massive spruce poles that served as the tower's legs would fall on either side of Eben, but the supporting members under the platform were going to crush me. There was no way I could get clear in time.

I dropped the axe and fell to the ground. I had just enough time to summon a kovet and will it to spread itself like a tent over me. The timbers struck the turgid kovet and splintered as the structure crashed down around me. A moment later, the kovet was gone, and the splintered members fell onto my back and legs.

I'd broken the momentum of the fall, so I was not crushed, but I was now pinned in place, with one timber across my upper back and two more on top of my legs. My right hand was pinned underneath me; with my fingertips I could feel the pommel of the knife on my belt. My left hand was free, but something had struck it during the fall; judging from the shooting pain when I tried to move it, several bones were broken.

I summoned another kovet to push the timbers off me, but the structure was too massive. The kovet succeeded only in pinning me more thoroughly before evaporating. Meanwhile, the cold continued to seep into my bones; Eben had not let up his attack. I wondered if I could summon enough tvari to start a fire. I certainly had plenty of wood to burn, and while burning to death is not a pleasant way to die, at that moment it seemed preferable to freezing. If I could get the fire going quickly, I might even kill Eben.

I soon realized, though, that it was hopeless. I was too exhausted even to create a small flame. As Eben climbed over the timbers toward me, I knew I'd been beaten. The lightning flashes and sounds of battle were drawing closer; Bolond had brought the Torzseki into the heart of the camp. The Torzseki had been outnumbered four to one, but they were still fighting. That gave me some encouragement: Bolond might still defeat Eben, although I would not live to see it.

Every part of my body that could still move was shivering. My fingers and toes had gone completely numb. Frost had formed on the ground around me. My breath came out in white puffs as I struggled to breath under the weight of the timber. It would make little difference in the end. I would not die from asphyxiation; I was moments away from freezing to death.

Eben stood on a timber near me, peering toward the blue-white flashes that grew ever close. "What the devil...?" he murmured.

An idea occurred to me. "B-B-Bolond," I gasped, barely able to make my lips form the name.

"Impossible," Eben said. "He is imprisoned in Delivaros."

"Es-s-s-scaped. K-kill you."

There was another bright flash, less than a hundred yards away, followed by screams.

"This is how you thought you would defeat me?" Eben said, turning back to face me. "You allied with that old fool?"

"W-working f-f-f-for Arn-y-y-kek."

"Bolond is doing the bidding of Arnyek?"

I found myself unable to formulate a coherent reply.

"Then it is as I suspected. Bolond has tired of trying to fix the mess he created. He fights me because he fears I have the power to prevent Arnyek from bringing the end of all things."

"K-k-kill h-him."

Eben laughed. "So that is your game. You allied with Bolond in an attempt to defeat me, but in the end, you fear Bolond more than you fear me."

"K-kill him. T-t-take b-b-brand."

The fighting was now just on the other side of a group of granite slabs to the northeast. The blue-white flashes were almost blinding. Barbaroki were running our way, trying to get out of Bolond's path. I wondered what would happen when Bolond got here. Had he needed me at all, or had he known from the beginning that it would come down to him and Eben?

I could see from Eben's—that is, Vili's—face that he was worried. He'd thought the Barbaroki were invincible, and he was not looking forward to facing a man who could lead an army to victory against such odds. Eben needed an edge, and I could give it to him.

"You do not intend to resist me this time?"

I could no longer speak, but I managed to shake my head slightly.

By this time, the battle had turned into a rout. Looking out through the cracks between timbers, I saw hundreds of Barbaroki fleeing toward the western mouth of the valley. To the north and east, I heard Torzsek battle cries. Distant shouts answered from the south. Even where the Torzseki did not have the aid of a sorcerer, the battle was going against the Barbaroki.

Eben climbed down from a timber onto the ground next to me. "Very well, then," he said, trying and failing to sound nonchalant. "I will take the brand from you. Be assured I will put it to good use."

He knelt down next to me, putting his hand on my forehead.
I felt the power begin to leave me, and I did not fight it. My body
was so numb by this time that I felt no pain. I barely even noticed
that Eben had stopped drawing heat from me. He needed me
alive for a little longer if he was going to take the brand.

My vision had begun to darken, but through the cracks in the
timbers I could just make out the shapes of scores of Torzseki
pursuing the fleeing Barbaroki. "Eben!" shouted the voice of
Bolond, less than a stone's throw away. "Show yourself!"

"In due time," muttered Eben, continuing to extract the
power from me. "In due time."

"I have defeated your army. Face me, and we shall end this at
last! Your sorcery against mine!"

If I'd been able to, I'd have laughed. I should have let Bolond
deal with Eben. I didn't belong here. I was no sorcerer. I was an
interloper, an impostor. A shepherd boy turned farmer who had,
through some joke of fate, happened upon a source of power he
could neither control nor comprehend. I couldn't possibly beat
Eben at his own game. So I took the obvious course of action: I
cheated.

I focused most of what little tvari I had left onto my left
hand, converting it to heat. It was a pathetic effort, but it was
enough. The warmth spread down through my fingers and up to
my wrist. The numbness disappeared, supplanted by a sharp ache.
I ignored it. My fingertips closed on the pommel of the knife. I
pulled it from its sheath and worked it into my palm. My vision
had darkened so much I could barely see Eben crouched over
me. I would only get one chance.

Silently asking Vili's forgiveness, I pulled the knife from
under my stomach and stabbed blindly toward the warm body
hanging over me. Eben gasped as the knife penetrated soft flesh,
and I kept pushing until it was buried inside him. Eben stumbled
away from me, falling onto one of the timbers. I felt a surge of
power as the brand returned to me once again.

"Damn you!" Eben shrieked, clutching at the knife still
embedded in his abdomen. "Damn you!"

"What is this?" I heard Bolond say from somewhere nearby.
"A meeting of sorcerers? There are so few of us left, it's a shame
not to be invited."

Suddenly the weight of the timbers lifted from me. My vision began to clear, and I saw the structure rise into the air above me. Eben slid off the timber where he was perched, falling to the ground a few feet from me. He emitted a groan, rolling onto his back, and then was still. Bolond stood a few paces from him, his right hand raised as he lifted the tower through sheer will. The structure floated sideways several paces and then crashed again to the ground.

My body still gripped by chills, I slowly pulled myself to my feet. Eben lay a few feet away, not moving.

"Konrad!" cried a woman's voice from behind me. I turned to see Ilona running my way. Rodric was not far behind her. Torzseki continued to stream past, pursuing the Barbaroki, but I no longer heard any fighting. It seemed the battle was over.

CHAPTER TWENTY-FIVE

I had stood too quickly, and my vision began to darken again. Ilona and Rodric caught me just before I fell. I could barely keep my eyes open. I was exhausted and felt like I would never be warm again.

Rodric gave a shout as a man staggered toward us. I realized dimly that it was Chief Csongor. He had been nearby when Eben had scattered his men, but apparently far enough way to have avoided having his bones shattered. He was unarmed and did not seem interested in us. He walked slowly to Vili's body and knelt over it, listening for breathing. He put his fingers to Vili's neck. After a long moment, he shook his head and stood up.

"Eben is dead," Csongor said. He seemed unmoved by the fact. Perhaps he'd started to rethink his alliance when he saw Eben kill six of his men.

My heart sank. I had thought I would feel elated when Eben was finally dead, but all I felt was numbness and pain. Vili had been my friend and protégé. He had trusted me. And because of me, he was dead.

"Then it's over," Bolond said. He sounded disappointed he didn't get to kill Eben himself.

Ilona and Rodric helped me over to Vili's body. I sank wearily to the ground next to him. His body was still warm, but he did not move. I took his hand in mind. "I'm sorry, Vili," I murmured.

Another man came out of the darkness. As the light of the torches hit his face, I recognized Nebjosa's right hand man,

Davor Sabas. He carried a massive battle axe and the furs he wore were spattered with blood. "The Barbaroki have been defeated!" he cried. "The Torzseki are victorious!" Howls and cheers went up from Torzseki who were converging on our location. Davor Sabas approached Bolond, and the two clasped hands.

"I concede your victory," Csongor said, when the clamor died. He turned toward Davor Sabas. "My warriors have fled. Do with me as you will."

Cries of "Kill him!" went up from some of the Torzseki. Davor Sabas held up his hand.

"I do not intend to beg for my life," Csongor said, "but I may yet be of use to you. I will swear my allegiance to your chief from this day forward."

Davor Sabas grimaced in disgust. "Take him away," he barked to a man standing nearby. "He will be executed tomorrow."

"Wait," said Csongor. "I will accept my fate. But first I would like to know how I was defeated. The Barbaroki were eight thousand strong, and by the looks of your men here you had less than half of that. Who is this sorcerer who is worth five thousand men?"

Bolond smiled, taking a step toward Csongor. "My name is Bolond," he said. "It is no surprise that you did not expect defeat, for you did indeed have far superior numbers. But I am the greatest sorcerer there has ever been, and you could not have stood against me even if you had twenty thousand men."

As Bolond spoke, I felt a slight pressure on my hand. My heart jumped. Looking at Vili's face, I saw his eyelids flutter. His lips moved, and I bent down to put my ear next to his mouth. "Konrad," he gasped.

"Vili?" It didn't sound like Eben, but I could not be sure. Had Vili somehow managed to return to his body for the last few moments of his life?

"Thank... you," he said, his voice was almost inaudible.

"I'm sorry, Vili. I'm sorry I lied to you. Sorry I let you down."

"It's all right," he gasped. "Now I... can rest."

The pressure on my hand disappeared. Vili's eyes stared into the distance. He was at rest now, along with his parents. Tears flowed down my cheeks. Somehow, Vili had managed to return to his body just long enough to say goodbye. "I'm sorry, Vili," I babbled. "Thank you."

Csongor took a step toward Bolond. "Bolond," he said, as if he'd heard the name before. "Strange that we have not crossed paths before, if you are such a powerful sorcerer. Are you sure there is no greater sorcerer?"

"None," Bolond said coldly.

"Where have you been while nations have warred for control of Orszag? Have you been sleeping?"

Bolond scowled. "I owe you no explanation. Davor Sabas, have your men take this savage away."

"Ah, wait a moment," Csongor said. "Now I remember. Bolond! Of course! You're the old fool who brought ruin upon Elhalad, are you not?"

"You know nothing of me, savage!"

Csongor smiled. "I know that you do the bidding of the Destroyer," he said. "And I know that you used up most of the power you had left moving that tower aside. Always the showman, eh, Bolond? Your vanity will be your downfall."

Terror seized me. Eben wasn't dead. He'd merely abandoned Vili's body for a less damaged vessel. Csongor raised his hand, and Bolond stepped back, his face white with fear. Davor Sabas stood by, unable to make sense of what was happening. Around us, hundreds of Torzseki dumbly watched the scene unfold.

With Rodric's help, I struggled to my feet. "Eben," I gasped. Rodric stared at me, uncomprehending, but Ilona understood. Gripping her fighting stick, she sprinted toward Csongor. She was nearly within striking range when Csongor turned toward her and unleased a blast of energy from his outstretched hand. Ilona's body stopped in mid-stride as if she'd hit a wall. She was thrown some twenty feet backwards and landed in a crumpled heap. I cried out. Tearing myself away from Rodric, I staggered toward Eben.

Csongor—that is to say, Eben—turned to face Davor Sabas, who had brought his axe over his shoulder and advanced toward the warlock. The axe handle burst into pieces and Davor Sabas yelped and staggered backwards, his face full of splinters. Eben turned to Bolond and unleashed another blast of the purple energy. By this time, though, Bolond had been able to get a shield in place. The blast struck the shield and Bolond fell to the ground.

Eben took a step toward Bolond, who was now on his hands and knees, shaking from exertion. Bolond clearly had nothing left, and Eben knew it. Eben smiled, and I knew he was reaching out to stop Bolond's heart. Still staggering toward him, I tried to summon enough tvari to block the attack, but I was too weak. A dozen Torzseki warriors were rushing toward him as well, but they would not reach him in time. Bolond would die, and Eben would rule Orszag—and a hundred other worlds as well.

From behind me, I heard the *thwick* of an arrow being loosed. Csongor—that is, Eben—screamed and fell to his knees, an arrow lodged in his right eye. Still he held up his hand, attempting to cast the spell to finish Bolond. Torzseki came at him with axes and spears, but I reached him first. I gripped his hand and intercepted the spell, absorbing the tvari as it left his body. Eben gasped, too weak to resist. Despite his bold talk, his own strength had been nearly depleted; he had been stalling for time.

I did not let go. A half-dozen Torzsek warriors encircled us, weapons raised, as I pulled the rest of the tvari from Csongor's body. Eben would not escape this time. I saw the terror in his eyes as the life left him. I stood, and Csongor's corpse crumpled to the ground. A Torzsek standing nearby plunged his spear through his chest. He did not stir. Eben was truly dead.

Somewhat revitalized with the tvari I'd pulled from Eben, I ran to Ilona. Rodric was already at her side. Her body was bloody and bruised, but her chest rose and fell with shallow breaths. She was unconscious, and I couldn't begin to guess how many bones she had broken. She would not live long.

"Konrad, help her!" Rodric pleaded. But all I could do is take her in my arms. I had great power, but I had never learned how to use it to heal. All I knew how to do was destroy.

"I can save her," said a voice from behind me. I turned to see Bolond approaching, looking somewhat recovered from his thrashing at the hands of Eben. Davor Sabas followed, still angrily picking splinters from his face.

"You couldn't even defend yourself against Eben," I snapped.

"I admit I let my guard down. But I can replenish my supply of tvari quickly. If you can keep her alive for an hour, I can begin to repair the damage."

"We will keep her alive," Rodric said.

"I will need some assurances from you, of course," Bolond said.

"Assurances?" Rodric asked. "What are you talking about, sorcerer?"

"I agreed to help you defeat Eben," Bolond said. "We have done so. Now you must pledge to leave this valley and never return."

I laughed bitterly, still holding Ilona in my arms. "I expected as much," I said. "I should have realized the truth when I saw the way you and Davor Sabas conferred at Kalyiba. As if you were old friends."

"What are you saying, Konrad?" Rodric asked.

"Bolond put the Torzseki up to wiping out Yenoom Nivek. When he realized his experiment to find another source of tvari had failed, his students became a liability. He had Davor Sabas kill them so they couldn't interfere with his plans. Vili's parents only escaped because they happened to be away at the time. They never knew their master had betrayed them."

"I have served Nebjosa for twenty years," Davor Sabas said. "He has grown old and weak. Even now, he sleeps comfortably in the palace at Nagyvaros while we rid his land of vermin. Our tribe is dying, and Nebjosa has betrayed us by settling in that place. The Torzseki were meant to fight and conquer, not to beg for scraps from the Barbaroki! Bolond presented me with an opportunity to reclaim the greatness of the Torzseki, and I took it."

"You betrayed your chief."

"I have betrayed no one. Nebjosa never asked me what happened at Yenoom Nivek, because he does not want to know. He allowed me to lead two thousand men to this valley because he is happy to have me solve his problems for him. But I am done fighting for Nebjosa. When the temple is rebuilt, the men here will be the seed of a new breed of Torzseki, and it will be I who leads them, not Nebjosa."

"Rebuild the temple!" cried Rodric. "I thought that is what we were trying to prevent!"

"Bolond and Davor Sabas planned this from the beginning," I said. "They never intended to stop the rebuilding of the temple. They just didn't want Eben in charge of it. Presumably Bolond promised Davor Sabas control over Nagyvaros."

"We will take Nagyvaros from Nebjosa," Davor Sabas said, "but we will not stand there. We will be conquerors of entire worlds!"

"As long as Bolond lives, you will be little more than a figurehead, just as Csongor was for Eben."

"I am true to my word," Bolond said. "And I trust that you will be faithful to yours, Konrad. Pledge to leave this valley forever, and I will save your friend."

"I should have let Eben kill you."

"Eben was no match for Arnyek. I can defeat him. But I must rebuild the Temple of Romok to do so. When the worlds are joined by a single gateway, tvari will flow freely. Veszedelem will be saved."

"And Orszag will become more like Veszedelem," I said.

"The price of sorcery must be paid."

"*Your* sorcery. And in the process, you will be loosing Arnyek upon a hundred worlds."

"It is inevitable that the worlds will be joined," Bolond said. "When that happens, someone must be prepared to stop Arnyek. I am the only one with the power to defeat him."

"So again, in defeating one enemy, we help another," Rodric groaned.

"We will deal with Bolond as well," I said quietly. "But the time for that has not yet come."

Rodric nodded wearily. "We must do whatever we can to save Ilona. I do not like it, but if you intend to acquiesce to the sorcerer's demands, I will not argue."

"Thank you, Rodric," I said, meeting his gaze. "I am sorry for what I must do, but I have no choice. Goodbye, old friend."

Rodric's brow furrowed. He opened his mouth to speak, but I did not hear him. I closed my eyes and pictured the room where I had met the Reverend Mother, wrapping Ilona and myself in a blanket of tvari. I hoped I had enough strength to do what I had to do.

A moment later, I opened my eyes to find myself in the Reverend Mother's chambers. Ilona lay across my lap, still breathing, but just barely. My clothes were soaked with her blood. Except for a sliver of light coming through the door, the room was dark. We appeared to be alone. Struggling to remain conscious, I gathered what strength I had left and shouted, "Help! Please, someone… help…."

Everything went black.

*****

I do not know how long I was unconscious. I woke in a room that was eerily familiar. It was dome-shaped, and the walls were made of blocks of salt. I'd destroyed the cell where the Cult had kept Bolond, but either they had another one ready or I'd been out long enough for them to build one.

I drank some water from a bottle that had been left next to my bed and gobbled down a half loaf of dry bread. Then I waited.

A few hours later, the slot in the door opened. A man barked at me to stand against the rear of the cell. I did so, and the door opened. Two guards stepped inside, brandishing short swords. They moved aside to make way for a woman wearing the same type of robe worn by the Reverend Mother and Myra. Black hair, worn in the style of the acolytes but a bit longer than usual, framed a stern but beautiful alabaster face. She looked to be only a few years older than I. She held something in her right hand.

"Hello, Konrad," she said, taking a step toward me. "My name is Katalinn. As of this morning, I am the Reverend Mother of the Cult of Turelem. These men have been ordered to kill you if you so much as raise a hand toward me, so please remain very still." She placed the object she had been holding onto the small table beside the bed. I saw now that it was a small hourglass. The sand had begun to pour. "I have a very busy week ahead of me, so I am going to get right to the point. You have until the sand runs out to convince me why I should let you live."

END OF BOOK THREE

Get Book Four Now!

The Throne of Darkness will be available on January 18, 2020. Order your copy today!

The Counterfeit Sorcerer series is:

The Brand of the Warlock
The Rise of the Demon Prince
The Book of the Dead
The Throne of Darkness (Release date: Jan 18, 2020)
The End of All Things (Release date: Mar 1, 2020)

Review This Book!

Did you enjoy *The Book of the Dead*? Please take a moment to leave a review on Amazon.com! Reviews are very important for getting the word out to other readers, and it only takes a few seconds.

Get Email Updates

Want to get the latest news about sales and new books by Robert Kroese? Sign up for email alerts at https://badnovelist.com/get-email-updates/!

Acknowledgements

This book would not have been possible without the assistance of:

- **My beta readers:** Mark Fitzgerald, Pekka Gaiser, Brian Galloway, Mark Leone, Phillip Lynch and Paul Alan Piatt;

- And the *Counterfeit Sorcerer* Kickstarter supporters, including:

    A.J., Chris DeBrusk, Lauren Foley, Kevin Mooney, Bruce Parrello, Christopher Turner, Karl Armstrong, Jason, Brent Brown, Philip R. Burns, Eric Stevens, Josh Creed, Lowell Jacobson, Ben Parker, Michael Wilson, Robert Jacobsen, Keith West, Travis Gagnon, Dennis Ruffing, Christopher Sanders, Emily Wagner, Jad Davis, Grant Morath, Phillip Jones, Sean Simpson, Kristin Crocker, Slater, Ryan McGuire, Pamela Crouch, and Joel Suovaniemi.

Cover art by Kip Ayers:
http://www.kipayersillustration.com/

Any errors in this book are the fault of the author. I did my best.

More Books by Robert Kroese

The Saga of the Iron Dragon

The Dream of the Iron Dragon
The Dawn of the Iron Dragon
The Voyage of the Iron Dragon

The Starship Grifters Universe

Out of the Soylent Planet
Starship Grifters
Aye, Robot
The Wrath of Cons

The Mercury Series

Mercury Falls
Mercury Rises
Mercury Rests
Mercury Revolts
Mercury Shrugs

The Land of Dis

Distopia
Disenchanted
Disillusioned

Other Books

The Big Sheep
The Last Iota
Schrödinger's Gat
City of Sand
The Force is Middling in This One

Made in the USA
Middletown, DE
06 January 2020

82628769R00135